LETHAL SECRET

SALLY RIGBY

TOP
DRAWER
PRESS

Edited by Emma Mitchell of @ Creating Perfection.

Cover Design by Stuart Bache of Books Covered

GET ANOTHER BOOK FOR FREE!

To instantly receive the free novella, **The Night Shift**, featuring Whitney when she was a Detective Sergeant, ten years ago, sign up for Sally Rigby's free author newsletter at www.sallyrigby.com

Chapter One

Whitney held onto the last note while the piano finished playing the accompaniment. When she stopped, applause from her fellow Rock Choir members rang around the room. Heat warmed her cheeks as she dragged in a much-needed breath. The last note was a killer and took every last ounce of energy she had. She loved to sing and felt privileged she'd been given a solo in the November concert being held in Birmingham, involving thirty Rock Choirs from the region. The theme of the concert was *Songs from the Shows*, and she was singing 'Defying Gravity' from *Wicked*. It showed off her whole range and had always been a showstopper. This rehearsal was a joint one with the Banbury choir, and there were over a hundred people there.

She slid her music back into the black folder she was holding and sat down.

'That was fantastic,' Liz, the choir leader, said.

'Thank you,' she replied, humbled by the praise.

Whitney had dreamed of singing professionally until falling pregnant at seventeen with Tiffany. Not that she regretted it. She couldn't be prouder of her daughter, who was taking an engineering degree at Lenchester University. The first person in their family to continue studying after school. Instead of singing, Whitney had pursued a career in the police force and had reached the rank of Detective Chief Inspector.

'Fifteen-minute break,' Liz said.

Whitney placed her folder on the chair and made her way towards the table where there were flasks of coffee and plates of biscuits.

'You have an incredible voice.' She turned to see who was speaking and came face-to-face with one of the few males there. As he wasn't from her choir, she assumed he was from Banbury. Out of habit, she scrutinised him, taking in the small details that were so much a part of her daily life. He wasn't very tall, maybe five foot six, though certainly taller than her. He had short dark hair, with hazel eyes and a cheeky smile.

'Thank you,' she said.

'Really, I mean it. You should take it up professionally. Your range is incredible and your tone beautiful and emotive.'

'That's kind of you to say so.' She sucked in a breath, trying to stop a beaming smile from crossing her face. She didn't want to come across as being full of herself.

'My name's Craig Robbie.' He held out his hand, which she shook.

'Whitney Walker,' she replied.

'I hope you don't mind me asking, but would you like to go for a drink after rehearsal?'

No. Her rules were simple. Don't get involved with anyone from work, and that extended to the choir. Because if it all went sour, it would make life difficult.

'Or is there a Mr Walker waiting for you?' Craig added, smiling.

'There's no Mr Walker, and yes a drink would be nice.' So much for her rules. It was the smile that did it. She hadn't been out with anyone in a long time. Even though this was just a drink and he probably only wanted to talk about the choir. 'There's a pub around the corner where we often go.'

'You'll have to show me the way, as I don't know the area.'

For the rest of the rehearsal, Whitney found it hard to concentrate, as out the corner of her eye she kept watching Craig. He intrigued her. Very few men joined Rock Choir. Why had he? Once they'd finished, she headed to where he was standing beside the door.

'You can leave your car outside, as it's not far,' she said.

She pulled on her coat, and they left the rehearsal room and walked to The Tavern.

'What can I get you to drink?' he asked once they were inside and standing at the bar.

As she was driving, she should have something non-alcoholic, like a lemonade, but she could murder something stronger. Singing did that to her.

'A white wine, please.'

The pub wasn't very busy, although following behind them would be other members of the choir. It was a typical city centre bar, with very little character.

It had been a good evening all-round. She loved singing and had also met a man. What would George make of it? And why on earth had she suddenly thought about the forensic psychologist who she'd worked with from time to time? Maybe it was because George had a new man in her life. Not so new, now, as they'd been together for a few months, and when George had phoned last week, she'd mentioned they were going on holiday together. Whitney had only met the guy once, but she approved. Very different from George. In a good way. How funny would it be if she got together with Craig and they could make up a foursome?

She pulled herself up short. She was having a drink with the guy and now suddenly she was arranging to double date. Before any more ridiculous thoughts entered her head, he'd been served and was handing her a glass.

'Thanks.' She took a sip and winced slightly.

'Is it no good?'

'A bit dry for me. It's fine, though.'

'I can get you something else if you'd rather,' he offered.

That was sweet of him, but not necessary. She'd drink it. She wasn't like George, who knew everything there was about wine. All Whitney knew was whether she liked it or not. George, on the other hand, would be sniffing and swilling it around her glass. She'd then proceed to tell you all about the different aromas coming through.

Whitney smiled to herself. She'd phone her friend and arrange an evening out soon. Just the two of them.

'No need. There's a table over there,' she said, pointing to the corner of the pub.

They went over and sat down.

'Tell me what you do when you're not singing,' Craig asked.

'You go first,' she said, knowing that as soon as she said she was in the police the whole dynamic of their evening would change.

Some men, thinking they were being funny, would make a quip about wanting her to handcuff them, or would hold up both hands and say *not guilty*. If she had a pound for every one of those comments, she wouldn't need to work again. Others would go all shifty, as if somehow she was able to know all about their illegal activities simply by looking at them, which in most cases would only involve running a red light, or claiming personal meals out on their tax return. Nothing major. That she knew of.

'I'm in business,' he said, his tone evasive.

'What sort of business?'

'I import supplements and sell them to the health-care industry.'

There was a huge amount of money to be made in the sale of illegal body enhancement drugs. Is that what he meant, or was she being needlessly suspicious?

'What sort of supplements?' she asked, unable to stop herself. Could she ever switch off from work?

'Not the sort you'll find in the local chemist. My products are upmarket, and I sell directly to nutritionists.'

'How did you get into that line of work?' she asked.

'I trained as a nutritionist and from there got interested in supplements and their effects. What about you?'

Her phone rang before she could answer. She glanced at the screen and saw Matt's name. If the detective sergeant was calling on her evening off, it must be something serious. 'Sorry, I have to take this. It's work.'

Disappointment flashed across his face, but he nodded. 'Okay.'

She reluctantly left the table and found somewhere quiet to stand.

'Walker.'

'I'm sorry to bother you, guv. I know you're busy this evening, but I thought you might want to know about a suicide that's been reported.'

'Why would I be interested in a suicide?' She frowned.

'Because it's the third identical suicide in the past two weeks.'

'How do we know that?'

'It seems the same officer was called to each of the deaths. She noted the similarities and raised the alarm. The third body has only just been found.'

'How did the victims die?'

'They hung themselves.'

'It sounds like a suicide cluster.' Whitney sucked in a breath. It wasn't uncommon for there to be a spate of suicides in the same area. If this was the case, it was both fascinating and alarming at the same time.

'Or murder. From what the officer told me, identical blue cord was used by the victims to hang themselves.'

'Give me the address of this latest victim. I'll meet you there.'

'It's 114 Brookfield Road East. I've already asked for a pathologist.'

'Is it Claire Dexter?' she asked, hoping it was, as she was the best pathologist in the area.

'I'm not sure who's on duty. They didn't say.'

'Okay, I'll see you soon.' She ended the call and hurried back to the table where Craig was waiting.

'I was beginning to give you up for lost,' he said.

'Sorry. I have to go. I'm needed at work.'

'At this time of night?' he said, checking his watch.

'It's only seven-thirty. This is nothing. Sometimes I work well into the early hours.'

'You haven't told me what you do,' he said.

'I'm a police officer,' she said, hoping he wasn't going to ruin everything by coming out with the usual response.

His eyes widened. 'I didn't expect that. You don't look like a copper.'

'Because I'm short?' It wasn't the first time she'd had that response.

'It's not just your height. It's … never mind. I wish we

could have got to know each other better. Would you like to try this again sometime?'

'Yes, that would be nice.' She pulled out a card from her pocket and gave it to him. 'Give me a ring.'

'Detective Chief Inspector. You didn't say you were such a high-ranking officer.'

'It's high enough for me.' She had no ambition for promotion; she liked real police work and wasn't interested in the politics and paper-pushing which occupied the time of the higher ranks.

'So, if you've been called into work, it must be something big.'

'I can't discuss it. It was good to meet you.' She walked away. Matt had better be right about these deaths.

Chapter Two

Whitney parked her car outside the front of the victim's house, a pebble-dashed semi-detached dating from the 1950s. She pushed open the white gate and walked up the path of the small garden to the open front door. Matt was standing in the hallway.

'What have we got?' she said by way of a greeting.

'The victim's name is Hayley Tennant, and she was found hanging in her bedroom by one of the other women living here. There are two of them and they're in the lounge.'

'Okay, let's go and see them first. Has the pathologist arrived yet?'

'Yes. It's Dr Dexter and she's upstairs.'

'Thank goodness for that.' If there was more to this than suicide, Claire would be the one to find it.

They headed into the lounge, where two women in their twenties were sitting in silence.

'This is Kiera,' Matt said, nodding in the direction of the woman with brown hair, hanging loosely over her shoulders. She was sitting still like a statue, her face ashen. 'She found Hayley.'

'Hello, Kiera. I'm DCI Walker. I know how hard this has been. Are you up to answering some questions?' she asked gently.

'Yes,' Kiera said, her voice barely above a whisper.

'And what's your name?' Whitney asked the other girl.

'I'm Sarah. I live here, too.'

'What can you tell me about Hayley?'

'She's only been living here three weeks. We don't know her very well at all,' Sarah said.

'So, you all rent?' Whitney asked.

'Yes,' Sarah said. 'I've been living here for two years and Kiera for six months.'

'You found Hayley in her bedroom, Kiera. Do you often go in there?'

'A package arrived for her, and I took it upstairs. There was no answer when I first knocked, so I tried again and gently opened the door, intending to leave it on the side. That's when I saw her … hanging … from the window latch. I ran over and tried to get her down … but I wasn't strong enough.'

'What did you do then?' Whitney asked.

'I called emergency services and—' Her voice broke. Tears rolled down her cheeks, and Sarah put her arm around her.

'We'll need to contact Hayley's family; do you have their details?'

'No, I'm sorry. We don't,' Sarah said. 'But the letting agency should. I can give you their number.'

'Where does Hayley work?' Whitney asked.

'I don't know,' Sarah said.

'Nor do I,' Kiera said, sniffing. 'She kept to herself and we hardly saw her. She left for work at eight in the morning and would come home around six. Occasionally I'd see her in the kitchen, but she'd always take her food back to her room.'

'What about weekends?' Whitney asked.

'I don't know, I'm usually with my boyfriend,' Sarah said.

'I'm in and out on Saturdays and Sundays, but I didn't see much of her,' Kiera said.

'What about visitors? Do you recall anyone coming to visit Hayley?' Whitney asked.

'Not that I know of, but as I've already said, I'm not here much,' Sarah said.

'I didn't see anyone either,' Kiera said.

'I know this has been a big shock for you, but we'll need to take statements when you're feeling up to it.'

'Okay,' they both said.

'Thank you for your help. I'm going upstairs. DS Price will stay with you until I return.'

She left the lounge and went up the stairs to the square landing. The door to the second room on the left was open and there was a rustle. She walked in and saw the pathologist kneeling next to the body, which was lying on the floor.

'Good evening, Claire.'

The pathologist looked up. As usual, Whitney could see some of Claire's weird and wonderful clothing peeping out from her coverall. This time, it was a fluorescent orange polo-neck jumper and a pair of huge wooden elephant-shaped earrings, which hung below her short red hair.

'Don't ask me anything, because I don't know yet,' Claire said.

'I wasn't going to.' The pathologist's abrupt manner didn't bother Whitney, because she'd been working with her for over a decade. Claire was the best pathologist in the country, but she was also difficult, awkward, and, sometimes, just plain rude.

'That's all right then,' Claire said.

'The officer who was called out to the victim attended two other suicides within the last two weeks, carried out in exactly the same way, and a similar blue cord was used.'

'I don't know anything about the other two. And there's not a lot I can say about this one until we get the body back to the lab, where I can run some tests and send bloods to toxicology.'

Whitney pulled on some disposable gloves and looked around the room. She opened the wardrobe and inside was a rail of exercise clothes and a yoga mat. On the bedside table were two yoga magazines.

'She obviously liked to exercise. Apart from that, there's not a lot I can tell about our victim from what's here in the room. It's rather bare. I wonder where she goes to classes?' Whitney said. 'Any idea how long she'd been hanging before she was found?'

'I'll let you know after I've got back to the lab. I'm not prepared to speculate,' Claire said.

'We need to find out where she worked, and her state of mind if she went in today. There must be something here to help the investigation.'

She caught sight of a tan handbag beside the bed and picked it up. She flipped open the purse. There was a business card for BATT, the British Association for the Talking Therapies, which had her name on it, and underneath, the title Senior Information Officer.

'If this is current, we know where she works. But before we go there, we need to inform her family. I've got her driving licence; we'll track them from that.'

'Are you thinking this might be a suicide cluster?' Claire asked.

Whitney was surprised the pathologist had decided to comment. It was very unusual.

'That was my first thought, but we need to look more into the other deaths. It could be the officer assigned to their cases jumped to conclusions. We don't know if these victims were connected in any way. There's also a chance it could be murder. We'll see what you come up with during your investigation.'

'I'll let you know as soon as I have something.' Claire looked away and continued working.

'I get the hint,' she said as she left the room and headed downstairs.

She walked back into the lounge, where the tension was palpable. No one was talking.

'I'd rather you didn't stay here until our investigation is complete,' she said. 'Do you have anywhere you can go for a few days?'

'I can stay with my boyfriend,' Sarah said.

'I've got a friend who will put me up,' Kiera said.

'Thank you. Give your contact numbers to DS Price and we'll let you know when it's okay to return. I noticed in Hayley's room that she's into yoga. Do you know where she went for classes?'

'I saw her going out early one Saturday morning, with a mat under her arm, and I asked where she went,' Kiera said. 'She said it was out in the country and she'd be gone all day. That was the most she'd said to me in all the time she was here.'

That might help. There couldn't be too many centres that far out of the city.

'Please go upstairs to collect your belongings. Would you like a lift?'

'It's fine. I can take us,' Sarah said as they left the lounge and went upstairs.

'What do you think?' Matt asked once they were gone.

'It's difficult to know at the moment. We need to compare the deaths, and not just have the police officer's word about it, to see if there are similarities. And that's down to Claire.'

'They could all be murders,' Matt said.

'Let's not even go there. We've had enough murders this year, and it would be nice to have some time off,' she said. 'Back to our victim. I've got her business card from work. We can check her out there. Obviously, we need to find out where her family lives and give them the news. Who's on duty? I don't suppose it's Ellie,' she said, referring to the Detective Constable who was their resident research guru. When they needed information, she was the one to find it.

'I believe it is, but not for much longer,' he said as he checked his watch. 'Shall I contact her?'

'No. I'll do it.' She pulled out her phone.

'Hello, guv. I didn't expect to hear from you tonight. I thought you had a rehearsal,' Ellie said.

'I got called away. I want you to track down the family of a Hayley Tennant. She lived at 114 Brookfield Road East but was only there for a few weeks. I'll text you her driving licence number. First impression is suicide, but we're not a hundred per cent sure until the pathologist has done her work.'

'No problem, I'm onto it.'

'Thanks. Let me know as soon as you've got the details. I want to speak to them this evening.'

She ended the call and texted the number to Ellie. Just as she'd finished, Sarah and Kiera came downstairs with their bags.

'Can we go now?' Sarah asked.

'Yes. Don't forget to give your details to DS Price.'

She left them giving their information to Matt and headed into the hall just as Ellie called her back.

'The next of kin listed on the victim's driving licence is Mrs Veronica Tennant, and she lives at 101 Joll Street, in Cowley.'

'Thanks. Matt and I will go there now.'

She ended the call. Cowley was about twenty-five minutes away, so they should make it there by nine-fifteen. Not ideal, but hopefully the woman wouldn't have gone to bed.

She waited until Sarah and Kiera had left before going back into the lounge where Matt was putting away his notebook.

'We're going to speak to the victim's family. They live in Cowley,' she said to the officer.

When they arrived at their destination, she was relieved to see a light on downstairs. It was a nice area of town and they lived in a modern detached property. After parking in the drive, they headed to the front door. Whitney rang the bell.

A man in his fifties answered.

'I'd like to speak to Mrs Veronica Tennant. I'm DCI Walker from Lenchester CID, and this is DS Price.' She held out her warrant card and Matt did the same.

'What's it about?'

'Who are you?' she asked.

'I'm Ken Tennant, Veronica's husband.'

'We'd like to come in and speak to you both.'

'Is it one of the children?' he said, panic in his voice.

'Please, Mr Tennant, if we could speak to you inside.'

Whitney hated this part of the job more than

anything else. She had to go in and totally destroy people's lives, knowing things would never be the same again.

He opened the door and ushered them in. 'My wife's in the lounge watching television.'

They followed him into the room.

'Who is it, Ken? It's very—' The woman, who'd stood as they entered, stopped speaking mid-sentence.

'It's the police,' he said.

'What's happened?' She clutched her hands to her chest.

'Please sit down,' Whitney said.

They did as she'd asked, and once they were both seated on the sofa, Whitney and Matt sat opposite on chairs.

'You have a daughter, Hayley?' Whitney said.

'Yes,' Mr Tennant replied.

'I'm very sorry to tell you, that earlier this evening, Hayley's body was found in the house where she was living.'

'Found? What do you mean? Is she dead?' Mr Tennant asked, colour draining from his face.

'Yes. I'm sorry, there was nothing we could do.'

'How did she die?' Mrs Tennant's voice was strained.

'The pathologist is with her now. We're not certain, but the initial indication is that she took her own life.'

The couple exchanged knowing glances, resignation etched across both of their faces. It was a strange reaction and not one Whitney had seen before.

'You don't seem surprised?' she said.

'Hayley's been distant from us for a few months. She stopped coming around. She stopped taking calls, and the occasional time we did see her, she was very withdrawn,' Mr Tennant said.

'Did this change happen slowly, over a long period of time?' Whitney asked.

'It was over a couple of months. We phoned her many times, but she never answered. We tried hard, but what could we do? She wanted nothing to do with us.' His voice cracked.

Mrs Tennant let out a groan and started to sob. 'I don't know what happened to her. Or why she changed so much. We couldn't get through to her. It was like she no longer cared about us. We should've done more. If we had then maybe this wouldn't have happened. We don't even know her new address. We only found out she'd moved after one of her sisters called to see her and was told.'

Mr Tennant took her hands in his. 'You can't blame yourself. We all tried.' He looked at Whitney. 'We have two other daughters, and they couldn't find out what was wrong with Hayley either. She cut herself off from all of us.' He visibly swallowed, obviously trying to not lose control.

'Had anything happened at work recently that might have explained the change in her?'

'Not that I know of,' Mr Tennant said.

'Do you know any of Hayley's colleagues? Someone we could speak to?' Whitney asked.

Mrs Tennant glanced at her husband, an anxious expression on her face. 'I'm sorry, she did sometimes mention her colleagues, but I can't remember their names. Can you?' she asked her husband.

'No.' He shook his head.

'Don't worry. We can find out,' Whitney said, reassuring them. 'What can you tell me about her hobbies? I understand she enjoyed going to yoga.'

Mrs Tennant frowned. 'Yoga? I had no idea she'd taken it up.'

'Maybe it was something she'd begun recently,' Whitney said.

'She'd become a stranger to us.' Mrs Tennant's eyes filled with tears and she began to shake.

Whitney had put them through enough. They needed to be alone with their grief.

'I'm afraid we need a formal identification of Hayley. Are you able to come in tomorrow? I can send an officer to collect you.'

Mr Tennant gave a grim nod, his efforts to retain control crumbling as his face distorted.

'Is there anyone we can phone to be with you?' she asked.

'No, thank you. We need to contact Hayley's sisters, but we'll do that ourselves.'

Their goodbyes went unnoticed as they let themselves out and drove back to Lenchester. George was due back from her holiday today. She'd give her a call. Whether they were dealing with a suicide cluster, or several murders, it was something the forensic psychologist could help them with.

Chapter Three

George headed upstairs with her suitcase, wanting to unpack as soon as possible. If there was one thing she couldn't stand, it was not putting everything away immediately. She'd left Ross downstairs making tea. They'd just arrived back from an impromptu week in Portugal. Someone Ross knew had offered them their holiday home, as one of the bookings had fallen through. When he'd asked her to go, she'd been reticent. Although they'd had a couple of successful weekends away, going overseas for a proper holiday was different.

But she'd been right to say yes. They'd stayed in a lovely fishing village, Cabanas de Tavira, in the Algarve, and had spent much of their time exploring. They'd walked through the salt pans and into the historic town of Tavira. In the evenings they'd dined alfresco in one of the many restaurants situated on the boardwalk of Cabanas, overlooking the channel which led to the beautiful sandy beach. The weather had been glorious and, because most schools had already started back, they'd avoided the craziness of peak season.

She'd go back there in a heartbeat. Being with Ross was relaxed and easy. Hopefully it was a good omen for her brother's upcoming wedding, where she planned to introduce him to her family. Once they'd discovered he was a sculptor, her parents weren't happy with her choice of partner. He was also from a working-class family with no connections to aristocracy, which her previous boyfriend had, and her parents had been ecstatic over. But seeing as she saw them rarely, what they thought was immaterial. It was her happiness that counted.

'What are you doing?' Ross called up the stairs.

'I'll be down in a minute.' She hurriedly unpacked her suitcase and joined him.

'I thought you must've fallen asleep,' he said.

'No. I just wanted to get everything sorted.'

'It's a shame we have to go back to reality. I had a lovely time. We've definitely got to go back there again.' He slipped his arms around her waist, dragged her close, and kissed her.

'Yes, it's a beautiful place,' she said as they finally parted. 'I've really enjoyed myself. I've been to Lisbon before, but never the Algarve, and I'm definitely a convert.'

'What are your plans tomorrow?' he asked.

'In the morning, I'll go into work to collect my mail and make sure everything is in place for when the new students start. I'll probably work from home in the afternoon, as I have some chapters to read from one of my PhD students. What about you?'

'I've just received a text confirming a new commission.'

'What is it?' She found Ross's work fascinating, and from their conversations and watching him work, she'd learned a lot more about sculpture than she'd known before. It was incredible the way he was able to sculpt recognisable faces out of different materials.

'It's a full-size bronze depiction of a Labrador who belonged to some farmers living near Oxford. Their family want it as a surprise for their golden wedding anniversary. I'll be working from several photographs.'

'Will you show it to me once you've finished?' she asked.

'I'd be happy to. The anniversary party is only a couple of months away, so I won't be able to see you much while I'm working on it.'

Her heart sank. She'd hoped they'd spend a bit more time together. But she understood. Work came first.

'That's not a problem. Remember, we have my brother's wedding soon, and we'll be away for four days.'

'Don't worry, it's in my diary. I'm looking forward to it.'

'I don't think you realise what you're letting yourself in for. If you did, you wouldn't be saying that.'

'Meeting your family isn't a problem. The service at Westminster Abbey will be cool. It's a once-in-a-lifetime opportunity. The same for the reception at the Imperial War Museum. I doubt I'll get the chance to go there again. I'm going to make the most of it. Plus, we've got our tickets to see *Hamilton*, and we'll have time to look around the art galleries. It's going to be a great few days.'

When he'd surprised her with the *Hamilton* tickets, she'd been thrilled. It was the hottest show in town, and one she'd wanted to see. He'd bought the best seats in the stalls, which was perfect. It would make enduring her family a lot easier. Whitney had persuaded her to buy a dress for the wedding that was totally different from anything she'd ever worn before. She wondered what Ross would make of it.

'Agreed. I think I might settle down with a book and have an early night, if you don't mind,' she said, suddenly feeling quite tired, as they'd been on the go all day.

'Okay.' He frowned.

Did he think he was staying overnight? She hadn't asked him to, and she could do with some alone time. 'You don't mind, do you?'

'Of course not. I need to get back as I want to make an early start.'

Was he just saying that? She didn't know. She did occasionally miss social cues. Actually, it was more than occasionally. Much to Whitney's amusement.

Her mobile rang, and when she picked it up from the kitchen table she stared at the screen. That was weird. She'd just thought of Whitney and now she was calling her. The officer would probably explain it away as being something to do with the law of attraction. George didn't believe in all that woo-woo stuff.

'Hello, Whitney,' she said.

'Are you back?'

'Yes, we've been here about an hour.'

'Good. I'm not disturbing you, am I?'

George glanced at Ross, who was sitting at the table, his hands around the mug of tea he'd made.

'Not really. Ross is with me.'

'I won't keep you long. We've had a death which I thought you might be interested in. It looks like a suicide, but—'

'Why would I be interested in a suicide?' she interrupted.

'If you let me finish … It looks like a suicide, but this is the third one, identical in nature. Well, we think it's identical. We've still got to check.'

'You're thinking suicide cluster?'

'We're not sure. It could equally be a murder, in which case it would be *murders*, as there are three of them, if they are linked. We need to wait for Claire's findings.'

'You're right. I am interested.'

'Can you come in tomorrow, so we can go through everything together? Unless you've got other things to do.' Whitney gave a laugh, and George realised what she was implying.

'Actually, Ross is about to go home, and I'll be on my own for the rest of the evening. So, yes, I can come in. I'd intended to call into work in the morning to get myself prepared for the onslaught of new students in a few weeks, but that can wait.'

'I'm sure you've already got everything prepared,' Whitney said.

'In principle, yes. But I want to go back over it all to double-check it's as it should be.' It was uncanny how the police officer knew so much about her. They'd known each other less than a year and, to the outside world, their relationship probably appeared strange, as they were such different people. But George found comfort in their differences, and she knew she could always rely on Whitney for support. She wasn't out to undermine her, as often happened in the university, when people were competing with each other for kudos in their research.

'What time will you be here?' Whitney asked, interrupting George's thoughts.

'First thing in the morning, if that works for you?'

'It does. I'd better leave you to it; I don't want to get in the way of your evening with Ross.'

'Goodbye, Whitney,' she said, ignoring the comment.

She ended the call and glanced at Ross.

'For someone who's tired and wants to have an early night with a book, you certainly became all animated and interested as soon as a case was mentioned.'

'Is that a problem?' she asked, not knowing what else to say.

'No. I'm not at all offended that you want to throw me

out in favour of a good book.' He laughed. 'All I meant was you clearly enjoy working with the police and have a great relationship with Whitney. She brings you out of yourself. I'm all for it.'

Could he be any more different from her ex, Stephen? *Stop it.* This was the last time she'd think about Stephen and Ross in the same sentence.

'I do enjoy working with the police, but that doesn't mean I don't enjoy my work at the university. I'm lucky I have the best of both worlds. Putting the theory into practice makes me happy.'

'I'm glad to hear that. Right, I'm off.' Ross finished the last of his tea and put his mug in the sink. 'You've got a busy day tomorrow, crime-busting.'

Chapter Four

'Good morning, everyone,' Whitney said the following morning as she walked over to the board in the incident room. Most of the team were already there, and they glanced up at the sound of her voice.

'Morning, guv.' Their voices echoed around the room.

'Just to get you up to speed, last night we were called to what initially appeared to be a suicide. But according to the officer on site, this was the third identical death she'd been to in two weeks. We have the names and addresses of the other two victims, but at the moment don't know anything else about them. The first death was two weeks ago, and the victim's name is Nicola Hurst.' She wrote the name on the board. 'Our second victim is Samantha Lyman, and our third, Hayley Tennant. Ellie, I'd like you to do a background check on victim one, Frank, you can do the second, and Doug, the third. We want to know everything about them. Where they worked, their family, friends, social media activity. We're looking for a possible link between the three of them.'

'I'm working on the spate of graffiti attacks in the city centre,' Frank said.

'This takes priority,' Whitney said to the older detective constable.

'Yes, guv,' Frank said.

'Once you have the information, pass it to me. I'll be visiting the other victims' homes and families as soon as possible.'

She was distracted by the sound of the incident room door opening. George walked in, and she did a double take. The forensic psychologist sauntered over looking relaxed and sporting a fabulous suntan, her shiny, blonde highlighted hair swinging in time with her steps. Whitney smiled to herself. No need to ask what that was all about.

'Good morning, Whitney,' George said as she approached.

'Carry on with what you're doing, I want to speak to Dr Cavendish,' Whitney said to the team. She took George to one side. 'Look at you, all tanned and relaxed. Did you have a good holiday?'

'Yes, thank you. It was very nice.'

'*Very nice.* Is that all you can say?' Whitney rolled her eyes. It was typical of George to underplay it.

'What do you want from me? Very nice is very nice, and that's what the holiday was.'

'I'm glad to hear it. Moving on, all we have on the deaths are the names of the victims and know their supposed suicides were committed in identical ways.'

'Have you definitely ruled out a suicide cluster?' George asked.

'Not yet.'

'Well, you know for them to be classed as clusters, we need three or more deaths.'

'I do.' Whitney's jaw tightened with impatience. Occasionally George would forget she wasn't talking to one of her students and that she did actually know plenty.

'So, first of all, we need to establish whether there are any connections between the victims. This could be in terms of location, or socially. Or even if they didn't actually know each other, they could have been subject to the same social circumstances, like the awful incident in Wales when an extraordinary number of people from the same small town committed suicide in one year.'

'I remember. Which is why the team are doing checks on them. We also need to speak to Claire and see what she's found.'

'Excellent. When do you want to go?' George asked.

'We'll go now, and after we've finished there we'll check the other two victims' residences. Have you got your car with you?' she asked.

'How else do you think I got here?' George replied.

'Ross could've brought you in.' She nudged her gently on the arm.

George frowned. 'I told you he wasn't staying last night. He went home.'

'You might have changed your mind, if you suddenly decided you couldn't keep your hands off each other.' George blushed, and Whitney grinned. 'When are you seeing him again?'

'I'm not sure. He's working on a new commission, and I'm busy with you and work.'

'You have to make some time for him,' Whitney said.

'We're going to the wedding in a few weeks. I'll see him then.'

'You could see him before, you know.'

'Whitney, give it a rest. The relationship is fine. Back to your question. I do have my car, and I assume you'd like to travel in it.'

'And here we have the George I've grown to know and love.' She smirked. 'Yes, to your car—it's much more comfortable than mine.'

'Attention, everyone. I'm going to see Dr Dexter. I've been discussing with George the possibility of the deaths being a suicide cluster. During your investigations into the women, check to see the types of background they came from. Remember, we're looking for anything they have in common.'

They left the station and headed into the car park. George's top of the range Land Rover Discovery stuck out among the majority of other cars parked there.

The drive to the morgue only took ten minutes. As they entered through the double doors, Whitney was hit, as usual, by the antiseptic odour. They walked down the corridor until reaching another set of double doors leading to the actual lab. Claire was sitting at her desk in the pathologists' office, staring at a computer screen.

'Good morning, Claire,' Whitney said.

'I assume you're here about last night's victim and the other two suicides?' the pathologist replied.

'Yes. What can you tell us?' Whitney said.

'Strictly between us, I'm not impressed by the job done on the other two victims,' Claire said.

'In what way?' George immediately asked.

'Both those deaths were investigated by a locum working here. I'd say he assumed suicide and looked no further. The post mortem was barely adequate. Nothing was investigated regarding the possibility of the victims having died of asphyxia by smothering, and their bodies hung afterwards.'

'What made you draw those conclusions?' George asked.

'In both cases, in the photos—which were also woefully

inadequate—there appears to be an indication of smothering. There were lesions in the lips on one of the victims and discolouration from bruising on the cheeks of the other.'

'How could he have missed this?' George asked.

'Very easily if he wasn't concentrating. This work is complex. A body doesn't arrive covered in Post-it notes marking where to look. We have to be methodical and experienced. Clearly he was neither.'

'Is the locum still working here?' Whitney asked.

'No. But I will be taking the matter further. It's not something you need concern yourself with,' Claire said in a cool voice. Whitney almost felt sorry for the incompetent chap.

'What about Hayley Tennant, the victim from last night?' George asked.

'Follow me, and I'll go through it with you.'

Claire led them into the lab area, and on one of the stainless-steel tables in the centre of the room was Hayley's body.

The pathologist swung the overhead lamp around, so it focused on the area around the neck.

'Do you see this raised dark brown mark? It's from the knot in the cord and is pointing upwards because gravity pulled the body down. Typical of hanging. Now look at the contusion on the lips.' She pointed to the purple bruise. 'A sign of smothering.'

'Are there any signs of a struggle?' Whitney asked.

'I was getting to that. I looked for evidence indicating an altercation, and there isn't any.'

'So, she could've been sedated before being smothered?' George asked.

'That we'll find out when the bloods are back from toxicology.'

'What do we know about the cord?' Whitney asked.

'It's a high strength nylon rope often used in sailing, as it has minimal stretch. I'm investigating the make.'

'Do we know whether the victim went sailing?' George asked Whitney.

'No. We'll look into it. What about time of death?' Whitney asked.

'Yesterday, between the hours of midday and four.'

'Do you have anything else for us?' Whitney asked.

'No. You can go now. I'll be in touch once I have the tox screen back.' The pathologist dismissed them with a flick of her hand.

They left the lab, and on the way down the corridor, Whitney's phone pinged.

'It's a text from Ellie. She's sent through further details of the other two victims. Do you have to get to work or are you okay to come with?'

'I'm free. Where are we going?'

'The first victim, Nicola Hurst, was a housing associa-tion tenant in a block of flats in Windsor Terrace. Ellie has arranged for someone to meet us with a key, as her belong-ings are still there. We'd better get moving,' Whitney said, trying to ignore the building fear that right now they had more questions than answers.

Chapter Five

George stared at the modern three-storey red-brick building in Windsor Terrace, where Nicola Hurst had lived. Judging by the design and the periodic gable ends, she'd put it at no more than ten years old. She wasn't a big fan of modern architecture; she much preferred older properties.

By the front door stood a man, who looked to be in his twenties, dressed in a dark suit, white shirt, and light blue tie.

'Are you from Leda Housing?' Whitney asked.

'Yes,' he said.

'DCI Walker and Dr Cavendish, who works with the police.' Whitney held out her warrant card.

'Mark Davies. I'm the housing officer in charge of the six flats belonging to Leda in this block.'

'How many flats are there?' George asked.

'Thirty in total.'

'What's the situation regarding Nicola Hurst's flat? Why are her possessions still there?' Whitney asked.

'The family put in a request to be allowed until the end

of the month to clear her belongings, as the rent had been paid up until then. We agreed, on condition that it was vacated by midday on the thirtieth of September, as the next tenant is moving in on the first of October.'

He used a swipe card to let them into the building's vestibule. It was a modern spacious area with some easy chairs and a small coffee table alongside one of the walls. They followed him to the lift.

'It's on the third floor,' he said.

The lift was silent, and within a few seconds the door had opened, and they walked out onto a wooden floor. When they reached Flat 3A, he pulled out from his jacket pocket a key with a large white plastic fob.

'You can leave it with us, and we'll lock up when we've finished,' Whitney said.

'This is a master key, and I'm not allowed to let you take it. I can wait.'

'This could be a crime scene, and we don't want anyone else in here. You can wait downstairs.'

'I thought she'd committed suicide,' Mark said.

'We can't discuss an ongoing investigation. We'll see you in the entrance hall when we've finished,' Whitney said.

He left, and they walked into the flat. The front door led immediately into a large open-plan room, with kitchen, dining, and living area. All the walls were painted a light shade of ivory, and there was no artwork on them.

George headed over to the big picture window in the living area and looked out. 'What a delightful communal garden,' she said, admiring the trees, the brightly coloured flower borders, and the large stone bird bath situated in the middle of the grass. There was a decked area with some outdoor furniture.

Whitney joined her. 'Yes, it's lovely. Maybe I should

move into a place like this and have someone do the garden.'

'What do we know about the family? Has she had her funeral yet?' George asked.

'Ellie will have all those details. I'll speak to her after we've left here. Come on, let's take a look around the bedroom first.'

It was a spacious room, again painted ivory, with a rainbow tree chakra poster on the wall, which used the seven chakra colours as the tree's foliage. The furniture was minimal, with a double bed, a bedside set of drawers, a dressing table, and a wardrobe. All of them white.

Whitney handed George some disposable gloves and she pulled them on before starting to look around. She opened the top drawer of the bedside table and found a leaflet about a four-day programme to stop smoking, together with a letter confirming a place on the course, which had taken place six months previously. George read the leaflet with interest. The retreats they offered took place in a large country house out of town.

'This looks interesting,' she said.

'What does?' Whitney said.

'There's a leaflet for a course to stop smoking that the victim attended. I might investigate it further. For me.'

'What's prompted this? I thought you didn't have any intention of giving up, seeing as you don't smoke much.'

'I've been smoking more since working with you. I should give up, and a course like this would help.'

'And it's nothing to do with Ross not smoking?'

'How do you know he doesn't?' she responded, frowning.

'Does he?' Whitney asked, arching an eyebrow.

'No,' George was forced to admit.

'There you are, then. Anyway, are you sure she actually went on this course?'

'Yes. There's a confirmation letter here. She went in March, six months ago.'

'Confirmation of her place doesn't necessarily mean she attended,' Whitney said. 'We'll need to find out. Put the brochure and letter into an evidence bag.'

George did as she was told and then continued looking around the room. On the dressing table was a small stack of books, including *The Secret*, *The Power of Now*, and *The Road Less Traveled*. There was also one she hadn't heard of called *Enlighten Your Spirit*, by Troy Randall. She glanced down the list of contents and then looked at the author's biography. On first impression, it seemed very much like all the other books of its ilk, pedantic and one-sided. After putting it down, she opened the small wooden jewellery box on the dressing table. Inside were several pairs of silver earrings for pierced ears and some silver chains, including one which had a chakra pyramid hanging from it.

'She was definitely into self-help and spirituality,' George said.

'What makes you say that?' Whitney asked.

'The chakra poster on the wall, her choice of reading material, and also this necklace.' She held it up.

'It's pretty,' Whitney said.

'Each one of these stones corresponds to one of the seven chakras in the body.'

'How do you know this stuff?' Whitney asked.

'From my reading.'

'Since when have you been all spiritual?'

'I'm not, but that doesn't mean I know nothing about it. It's an interesting phenomenon,' she said.

'Is there anything you don't know?' Whitney shook her head.

'Plenty. Let's get on.'

Whitney opened the wardrobe drawer. 'Interesting. A yoga mat. Hayley Tennant went to yoga. We should check to see if they went to the same studio. It could be a link, however tenuous. In the meantime, we need to know more about Nicola Hurst.'

'Maybe her neighbours will be able to help?' George said.

'We'll see if there's anyone at home after we've finished looking. It's very sparse here. It's like she only used it as somewhere to sleep, and nothing else.'

Once they'd completed their search, finding nothing else of interest, Whitney knocked on 3B, the next door flat, but there was no answer. She crossed over to the other side of the corridor and pressed the bell for flat 3F. The door was answered by a small elderly woman with short grey permed hair.

'Good morning, I'm DCI Whitney Walker from Lenchester CID, and this is Dr Cavendish. We'd like to talk to you about your neighbour, Nicola.'

'It was so sad,' the woman replied, tears forming in her eyes. 'Such a young woman. No one should die at that age. Come in. I don't know if I can help, but I'll tell you what I can.'

'What is your name?' Whitney asked.

'Dorothy Fletcher.' She opened the door and ushered them in. 'Would you like a cup of coffee? I was about to make one.'

George looked at Whitney, noticing how her eyes had lit up. She never turned down a coffee when offered. If the detective didn't have her caffeine fix every few hours, she turned grumpy.

'That would be lovely. Milk, no sugar, please, Mrs Fletcher,' Whitney said.

'Call me Dorothy.'

'Same for me, too, please,' George said.

They walked further into the flat, which was the same layout as Nicola's. Only that was where the similarity ended. This was full of life and looked lived in. Photos adorned every surface and there were country scene paintings on the walls.

'Take a seat,' Dorothy said.

They sat on the grey and white patterned sofa.

'Have you lived here long?' Whitney asked.

'I moved in when the flats were first built ten years ago, after my husband died. It's a lovely place to live. Everyone is very kind and we all look out for each other.'

'How well did you know Nicola?'

'She was here for eighteen months, maybe longer. Time goes by quickly when you get older. For the first twelve months we'd see each other regularly. She'd call around for coffee and cake. She'd tell me all about her work and what was happening in her life.'

'Where did she work?' Whitney asked.

'In the office at a courier company, but she got made redundant in January. She couldn't get another job and had been on benefits ever since.'

'That must've been hard for her,' Whitney said.

'Yes, but it got worse once she finished with her boyfriend a few weeks after losing her job. They'd been together for two years. He found someone else. She was devastated.'

'It was fortunate she had you to talk to,' Whitney said.

'We spent a lot of time together after that. At least, we did for a while.' The woman hung her head.

'We found a leaflet for a stop smoking programme she went on in March. Do you know anything about that?' George asked.

'I can't tell you about the actual course, but I do know that after she returned, she'd totally changed.'

George nodded in Whitney's direction. They now had confirmation Nicola did actually attend the programme.

'In what way?' George asked.

'She stopped coming over for coffee, and every time I knocked on her door, when I knew she was in, she wouldn't answer. If I saw her in the corridor and invited her in, she turned me down, saying she was busy. It was very strange.'

'But the course was only for four days. Did she really change so much in such a short space of time?' Whitney asked.

'I didn't see her until three weeks after it had finished. I was on holiday when she got back.'

'Were you away for a long time?' Whitney asked.

'Four weeks. I went to Canada, to see my cousin. I knocked on Nicola's door the day I returned, but there was no reply.'

'Did she talk about the course before she went?' George asked.

'Yes, she was excited about it because she'd been wanting to quit for a long time. Someone had recommended it to her.'

'Do you know who?' Whitney asked.

'I don't. It might have been someone she used to work with.'

'How could she afford to go if she was on benefits?' George asked.

'I gave her the money because I could see how important it was to her,' Dorothy said, her cheeks going pink.

'A loan?' George asked.

'No. It was a present. I knew she wouldn't be able to pay me back. I didn't mind. I've got plenty of money. After my husband died, I was able to buy this flat outright. We didn't have children. Nicola was like a daughter to me until she cut me out of her life.'

'You must have been very upset when that happened,' Whitney said.

'Of course. But I wish I'd made more of an effort to find out what was wrong. If I had, she might still be alive. I had no idea she'd been depressed enough to take her own life.'

'You can't blame yourself,' Whitney said gently.

'I know, but it doesn't make it any easier.'

Dorothy walked towards them, carrying a tray with coffee and a plate of home-made biscuits.

'We noticed from Nicola's possessions she was quite spiritual,' George said.

'What do you mean?' Dorothy frowned.

'The books she was reading and several other items we found,' George said.

'That's very strange. She wasn't like that before,' Dorothy said.

'She had a yoga mat. Do you know which studio she used?' Whitney asked.

'Yoga? She didn't do yoga. We used to go walking, but that was the extent of her exercise.'

'What about her friends and family? Do you know them?' Whitney asked.

'She used to spend a lot of time with her boyfriend. After they finished, she didn't go out much, other than with me. Her family are in Rugby. She rarely mentioned them. All I know is her parents divorced when she was younger. She occasionally spoke to her mum, who still lives there and remarried.'

'Who found Nicola's body?' Whitney asked.

'One of her new friends.'

'I thought you didn't know any of her friends?' Whitney said, a small frown creasing her brow.

'I don't, but I did notice a young woman visiting her regularly. They'd often go out together.'

'When they went out, were they carrying yoga mats?' Whitney asked.

'I'm not sure. I'd see them through the peephole in my front door. All I could see was their heads.'

'What happened on the day she found Nicola?'

'I heard a scream and hurried out of the flat. The girl was standing in the doorway of Nicola's flat. She said Nicola had hanged herself, but she wouldn't let me in. I rushed back here to phone for an ambulance. They arrived fifteen minutes later with the police.'

'Did you go back to Nicola's flat to wait with the woman who found her?'

'Yes, but she'd gone. I wanted to go to the funeral but didn't know how to find out when and where it was.'

'Thank you, you've been very helpful.' Whitney stood, indicating she'd heard enough, and George followed.

'If you'd have asked me six months ago, I'd have said Nicola wasn't the type of person to commit suicide. But she'd changed so much I could've been wrong,' Dorothy said.

'If you think of anything else, please contact me.' Whitney pulled a card from her pocket and handed it to the old woman.

They left the flat and took the lift to the ground floor.

'We definitely need to find out more out about this course,' Whitney said. 'And how come she'd suddenly changed afterwards. Totally blanking the person who paid for her to attend doesn't make sense.'

They returned to the reception area, where Mark was waiting. Whitney handed over the key.

'Now where?' George asked, as they walked over to the car. 'Do we talk to Nicola's family or go to the second victim's house?'

'I'll speak to Ellie and decide.'

George drove while Whitney spoke to the officer.

Whitney finished the call and turned to her. 'Our second victim, Samantha Lyman, lived with her parents, and Nicola's mother is still in Rugby. I'm going to send Matt to visit her, and we'll go to Samantha's home. Then it's back to the station to get this investigation underway.'

Chapter Six

While George drove, Whitney pondered the case. It was very strange. Two women who didn't interact with others. Both had become withdrawn over the last few months. Could they be linked? They needed more information.

She had choir rehearsal tomorrow, but if they didn't sort this out, it would be unlikely she'd get there. She'd been looking forward to seeing Craig again. Maybe she'd be able to nip out to it. Her phone ringing distracted her.

'Walker.'

'It's Claire. I've got something for you.'

'I'm driving with George. I'll put you on speaker, so she can hear.'

She rested the phone on the dashboard.

'I've had the bloods back. The victim had been sedated.'

'I was right,' George said. 'What did they use?'

'Flunitrazepam. You'll know it as Rohypnol. There was also alcohol in her bloodstream. Red wine,' Claire said.

'There was nothing in her room to indicate she'd been drinking,' Whitney said.

'The wine could have been consumed elsewhere,' George said.

'Maybe downstairs in the lounge, although the two girls she lived with said she didn't ever go in there,' Whitney said.

'She could have been drugged while in a bar. Or the offender took away the glasses and bottle,' George suggested.

'Excuse me, I do have work to do,' Claire said. 'I can't sit here while you two debate the victim's movements.'

Whitney exchanged a glance with George, and they both smiled.

'Sorry, Claire. Was anything found in the blood of the other two victims?' Whitney asked.

'Nothing was sent to toxicology in either case.'

'Shit,' Whitney said. 'With the other two victims, if you took blood samples now, would you be able to find anything?'

'There wouldn't be any sign of this particular drug. It doesn't stay in the system for long. But I could still look for needle sites, in case they were drugged with an injection rather than orally.'

'We need you to examine them again,' Whitney said.

'The coroner has released both bodies to the families, so we don't know if they've been buried or cremated,' Claire said.

'If buried, we can ask for the bodies to be exhumed,' George said.

'You've more chance of finding unicorn poo than being allowed to do that, especially this early in an investigation when we have no hard evidence to back up our theory,' Whitney said.

'But surely they happen sometimes?'

'In extreme circumstances. We'd need permission from

the coroner if we were to request one, as it's part of a criminal investigation,' Whitney said.

'What about the cords used in the other two deaths, do you have them?' George asked.

'I've asked for them to be sent over. That's assuming the locum actually put them into the evidence store,' Claire said.

'Well, if the officer who found the bodies is correct, the cords should be identical to this one,' Whitney said.

'If it is murder, what can you tell us about the offender?' George asked.

'They were strong enough to lift the body and put it into the noose. They knew how to stage the scene and make it convincing. When I was there yesterday, there was a wastepaper bin on its side a few yards from the window. It was made to look like the victim had kicked it away so her body would drop,' Claire said.

'Do you think the offender is male?' George asked.

'Not necessarily, but it's likely, as men are usually stronger than women.'

'What about the other two deaths? Are there any similarities?' Whitney asked.

'I have the photos in front of me. On both bodies there was only a single ligature mark on the neck. A mark of a slip knot, the same as the latest one, which is suspicious, as not everyone knows how to tie a knot like that.'

'Nicola Hurst was found hanging on the back of the door. Do we know about Samantha Lyman?' Whitney asked.

'On a window latch, the same as the latest victim,' Claire said.

'Thanks. Whether that's enough to obtain permission to exhume the bodies remains to be seen.'

'Assuming they haven't been cremated,' Claire said as she ended the call.

'Okay, change of plan,' Whitney said. 'We need to get back to the incident room. After we've sorted everything out there, we'll go to see Samantha Lyman's parents.'

'Listen up, everyone.' Whitney didn't slow her pace until she'd reached the board. 'We're not dealing with suicides or suicide clusters. We now believe we have three murders on our hands.' She wrote Rohypnol under Hayley Tennant's name. 'Claire has confirmed the third victim was drugged and the suicide scene was staged.'

'What about the other two, guv?' Frank asked.

'Both bodies have been released to the families. What we don't know yet is whether they've had their funerals and, if so, were they buried or cremated? Ellie, I want you to find out straight away.'

'Yes, guv,' Ellie said.

'Unfortunately, Claire didn't do the PMs on the other two bodies, as there was a locum, and we don't have as much information as we'd like. In particular, bloods weren't sent to toxicology, so we have no idea whether they were given a sedative. However, judging by photographs of the bodies, the deaths were suspicious. There was bruising and lesions on both victims, which hadn't been picked up. Also, a similar knot was used on the noose for all of them. Claire will analyse the locum's findings and undertake further PMs on the other two bodies once we know whether they're available.'

'Do we know when she'll have any information for us?' Matt asked.

'You know Claire. It will be in her time. But I'm sure

she'll get it to us as soon as possible. For now, we have a lot to do. Matt, I'd like you to go to Rugby and speak to the family of Nicola Hurst. Take Sue with you. According to the neighbour, Nicola was only in contact with her mother. Ellie will give you the details. Also, the same neighbour commented on how much Nicola had changed over the last six months. She kept to herself and ended their friendship.'

'What happened six months ago?' Matt asked.

'She went on a stop smoking programme. Ellie, after you've found out about the bodies, I'd like you to look into this course. We've got a leaflet advertising it. We know from Hayley's family that she'd also become withdrawn from her loved ones over the last few months, and they had no idea why. She'd recently moved into a new house and her flatmates didn't really know her, so weren't much help. All we do know is, at the weekends, she spent the whole day doing yoga.'

'Yes, guv,' Ellie said.

'We believe Nicola Hurst also went to yoga classes, as we found a mat in her flat. Let's see if we can find anything connecting the two of them, other than them both becoming withdrawn and distant from their family and friends, and taking up yoga. Nicola had a new friend who we know nothing about. She'd disappeared before the police and ambulance arrived. Where are we on the background checks?'

'Nicola Hurst was on the Jobseekers Allowance. She worked at Express Couriers until being made redundant in January. I've looked at her social media presence, and up until about six months ago she regularly contributed. Since then there's been nothing, apart from a recent post where she was talking about how her life had changed spiritually and she believed today's secular society had no moral compass,' Ellie said.

'She used those exact words, did she?' George asked, her curiosity obviously spiked.

'Yes,' Ellie said.

'Why?' Whitney turned to study her.

'When I was looking at Hayley Tennant's books, I came across one called *Enlighten Your Spirit* by Troy Randall. I'm sure those words came from the description on the back.'

'Reading the same book doesn't seem like a strong link,' Matt said.

'Under normal circumstances I'd agree with you. It could be a coincidence, but you know my views on that. Can you quickly look up the book on Amazon, Ellie?' George asked.

The officer's fingers ran across her keyboard. 'I'm in his author's page. He comes from Dorset and now lives in the Lenchester area. He published the book himself in 2017.'

'Interesting. His is a rather specific genre of self-help, and the author isn't one I've heard of. If he was reputable in his field, particularly as he's local, I'm certain the university would have had him in for some seminars. Or he'd have done a signing in the campus Waterstone's, as students would be high on his target audience list. As it is, I think there's something here given the lifestyle changes the victims have made.'

'It's certainly worth checking. Look deeper into this Troy Randall chap ready for the next briefing please, Ellie. Frank, what have you got on Samantha Lyman?' Whitney asked.

'She taught at Oakford, the private girls' school in Lenchester.'

'Contact them and arrange for me to speak to the head teacher tomorrow. Anything else?'

'Her parents have retired and, according to the files, they didn't seem surprised by the suicide because she'd become withdrawn leading up to her death.'

'We had similar comments from the parents of Hayley Tennant. Doug, you did a check on Hayley. We know she worked for a professional association. What else did you find?' she asked the detective constable.

'Her social media accounts had photos of her with friends and family from a while ago, but nothing recent,' Doug said.

'Did she mention anything about yoga?' Whitney asked.

'I'll go through her pages again and check.'

'Frank, we need to look at CCTV footage in and around where all the victims lived, on the dates of their deaths. For Nicola Hurst, we're looking at the twenty-seventh of August. Samantha Lyman, the fourth of September, and Hayley Tennant, the eleventh. You can get their addresses from Ellie. Also, check whether there have been any other suicides in the Lenchester area recently. George and I are going to visit Samantha Lyman's family.' She checked her watch. It was almost lunchtime. 'Okay, we'll meet back here for a briefing at four. Any questions?'

No one had, so she left with George. 'I take it you're still okay to come with me?' she asked.

'Yes.'

'Good. I need your expertise on this. We have no idea whether there'll be more murders. The sooner we make a connection between all of them the better.'

Chapter Seven

On the way to the Lyman's house, in the Forest March area, Whitney heard from Ellie that Nicola Hurst's funeral was scheduled for the following week, which meant the body didn't need exhuming. The coroner had approved a second post mortem, and the funeral home would be delivering her body to Claire. She breathed a sigh of relief. It made their lives much easier.

The Lymans lived in a stone semi-detached Victorian property with a large, grassed, front garden. Whitney pushed open the dark green wooden gate and they walked up the path to the front door. She knocked using the brass knocker and within a few moments could hear footsteps. A man in his late sixties answered.

'Mr Lyman?' Whitney asked.

'Yes,' he replied.

'I'm DCI Whitney Walker and this is Dr Cavendish. We'd like to speak to you about your daughter Samantha.'

'Come in.' His face clouded over, and she could see him blinking away the tears.

He ushered them into the hallway and led them into a

beautiful, spacious sitting room with high ceilings and a large bay window. Floor to ceiling heavy red and gold curtains were secured by ornate brass holdbacks. A wrought iron fireplace was situated in the middle of the longest wall and, on top of the parquet floor, there was a thick oriental rug.

The woman sitting on the deep red and black upholstered sofa stood. She was tall, with blonde highlighted hair framing her strained face.

'The police are here to speak to us about Samantha.'

'Please sit down,' she said, gesturing to the two empty chairs. 'I'm Marj Lyman, and you've met my husband Peter.'

'I'm very sorry for your loss.' Whitney tensed, anxious to get this over with. It was hard for her to remain detached when facing distraught families. She waited as the couple collected themselves and then spoke. 'I'd like to ask you some questions about Samantha, if you feel up to it?'

'As we've already told the other officers, Samantha had been acting out of character for quite a few months,' Mrs Lyman said. 'I keep going over everything. Could I have done more to stop it from happening? I thought maybe she'd been having trouble at work which she didn't want to share. I had no idea she'd considered taking her own life. I'll never forgive myself for not doing more.'

'You have to stop blaming yourself,' Mr Lyman said.

'How can I not? We were on holiday at the time it happened. If we hadn't gone away, she might have confided in us, and we could've stopped her.' Her voice cracked, and her husband put his arm around her shoulders.

'Have you had Samantha's funeral yet?' Whitney asked gently.

'It's on Saturday at the crematorium, just a small family affair,' Mr Lyman said.

'I'm sorry, but we have to ask you to delay it,' Whitney said.

'Why?' Mrs Lyman asked.

'Due to a recent suspicious death, we have reason to believe Samantha may not have committed suicide. We need our forensic pathologist to carry out a second post mortem to ensure nothing was missed during the first. Two other women have died in almost identical circumstances to Samantha within the last two weeks, and we want to make sure her death is investigated properly.'

'Are you saying she was murdered?' Mr Lyman asked.

'That's what we're investigating. You mentioned Samantha had changed recently. Can you pinpoint the exact time this happened?'

'Yes,' Mrs Lyman said. 'A few months ago, she went on a wellness retreat. She'd always carried a few extra pounds and thought something like this would help her change her lifestyle choices and she'd lose weight.'

'How long was the retreat for?' Whitney asked.

'Two weeks. She was a teacher and she went during the Easter holidays.'

'Can you explain the difference in Samantha when she returned?' Whitney asked.

'She didn't want to talk about the retreat when she got back, even though she'd talked about nothing else beforehand. She'd definitely lost some weight and continued taking yoga classes at the centre where the retreat was held. She went every weekend.'

Yoga. The link had to be yoga.

'Was it a continuation of the retreat?'

'I don't know. Possibly. She didn't say.'

'When you say she became reclusive, can you describe exactly how her behaviour was?' Whitney said.

'She stopped going out with her friends. She stopped laughing and telling jokes. It was like she'd been brainwashed. Apart from work, she didn't go out during the week and spent the evenings in her room meditating or reading. At the weekend, on both days, she'd go out first thing and come back around nine at night.'

'Which books did she read?' George asked.

'Not her usual reading material. She'd always loved crime thrillers, but she'd started reading all this new age stuff,' Mrs Lyman said.

'In the past, she always laughed at people who were into that,' Mr Lyman added.

'Do you know the names of these books?' George asked.

'They're in her bedroom; I can't tell you what they are,' Mrs Lyman said. 'I don't go into her bedroom often.'

'Who found Samantha?' Whitney asked.

'It was our cleaner, Lottie, who comes in on a Wednesday morning. She went into Samantha's room expecting her to be at work and found her. She phoned the police and they contacted us. We came straight home.'

'Would you mind if we went up to Samantha's bedroom to take a look? We'd also like to interview Lottie if you can let me have her telephone number.'

'It's upstairs, first on the right. I'll have Lottie's details when you come back down,' Mrs Lyman said.

'Another retreat and yoga. Is that the link?' Whitney whispered to George as they climbed the stairs.

'It appears to be. We need to find out all we can about the place,' George replied.

She handed George some disposable gloves, and they started looking through Samantha's bedroom. It was a pleasant square room with an open fireplace. She had an oak, queen-sized bed with a matching wardrobe, dressing table, and chest of drawers. On the windowsill were two photographs, one of Samantha in her graduation cap and gown standing between her parents. They all appeared relaxed and happy. The other looked more recent, and she was standing with a group of people.

'I wonder if this is from the retreat?' Whitney picked up the photograph and put it into an evidence bag.

George was standing by the bed with a book in her hand. 'This is the same book Nicola Hurst had. *Enlighten Your Spirit* by Troy Randall.'

'Put it in an evidence bag and I'll get forensics onto it. If this is the link, our killer could have given it to her,' Whitney said.

They continued searching the room. From under the bed George pulled out a box file. 'Here are all her receipts and invoices. She wasn't very methodical, everything's thrown in, but there's a brochure for the retreat her parents mentioned.'

Whitney walked over and took it out of George's hand. The brochure showed 'before' and 'after' photos of attendees. A beautiful country home stood proud in the background. The same house as in the brochure for the programme to stop smoking.

'I wouldn't mind going here for some healthy living advice,' Whitney said.

'Why?'

'Because you could hardly call my lifestyle healthy. Then again, to have one would mean learning how to cook, and I don't have the time. Perhaps I won't go.'

'I could teach you,' George said.

'I still don't have the time.'

'You could make time,' George pushed.

'Not at the moment.' By the side of the bed there was a laptop leaning against the drawers. She picked it up and put it into an evidence bag. 'We'll take this with us. I wonder where her phone is?'

'The dressing table.' George handed it to her, and Whitney placed it into a different evidence bag.

Once they'd finished going through the room, they went downstairs to speak to Mr and Mrs Lyman and collect the cleaner's details.

'We'll be in touch and let you know what's happening with our enquiries. We're taking Samantha's phone, laptop, a photograph, and the wellness retreat brochure with us,' Whitney said.

'Will someone be coming here to take fingerprints?' Mr Lyman asked.

'No. You've had the cleaner in and it's been over a week. We're unlikely to find any usable evidence. Here's my card. Please feel free to contact me at any time if you have any questions or think of anything else that might help us. We'll let you know as soon as we can release Samantha's body back to you,' Whitney said.

'Thank you,' Mr Lyman said, taking it from her.

'Will they feel better knowing it's murder and not suicide, do you think?' Whitney asked once they'd reached George's car.

'It's not going to bring her back, but it will certainly help them stop blaming themselves.'

'Come on. Let's get back and start putting some of this together.'

Chapter Eight

George removed her jacket and left it with her handbag on the desk in front of the board. She scanned the room for Whitney and saw her heading in the direction of Ellie's desk. She followed her over.

'Here's Samantha's phone,' Whitney said. 'See what you can get from the self-service kiosk. I want to know who she'd been in contact with in the months leading up to her death. Especially from when she went on the wellness retreat. Also, here's her laptop. Send it to Mac in Digital Forensics.'

'Yes, guv,' Ellie said.

'What have you discovered about the stop smoking course?'

'I've checked it out and it's held at the Wellness Spirit Centre about ten miles out of the city.'

'And what do we know about the centre itself?'

'I'm looking into it at the moment, guv. I've been on their website and they offer lots of programmes, from healthy lifestyle and weight loss to stopping smoking and yoga. They use hypnotherapy treatments in all of their offerings. I tried to contact them, but there's an out-of-hours message saying the centre is closed until Tuesday next week, as they're on their annual staff retreat. They didn't say where it was.'

'Well, it's looking like that's our link. We found this health and wellness retreat brochure in Samantha Lyman's room. All three victims attended a programme there. Does the site give any information on the owners or event organisers?'

'It was setup by a guru called Troy Randall … the author of the book *Enlighten Your Spirit*,' Ellie said.

'Listen up, everyone,' Whitney said. 'We've made a positive connection between our victims. Two of them attended a programme at the Wellness Spirit Centre, which Ellie has discovered is run by Troy Randall. All three have knowledge of his book. We need to confirm whether the centre was where victim three went to yoga classes. I want someone to help Sue with checks on Troy Randall, the leader of the centre.'

'I'll do it, guv,' Ellie said.

'Thanks. Where are we with the CCTV footage, Frank?' Whitney asked the officer.

'There are quite a few cameras close to the block of flats where Nicola Hurst lived. It's a busy area, and there were people coming and going all the time around the date of the murder. With the other two victims, because they lived in relatively quiet streets, we weren't able to get so lucky. The closest CCTV cameras were on the main roads.'

'See if you can identify any similar cars close to each area a few hours leading up to their deaths, probably up to twelve, as we don't yet know time of death for the first two victims. We're waiting on Claire for that information.'

'Do we have a time of death for Hayley Tennant?' Frank asked.

'Yes, it's yesterday between the hours of midday and 4 p.m.,' Whitney replied. 'Did you arrange for us to visit the school where Samantha Lyman taught?'

'Yes. It's fine for you to go tomorrow, but the head teacher did say all the staff are in now for a training day, if you wanted to go over. School doesn't officially start until Monday.'

'I thought schools had already gone back,' Whitney said.

'Private schools have longer holidays,' George said.

'So, you pay for the privilege of having shorter terms. How ironic is that?' Whitney said, a wry grin on her face.

'It's how it's always been,' George replied, not rising to the bait, knowing it was just Whitney being her usual self.

'I have time to go now. What about you, George? I'd rather you were with me, as you're the expert on these sorts of places.'

'Yes, I'm available,' she said without giving it much thought. It looked like she wasn't going to make it into work today. She'd go in tomorrow. At a meeting she was at recently, one of her colleagues had made a sarcastic comment about her being a part-timer. She'd ignored it, but she still needed to tread carefully. Her activities with the police could be curtailed if her superiors deigned. But if they tried, she'd put up a fight. None of her work had suffered. Her students were doing well, and her research was making an impact on the national stage, which meant kudos to both her and the university.

'And definitely in your car,' Whitney said, cutting across her thoughts. 'It's such a posh school we don't want to stand out in my crapped-out old Ford.'

She debated explaining that Whitney's car would be

fine but changed her mind. Whitney wouldn't believe her that not all rich people drove new cars and wore designer clothing.

'Of course,' she replied.

'Okay, let's go. I'll see you all later,' Whitney said to the team.

As they headed out of the station, George's phone rang. She glanced at the screen. 'It's my brother. I'll keep it brief. Hello, James,' she said.

'Deanna and I would like to meet your sculptor guy before the wedding,' his voice boomed into her ear. He couldn't sound more like her father if he'd tried.

'I'm not sure that's going to be possible. Ross is very busy at the moment. As am I.'

'I'm sure you can fit in a lunch. Are you free a week on Saturday? We'll drive to you. We can go to the restaurant owned by Father's patient. My assistant will book us a table.'

George knew the place well. It was where she'd met Ross. He'd been helping out his friend, the owner, and had been their waiter when she was there with her parents.

'Have Mother and Father put you up to this?' she asked, knowing how they operated.

'It doesn't matter. We'd like to meet him.'

'I'll confirm after speaking to him.' She ended the call.

'Trouble?' Whitney asked.

'This bloody wedding. My brother and his fiancée want to meet Ross beforehand. It's my parents interfering, wanting to make sure he's not going to let the side down.'

'Are you going?'

'I'll check with Ross. As much as I don't want to, the fall out if we don't would be worse. I'll quickly text him.' Almost immediately he responded, agreeing. 'He's said yes. I'll confirm with my brother and then we can leave.'

She texted James, and then they left the station, driving the ten miles to Oakford School, which was situated in large grounds in a rural area outside of the city. The campus was attractive, with grounds looking remarkably like Capability Brown had designed them, with their natural style and sweeping lawns. The main building was an old castle dating back to the 1600s. As they drove up the long drive, they could see the sports fields in the distance to the right, a chapel to the left, and the commanding castle facing them.

'Wow. I can't believe this is a school,' Whitney said. 'It beats North Lenchester Comprehensive, where I went, which was built in the sixties and is an ugly, characterless building. Did you go somewhere this grand?'

'My school had a rich history, stretching back hundreds of years, and was also a castle before being turned into a country home, and then a school. The façade was magnificent, but in my time it was in need of extensive modernisation. There was no heating in the dorms, and we'd freeze in winter.'

'I thought it was where the really posh sent their kids.'

'They relied on their reputation in attracting students. Plus, living like that was meant to be character building.'

'I wonder what it's like here?'

'I don't know; I haven't been before. But I agree with you, the setting is magnificent.'

When they arrived, they walked up the stone steps through a large white wooden door into a stone-floored entrance hall, lined with portraits with name plaques underneath. They were the school's head teachers going back two hundred years. A huge mural was on the wall facing them.

'That's amazing,' Whitney said.

'It looks like a Pellegrini to me,' George said, staring at

the painting of a seventeenth century woman in fine costume, next to a young child. 'Even though it's oil on plaster, its quality is undeniable.'

'Seriously, is there anything you don't know?'

'I've seen his work before. He painted murals in quite a few castles and country homes in England during the eighteenth century.'

'I didn't expect to visit a school and have an art history lesson.' Whitney laughed. 'Then again, this is you.'

They followed the directional sign to the school office and, when they got there, Whitney knocked on the open door and they walked in. An older woman with auburn hair cut into a long bob was sitting at a desk in front of a computer screen.

'I'm DCI Whitney Walker and this is Dr George Cavendish. We've come to see the head teacher.'

'If you'd like to take a seat, I'll let Mrs Richardson know you're here.'

The woman gestured to two chairs against the wall in her office and then walked through the adjoining door.

She returned shortly. 'Please come through,' she said, stepping to the side for them to walk past. She closed the door behind them.

The office was large, with wood panelling and a high ornate ceiling. Large picture windows overlooked the grounds of the school. A woman sitting behind an antique desk stood and walked towards them.

'Good afternoon, I'm Mrs Richardson.'

'I'm DCI Walker and this is Dr Cavendish. We'd like to speak to you about Samantha Lyman.'

'Such a tragedy. The entire school was shocked. Take a seat over there.' She gestured to a low round table, situated by the window, with four easy chairs around it.

'How long had Samantha worked here?' Whitney asked once the woman had sat opposite.

'She'd been here six years and taught history in the senior school. She was also form mistress to the first years. She was very good with the new entrants.'

'What was she like as a teacher?'

'Exceptional. Both students and staff loved her. She always worked over and above what was required. She had time for everyone until …' She paused.

'Until what?' Whitney asked.

'After the Easter holidays this year, she was different.'

'In what way?'

'Not with the children. She was still excellent with them and worked hard. She was different with her colleagues. She started keeping to herself and didn't go out on any of our *jollies*.'

'Do you know she went on a wellness retreat at that time, during the holidays?' Whitney asked, looking like she was trying not to roll her eyes at the mention of the word "jollies".

'I didn't know personally, but after she'd died, those who'd been close to her mentioned it. I remember noticing when she came back for the start of the summer term, how healthy and in good shape she looked. We were all devastated when we heard the news. Although she'd distanced herself, we had no idea she was suicidal. A number of us felt very guilty for not recognising it.'

Whitney bit down on her bottom lip. George wondered if she was going to mention they were treating it as murder? It might be a good idea, as someone at the school could have relevant information. She wasn't entirely sure of the protocol.

'We're no longer treating Samantha's death as suicide. New information has come to light, and we now believe it to be a murder. This isn't public knowledge, as we're waiting for conformation from the pathologist,' Whitney said.

Mrs Richardson drew in a sharp breath. 'Murder? That's dreadful.'

'We'd like to speak to the colleagues you mentioned she was close to.'

The head teacher got up from her chair, walked over to the door, and opened it. 'Mrs Browne. Please could you ask Miss Latimer and Mrs Frost to come to my office, as DCI Walker would like to speak to them.'

'While we're waiting for the other staff members, please could you explain more about how Samantha had changed,' Whitney asked.

'When I said she was distant, it was because of the difference between how she was before the holidays and when she came back. She still spoke to people, attended meetings, and contributed when necessary. And, as I've already said, she was very good with the children. But that aside, her whole demeanour had changed. Before, she would engage you in conversation if she saw you and would always be smiling and happy. After the holidays she didn't seem unhappy, but instead she was more reserved and thoughtful. In a way she looked peaceful, and certainly not troubled.'

'Did she have a partner?' Whitney asked.

'Not as far as I know. She certainly didn't bring anyone to school functions. Her colleagues may be able to tell you more. As head, I don't get to know everything that goes on.'

There was a knock at the door. 'Come in,' Mrs Richardson called.

Two women walked in. A younger one wearing jeans and a shirt, her light-brown hair hanging loose over her shoulders, and one in her fifties, wearing a floral print dress.

'You wanted to see us?' the older woman said.

'Yes, this is DCI Walker and Dr Cavendish. They would like to speak to you about Samantha. Should I leave?'

'Yes, please,' Whitney said.

The head teacher left, and the two teachers sat next to Whitney and George.

'Please could I have your names?' Whitney asked.

'I'm Ruth Latimer,' the older of the two said.

'And I'm Lisa Frost,' the younger one said.

'We're investigating the circumstances surrounding the death of Samantha Lyman, and Mrs Richardson mentioned you were both close to her.'

The teachers exchanged a glance.

'What do you mean *circumstances*?' Lisa said. 'She committed suicide.'

'We're not sure that is the case, now. We've been informed Samantha changed after going on a wellness retreat during the Easter holidays. What can you tell us about it?' Whitney looked at the younger teacher.

'She'd been excited about going. She wanted me to go too, but my husband had already arranged a holiday. We spoke on the phone the evening before she went. For the first couple of days she texted, telling me what they'd done. After that, the texts stopped. I still texted her every day until she'd been there for ten days.'

'What happened to make you stop?' Whitney asked.

'She asked me not to contact her and said she'd see me on her return. It was very terse and not like her usual chatty texts, which were full of emojis.' The young teacher paused, a distant expression on her face.

'And when she came back?' Whitney asked.

'On the first day we returned to work, I spoke to her. But she didn't want to share anything about the retreat other than to say it was life changing. I asked her how, but she wouldn't elaborate. From then on, she was always polite, but never chatty, and certainly didn't confide in me like she used to. I wondered if she'd met a guy there, but when I asked her, she said no. I wish I'd never told her about the place.'

'How did you find out about it?' Whitney asked.

'I saw an advert in *Looking Good*.'

George knew the magazine. An upmarket, monthly glossy which was attached to the local newspaper.

'Why did you show it to Samantha?'

'She'd been complaining about putting on weight, saying she wanted to get herself fit. The retreat seemed perfect. Like I said, she wanted me to go with, but I couldn't. Do you think her death was connected to the retreat?'

'We have several lines of enquiry, so it's too early to say,' Whitney said.

The teacher slumped in her chair.

Whitney turned to the older woman. 'What can you tell us about Samantha?'

'I don't have a lot to add. Everything Lisa said, I found, too. She was a lovely girl. Whatever happened at this retreat wasn't good. Yes, she came back looking great, but it wasn't worth it when you consider the outcome.'

'Thank you, you've both been a great help, and if you think of anything else you'd like to tell us, please get in touch. Here's my card.' Whitney handed it to Lisa.

The two women left the room.

'What do you think?' Whitney asked George.

'Something's going on at this Wellness Spirit Centre, and Tuesday can't come soon enough.'

Chapter Nine

The following day, Whitney left work at two to attend an afternoon choir rehearsal. She'd left Matt and Ellie at the station examining the bank accounts of the three dead women. She wanted confirmation they'd all paid into the account belonging to the wellness centre to strengthen the link between them. Ellie was looking at the women's social media accounts. Had they added new friends recently, and if so, who were they? Also, did they have any friends in common?

Conscious of the overtime budget at this early stage, and without anything concrete to help them, she'd given the rest of the team the day off. Once they'd visited the centre on Tuesday, she'd be better placed to allocate their resources, and she knew that days off would be a distant memory.

It was a joint rehearsal with Banbury again, arranged at the last minute because so many had missed the one earlier in the week. Hardly surprising seeing as it had started at five and many of them worked and weren't able to get away. Was Craig going to be there? Not that it mattered. Well, that's what she told herself. She headed to her position in the front line because of her solo.

Craig wasn't there. Her heart sank a little until she told herself not to be stupid. He wasn't the reason for her going. She wanted to sing. She took out her folder and placed it on her lap. The room had filled up and Liz called them all to attention. She wanted to run through Whitney's solo first.

A bang of the door distracted her, and Craig came running in. He apologised and took his place on the right-hand side of the group with the bass section. He caught her eye and smiled.

The conductor coughed and signalled the start of the song. She took a deep breath and focused on the first note. And then everything was forgotten as the music took over. Once she'd finished singing, she stupidly glanced at Craig. He was smiling broadly and clapping. Warmth rushed up her cheeks. Crap. She hadn't blushed since being at school. This was ridiculous. She pulled herself together and from then on kept her eyes firmly fixed on Liz.

After the rehearsal, she grabbed her bag and was heading out of the door when Craig came up beside her.

'Hi,' he said, smiling.

'Hello,' she replied casually, not wanting to show how pleased she was he'd turned up.

'Do you have time for a coffee, or are you going to be called back to work?' he asked.

She'd hoped he'd ask her, even though she didn't have much time.

'Yes, that would be nice,' she said, glancing at her watch. 'I can spare half an hour.' She'd planned on taking her brother, Rob, who was in a home for people with learning difficulties, to visit their mum, who had dementia and was in a care home. Tiffany was away camping with friends, so she couldn't ask her to take him instead.

She hated that she wasn't able to have her mum and brother living with her, but they needed twenty-four-hour care, and with her job it was impossible. They were in wonderful places and were both happy. That didn't stop the guilt, though. George would tell her to get over it because they were in the right places. But it was easy for her to say. She'd never been in that situation.

'We'd better get going, then. I don't want to get in the way of your busy lifestyle,' Craig said.

Was he being sarcastic? She glanced at him and saw he was grinning.

'I've got family commitments,' she said, for some reason deciding to qualify her comments.

'Is there a café nearby?' he asked.

'Yes, this way.'

They left the rehearsal room and crossed the road to a small café opposite. It was one of her favourites and dated back to the fourteenth century. It had a curved vaulted ceiling. It stood next to St Benedict's Church, which had long been a tourist attraction for being the oldest church in the area to have a pointed spire. She pushed open the heavy dark wooden door and the smell of fresh coffee invaded her senses. She stopped herself from groaning in ecstasy just in time. She didn't think it would look good.

'Grab a table and I'll order,' Craig said.

'Okay, I'll have …' He'd already gone to the counter before she could tell him. How did he know what she wanted? He wasn't to know that coffee in any shape or form would hit the spot.

She found a table by the window and sat down, hanging her handbag on the back of the old wooden chair. This had always been a popular café, and had become even more so since the latest owner, from Italy, had taken over. The cakes they baked on the premises were to die for.

After several minutes, he returned holding a wooden spoon with a number on it. He sat opposite.

'I ordered you a flat white, is that okay? So many different coffees to choose from. I didn't realise.'

What planet was he from? He sounded like her mother.

'Yes, that's fine,' she replied.

'Tell me about your family. You mentioned having family commitments,' he said.

She didn't want to go into too much detail, as she hardly knew him. And she certainly wasn't prepared to discuss her guilt regarding her mum and Rob, even though she understood their needs came first and it wasn't all about her.

'I'm going to see my mum. She's in a care home, and I'm taking my brother with me.'

'How old is your brother?'

'He's thirty-five.'

'Does he have any family? Do you have any nieces and nephews running around?'

'No, I don't. Unfortunately, Rob has learning difficulties and is in a special care facility.'

So much for not telling him.

'I'm sorry to hear that. It must be hard with both of them in care. Especially as you have such a demanding job.'

'It has its moments, but I manage to juggle everything,' she said, crossing fingers behind her back.

'What about your father?' Craig asked.

'What's this? Twenty questions? I thought I was the police officer and good at interrogation.'

He held his hands up in mock surrender. 'I'm sorry.

I'm just interested. Sometimes I do come across as being nosy.'

'That's the first time I've heard a man describe himself as nosy.' She laughed. 'It's fine. Why don't you tell me about you and your family?'

'Okay, I was born in Guildford and have four sisters. My mum and dad still live there.'

'Four,' she exclaimed. 'That must've been interesting when growing up.'

'Yes. They're older than me, and I would hear all about their boyfriends and social life. Being surrounded by females is what got me interested in nutrition. There was always talk of diets and food.'

'I wish I had time to take more care of myself, but with my lifestyle it tends to be fast food most of the time. I don't think about supplements, apart from in winter when I occasionally take vitamin C to stop me from getting a cold.'

'I can sort you out some supplements. The ones I import are the very best.'

'We'll see,' Whitney said, not wanting to commit herself. 'Tell me how come you joined the rock choir. It's mainly women.'

'Two of my sisters belong to the one in Guildford and thought I'd enjoy it. I love singing, and decided to give it a try. I've been in the choir for about twelve months.'

'And getting lots of attention from all the women members,' she said, laughing.

'There are hardly any men in the choir, so yes, that's true. I also have the occasional solo if there are any for bass voices. I can't be compared with you, though. I'm in awe of your talent.'

'Well, I'm sure there are things you excel at.' She smiled at him.

'Tennis is my thing. Do you play?'

'A little, but not much since school.'

'Would you like to play again sometime?'

Would she? When she'd said she played a little, that was an exaggeration. She'd rarely played racket sports. At school she was more interested in playing hockey. She'd whack the bigger girls on their ankles when they got too close.

'I don't have the time. We're currently very busy at work.'

'Ah, yes. The last time we met, you were called away. What case are you working on?'

'I can't discuss ongoing investigations.'

'Do you have many murders around here?'

She looked at him and frowned. It was an odd question to ask. Although people liked to know about her work, they didn't automatically think of murders.

'Lenchester is the same as any other big city. We have our serious crimes.'

'Banbury does, too. Although on a lesser scale because it's not as large. If you're in CID, you must deal with all the murders.'

'Yes, murders do come under our remit.'

'I bet it's interesting work. I love the documentaries on Netflix which look into the minds of killers. I don't suppose you watch anything like that because it's too close to home.'

'I don't have Netflix, or the time to watch television, as we work long hours. But—' Her mobile ringing interrupted her. She glanced at the screen. It was her boss, Jamieson. What the hell did he want? 'Sorry, I have to take this.'

She headed outside.

'Walker.'

'It's Tom,' Jamieson said.

Tom? He'd never referred to himself by his first name before. And what was he doing phoning on a Saturday? She hadn't seen him at the station.

'Yes, sir?'

'I've just come into the office. I thought you'd be here, as we've got a murder enquiry. I—'

'I took a couple of hours off,' she said, interrupting him. She waited for the bollocking.

'This isn't a reprimand, Whitney.'

Whitney? She pinched herself on the arm to make sure she wasn't dreaming.

'How can I help you, sir?'

'I'd like to talk to you away from the station. Can you meet me at the Crown pub?'

She glanced at her watch. She could hardly say no … he was her superior officer. She'd have to leave Craig and hope the meeting didn't take long. She wanted to be at her mum's before dinner was served.

'I can be there in half an hour.'

The pub Jamieson wanted to meet at was a couple of streets away from the station. It was quiet and where the team went when they didn't want a lot of noise. She hoped it wasn't anything serious, like an illness.

'Thank you. I'll see you there soon.' He ended the call and she stood staring at her phone. It had to rank as one of the weirdest calls she'd ever had.

She went back into the café and over to the table. The coffee had been delivered. He'd also bought them both a chocolate muffin. She certainly wasn't going to waste that, either.

'Work?' Craig asked.

'Yes. I've got to go in.'

'Straight away?'

'Not until I've drunk my coffee and eaten the muffin.' She smiled.

'Would you like to come out to dinner with me sometime?'

'I've been called away both times we've been together. Are you sure you want to risk it happening again?' She didn't know why she'd said that because, actually, she would like to go out with him.

'I'm hoping it's third time lucky.' He flashed a cheeky grin, and she found herself returning it.

'In that case, yes. I'd love to.'

'When?'

'Give me your phone number and I'll check my diary and text you.'

She finished her coffee and cake and got up to leave.

'Let me see you to your car,' Craig said.

They walked past the rehearsal room and down the adjacent side road where she'd parked.

'This is my old banger,' she said, feeling somewhat embarrassed at the state of her old Ford. She couldn't afford a new one as she had a mortgage to pay and Tiffany's university expenses to help with.

'As long as it gets you from A to B,' he said, patting it on the roof.

'I really must go. I'll text you the dates I'm available.'

He leaned forward and kissed her on the cheek. 'I'm looking forward to it.'

Feeling the heat rise up her cheeks, she quickly unlocked the door and got in. She didn't want to blush in his presence. She'd never been one for blushing, and she didn't want to start now.

She drove away and could see him watching in her rear-view mirror. What would George make of her arranging a date?

Chapter Ten

As Whitney arrived at the pub carpark, Jamieson pulled up behind her.

'Hello, sir,' she said, once they'd got out of their cars.

'We're away from work, so please call me Tom.'

They walked in silence into the pub and up to the bar.

'What would you like?' he asked.

'A lemonade please, sir. I mean Tom.' His name stuck in her throat. Saying it out loud was most odd.

He ordered their drinks, and they headed to a table in the corner.

'Cheers,' he said, holding up his pint glass and then downing half of it in one go.

'What's this all about?' she asked, unable to keep quiet any longer. *Or* call him Tom.

Nothing about this situation was normal. Their relationship had only been conducted in the office before.

'Can't I take my DCI out for a drink?'

'You've never done it before. Nor have you asked me to call you Tom. Neither have you ever called me Whitney. So, what's going on?'

His eyes momentarily flashed with guilt. Then he coughed, as if trying to pull himself together.

'I want to ask you a favour,' he said.

'What?'

'As you know, my wife left me and the girls earlier in the year.'

She remembered clearly when he'd told her. She'd been taken aback that he'd confided in her about his personal life. He'd never mentioned it again. She didn't envy him having two hormonal teenage girls to deal with.

'Yes.'

'I'm having a lot of difficulties with my younger daughter, Alex.'

'What sort of difficulties?'

'She refuses to eat because she's on a diet. She thinks she's fat, but she isn't. I need to be at home more, to sort this out. I want to take her to see someone. But it's hard in this job, as you know.'

'I'm sure if you explain to the Deputy Chief Constable, she'll understand if you need to take time off. Some parental leave.'

'I can't let her know. I want to start applying for Chief Superintendent positions, and if I have time off with family issues, it could get in the way.'

'How do I fit into this?'

The irony of the situation didn't escape her. He was always criticising her ability to divorce her family life from her work and on several occasions had questioned her ability to lead investigations because of it.

'I thought you could help. That you'd understand because of your family situation.'

'I don't let it interfere with my work,' she said in a sharp voice.

He flinched. 'That wasn't what I meant. Sorry.'

And now he was apologising to her. The whole situation was getting more bizarre by the second.

'That's fine, sir. How can I help?'

'I'd like you to take over some of the administrative tasks I have on at the moment. There are several reports that need writing, and the occasional meeting to attend. I can make myself available to advise you if necessary. But I'm too stretched to do them myself.'

So, despite the fact he'd complained she didn't have the time to do her job properly, he was now doubling her workload.

'You do know we're in the middle of a murder investigation, which will take up all my time?'

'Slight exaggeration. You weren't at work this afternoon.'

Boom. Back to the old Jamieson in a matter of seconds.

'It's my day off,' she reminded him. 'I had a choir rehearsal.'

'You sing in a choir?'

'When I can get there. We're rehearsing for a big concert in November.'

'Well done.' Did he mean to sound so patronising?

'Thank you.'

'Do you have capacity?'

What if she said no?

'How many hours a week are we talking about?'

She wasn't being entirely unselfish. She'd love for him to be promoted and out of her hair. If she could help, she was all for it.

'It's difficult to quantify. I do have on my desk a report that needs to be done by next week. I've made some preliminary notes, which I will pass on to you.'

'And this is to go out in your name, I assume?'

He averted his gaze, for once looking embarrassed. 'Yes, it will bear my name, but I'll make sure you're credited for assisting me.'

Perhaps she should get that in writing.

'Okay, I'll do it.'

She hoped this wasn't a decision she'd regret.

Chapter Eleven

George walked into the station, her mind focused on Troy Randall's book *Enlighten Your Spirit*, which she'd ordered online and had been reading. It was far more than the pedantic diatribe she'd first thought. Embedded in the language were hypnotic cues which acted as commands, repeated throughout the text. It was extremely manipulative.

Someone behind her was whistling a bar of a song she didn't recognise, and she slowed her pace as she turned to see a familiar figure striding towards her.

'Whitney,' she called.

The whistling stopped, and Whitney gave her a broad smile. 'Hello. I didn't notice you there.'

'You're very cheerful today,' George said.

'Am I?'

'Yes. The whistling. The smile. The bright eyes. Even I could tell, and you know my struggle with social cues. How was your weekend?'

'Let's just say it was good.'

'I'm glad,' George said.

'Only you would be happy with that response,' Whitney replied. 'Most other people would push to find out more.'

'It's up to you if you want to tell me.'

Whitney sighed. 'Of course I want to tell you. I've met someone.'

'What do you mean?'

'I met a guy at choir rehearsal last week, and we got together afterwards, but I got called away. On Saturday he was at rehearsal again, we went out afterwards, and the same thing happened.'

'How frustrating.'

'It was, but he's asked me out to dinner, and I've agreed to go. We haven't set a date yet.'

'That's very nice.'

'Is that all you've got to say? Don't you want to know what he looks like? What he does? Anything else?'

'That seems to be the way you operate. Tell me: what does he look like?'

'He's not very tall, but taller than me. He's got lovely smiling eyes and, from what little I've seen of him, I think it's going to be fun. One thing in his favour is he didn't crack those awful police jokes when he found out about my job.'

'I'm happy for you. How are you going to fit seeing him in between the murder enquiry and your family?'

'What are you, my conscience?' Whitney said.

'I just wondered.'

'I'll manage, don't you worry.'

They arrived at the incident room and pushed open the door. Many of the team were already sitting at their desks working.

'What are the plans? I need to go into the university at some point. If only to be seen,' she said.

'Are you having issues?' Whitney asked.

'Juggling the university with our work here isn't always easy.'

'I thought you had permission to be with us,' Whitney said, her brow furrowed.

'I do, but not at the expense of everything else.'

'After the briefing, we'll go to BATT and interview Hayley Tennant's colleagues. I want to see how it fits in with what her parents told us. I think that's the best use of our time, as we can't go to the Wellness Spirit Centre until tomorrow. I'm interested to hear your reaction to the place.'

'Unfortunately, I can't go with you as I'm tied up until four. Unless you wait until then to go?'

'That will be too late. I'll take Matt instead,' Whitney said.

'While you're there, see what you can find out about the stop smoking course.'

Whitney stared at her. 'This isn't a social visit, you know.'

'I realise that. I just want to know more.' She guessed that did come across as being rather unprofessional. But now she'd made up her mind to quit smoking, she wanted to get onto it, and the course at the centre seemed ideal.

'I can imagine Jamieson's response if he knew we were signing you up to a course run by a place under investigation. Speaking of Jamieson, you'll never guess what's happened.'

'He's been promoted,' she said. That could be the only thing which would produce such glee in Whitney's voice.

'Not yet. Although we can but hope. He's got trouble at home and he's asked me to step in and cover for him. Can you believe it? After all the stick I've endured over the time he's been here, he's doing the exact same thing he's been accusing me of. Putting family first.'

'What did you say?'

'I agreed. He doesn't want to be seen as slacking because of his promotion chances. Of course I'm going to help.'

'That makes sense.'

Whitney turned away from her. 'Listen up, everyone. Let's start the briefing. From what we know so far, our three victims all changed in personality over the last few months. They're all connected to the Wellness Spirit Centre, and we'll be visiting them tomorrow. Matt, what did you find out over the weekend?'

'All three victims have made regular payments to the Wellness Centre,' Matt said. 'The initial ones for Nicola Hurst and Samantha Lyman were large, and were for the courses they attended—the dates and website prices match. Then there were regular monthly payments after that, which could be for the yoga classes, although that would make them very expensive.'

'What else did they spend their money on?' Whitney asked.

'Not much. They both started to live frugally. No form of entertainment like cinema, pubs, and clubs. Their major expense was the centre.'

'Thank you. Ellie, how did you get on?'

'I took a deeper look at their social media accounts, comparing the friends, and found none in common, a few shared mutual friends, but no direct links. Also, each woman took a step back from their posting habits within a week of attending the retreat, and when they did post, it was similar to the quote from Troy Randall's book Hayley posted.'

'Everything's pointing to that damn centre. Do we know the names of the staff there?' Whitney asked.

'No. The website only mentions Randall. I started looking yesterday, and will continue with that today,' Ellie said.

'Good. George and I are going to Hayley Tennant's workplace. I'll see you all back here later. Let's go,' she said to George.

George picked up her bag from the desk and followed Whitney out of the incident room.

The BATT offices were situated on the top floor of a five-storey building, housing a number of other companies.

They took the lift and walked out into the reception. On the wall was a large mural of two clasped hands.

'I'm DCI Walker and this is Dr Cavendish. We'd like to speak to the most senior person on the premises,' she said to the receptionist.

After a few minutes, a woman in her thirties, dressed in a navy trouser suit, walked up to them. 'Good morning, I'm Deirdre, Executive Assistant to Andrew Carver, our Chief Executive. He's currently in a meeting with our senior managers. Can you tell me what it's about?'

'We'd like to speak to him urgently about one of his employees. Please go and get him,' Whitney said in her no-nonsense voice, which George had come to recognise she used when not prepared to be fobbed off.

Deirdre left them, and Whitney strolled over to where there were several easy chairs around a coffee table and sat down. George followed suit. She picked up a magazine from the table. It was the BATT quarterly journal, which gave details of the association.

'Mr Carver will see you now,' the assistant said as she came back to where they were sitting. 'Please come with me.'

She led them down the corridor until reaching a large meeting room. 'He'll be along shortly.'

'This is a nice meeting room. In fact, the whole place looks very swish. I thought associations like this were classed as charities,' Whitney said.

'According to the magazine I looked at, you're right. They are a charity. All this would be from their membership fees which might be high, or they have a lot of members,' George said.

The door opened and in walked a man of medium height, who looked to be in his fifties. He had grey wavy hair that flicked over his ears. He was wearing a suit, with an open-necked shirt. No tie.

'Good morning, I'm Andrew Carver.'

'We'd like to speak to you about Hayley Tennant.'

He frowned. 'Hayley. She's a strange one. She hasn't been in work since last week, and we've been unable to contact her.'

'I'm sorry to have to tell you, Hayley died on Wednesday,' Whitney said.

Carver paled. 'Dead. What happened?'

'We can't give you the exact circumstances as we're still investigating. But we'd like to ask you a few questions.'

'Yes, of course. Let me know how I can help.'

'I understand she'd worked here for three years.'

'Yes. As part of our information team.'

'What does the work involve?'

'The team are the association's front line. They're our call centre, taking enquiries from members of the public who want information about us, or if they want to know about any training courses we recommend. They also take calls from people wishing to complain about any of our members and forward the details onto our legal department.'

'Was she good at her job?'

'She used to be one of our best. She was a senior officer and part of her remit was to train new staff members. She had a good way with her.'

'When you say *used to be*, what do you mean?'

'She'd changed recently. We'd all noticed.'

'How?' Whitney asked.

'Her manner. She'd become quieter and unresponsive. She'd never been loud and outspoken but did have a quiet confidence which inspired the others in her team. That's what made her such a good supervisor and excellent on the phone with the public. She was always considered in her responses.'

'After she'd changed, was her work affected?'

'Not exactly. The best way to explain it is that she was less open and forthcoming when she was with her colleagues. I'm going to have to make an announcement about her death. What can I tell the staff and association members?'

'Just inform them of her death, but that you have no further details. As soon as we have something concrete, we'll let you know. We'd like to speak to anyone here who she was close to.'

'I'll ask my assistant to come in and speak to you. She was friendly with Hayley and can give you more information than I can.' He pulled out his mobile phone and called her.

After a couple of minutes, the conference room door opened.

'Sit down, Deirdre,' Andrew said gently. 'I'm afraid we've had some bad news.'

A worried expression crossed the assistant's face as she sat next to him. 'What is it?'

'It's Hayley. She's dead,' he said. He reached over and covered her hand with his. 'I'm sorry.'

Tears filled her eyes. 'What happened?'

'We're investigating at the moment,' Whitney said. 'We understand you were friends with her. We're sorry for your loss. We'd like to ask you some questions, if you're up to it.'

'Y-yes.' Her voice cracked. 'Sorry. I can't believe it. When did it happen?'

'Her body was found last Wednesday.'

'That's why she wasn't in work. I called when she didn't ring in her absence, but there was no answer. I didn't pursue it because of the way she'd been acting recently.'

'That's what I'd like to ask you about,' Whitney said. 'Mr Carver has explained how she'd become quieter over recent months. As her friend, could you tell us more?'

'It was very strange, and it happened almost overnight. A couple of months ago she went on a yoga retreat.'

George and Whitney exchanged a glance. Was it the Wellness Spirit centre?

'What can you tell us about it?'

'It was at a wellness place in the country. She went away for a weekend, and when she came back, she'd changed.'

'Can you be more specific?' Whitney asked.

'She told me what a fantastic experience it had been and urged me to come with her. We used to go to yoga together, but I had to give up because I damaged my knee. She said how wonderful the leader of the centre had been and that he could help with my injury. She seemed almost star struck by him. When she couldn't persuade me to go, she wasn't the same.'

'Did she stop talking to you?' Whitney asked.

'Not exactly. We still had to work together, but we stopped having our lunches. Initially, she'd make up an excuse as to why she couldn't be with me, saying she had to go shopping, or had to be somewhere. After a couple of weeks, I no longer asked. If I saw her in the lunchroom, which was rarely, she would always smile and answer when I asked how she was, but she wouldn't engage in further conversation. She spent most of the time at her workstation answering the phone, even when she was on a break. I can't believe she's dead.'

'We'd like to take a look at her desk, if you could take us,' Whitney said.

Deidre looked at the Chief Executive and he nodded.

'Come with me,' she said.

They left the meeting room and went down the corridor into an open-plan office, where there were about ten people sitting in front of computers with headsets on.

'This is the Information Centre. Hayley's desk is over in the corner.'

'It's very tidy,' George said once they'd crossed the room. All that was on show was a computer screen, keyboard, and a calendar.

'Yes. Everything was always put away before she left work for the day.'

Whitney opened the top drawer. It was also neat and tidy. George peered over her shoulder and saw the book written by Troy Randall, *Enlighten Your Spirit*. She leaned over and took it out. How come she had two copies?

'Have you seen this before?' she asked Deidre.

'Yes. After she returned from the retreat, she gave it to me.'

'Did you read it?' George asked.

'I started to, but found it too dogmatic, so stopped and gave it back to her. She said I should keep it because there was much in there that could help me live a good life. But I said no. Is it something to do with how she died?'

'What made you ask that?' Whitney asked.

'Because of what you've been asking me. I'm assuming she didn't die of natural causes or you wouldn't be here.'

'We don't know at the moment. We're looking into all areas of Hayley's life,' Whitney said. 'Thank you for your help. Here's my card if you remember anything else.'

'Do you want to speak to other members of her team?' Deidre asked.

'Not at the moment, thank you,' Whitney said.

They left the offices, went down in the lift, and onto the street.

'Why did you decide against speaking to more of Hayley's colleagues?' George asked.

'I think we've gleaned everything we needed to know from Deidre. We're certainly finding a pattern of behaviour among the three victims. They go to the Wellness Spirit Centre and come back changed people. Irrespective of what course or retreat they were doing. What do you make of it?' Whitney asked.

George pondered for a moment. There was only one thought in her head.

'It's confirmed my suspicion that what we have here is more than just a wellness centre. We're dealing with a cult.'

Chapter Twelve

'Can I have everyone's attention,' Whitney said once they'd arrived back at the station and had settled into the incident room. She stood by the board with George at her side. Her team stopped what they were doing and looked at her. Above the names of the three victims she had written "Wellness Spirit Centre".

'We've just come back from visiting Hayley Tennant's workplace. They informed us how she'd changed after going on a yoga retreat, which we believe was at this centre.' She pointed to the name on the board. 'All of our victims had visited this centre and had changed in their demeanour afterwards, according to people who knew them well. Dr Cavendish has come up with a theory that this wellness centre is a lot more than that. She believes Troy Randall is running a cult. I'm going to hand over to her, and she'll give us more information about cults and how they operate.'

She nodded at George. The forensic psychologist smiled and stepped forward.

'Thank you. Cults are fascinating organisations.'

'Aren't they an American thing?' Frank asked.

'Absolutely not. What you might not know is we have over one thousand cults in the UK, and more are springing up every day.'

'Bloody hell. That's a lot. How come we don't know more about them?' Frank said.

'They fly under the radar and purport to be something they're not. They're very often hidden behind what is viewed as legitimate endeavours. The Wellness Spirit Centre offers yoga classes, lifestyle retreats, meditation classes, and a programme to stop smoking. All things that are appealing to people, and on the outside don't appear to be dangerous to anyone who attends. If we investigate the centre further, there's a very good chance that, behind the scenes, we'll find once people get involved with them, they're manipulated into joining on a permanent basis. It's brainwashing.'

'What do you mean, exactly?' Whitney asked.

'They control the environment a person is in,' George said.

'How?'

'Through isolation from everyone apart from cult members. By using a system of reward and punishment. Instilling a sense of powerlessness in their members, using fear and dependency. Reforming behaviour and attitudes. Controlling human communication. These are well documented brainwashing techniques.'

'What sort of people are members of these cults?' Matt asked.

'Weak willed, who are down on their luck and can be easily persuaded,' Frank said.

'I hate to tell you this, Frank, but the people most susceptible to converting to a cult's way of thinking are intelligent, logically minded, and strong willed,' George said.

'How can that be?' Whitney asked, frowning.

'Research indicates the easiest people to recruit are those who want to debate issues. Intelligent, strong-willed people can quickly fall victim to the techniques designed to break people down and control them.'

'What sort of techniques?' Whitney asked.

'Hypnosis, repetition, constant wearing down with arguments. There are a variety of methods that can be used,' George said.

'It all seems a load of rubbish to me. There's no way anyone could convince me to join a cult,' Frank said.

'If it's anything to do with wellness, they're hardly likely to get the chance, are they?' Doug said, laughing.

'I don't know what you mean. I'm very healthy, just ask the wife. I regularly walk around the supermarket,' Frank said, joining in with the laughter.

'Especially the biscuit aisle,' Doug said.

'How can people be part of a cult if they're living at home?' Whitney asked, cutting across the office banter. If she didn't, they'd be at it all day, and if what George said was right, there was a chance more people might be at risk.

'People have a misconception that when you join a cult you all live together, in a commune, but it's not like that nowadays. There are many cults where people don't actually live-in. They carry on with their paid work and spend their free time with others in the cult, neglecting their family and friends in the process.'

'That makes it much harder to identify whether people have joined one, I would've thought,' Whitney said.

'There are certain things you can look for in a person's demeanour,' George said. 'The most obvious being an unexplained change in their behaviour, which is what we found in our victims. Also changes in diet and reading materials are indicators, together with a change in the people they spend time with. You'll often find members of cults lose their personality and are different from how they used to be. These things individually are not warning factors. But taken together they should be considered as problematic.'

'I don't understand how people can allow themselves to be indoctrinated,' Whitney said.

'They might not realise. They lose their ability to critically evaluate, and accept everything they're told. They can't step away and take an objective look at what's happening.'

'Why do people start a cult?' Whitney asked.

'Two reasons. Power and money. Leaders of cults, or gurus, as they like to think of themselves, enjoy having power over people. They're very often able to amass great wealth, especially when they insist people pay their earnings into the cult bank account. Often people will donate money they have saved or inherited. There are many cults, especially in America, that are extremely wealthy.'

'That could be the case with Nicola and Samantha, because they made monthly payments to the centre that were considerably more than yoga classes would normally cost, plus they'd changed their spending habits,' Whitney said.

'What about these religious cults?' Frank asked.

'Some cults are more religious, although from what I can tell, the Wellness Spirit Centre isn't based on religious principles.'

'How do they recruit people?' Whitney asked.

'By offering courses and retreats. Also, members recruit other members. For example, when we went to Hayley Tennant's workplace, we know she tried to get a colleague to come to yoga with her. If every member of the cult got one more person to join, it would double in size every time. So, you can see how quickly these organisations can grow.'

'Any more questions?' Whitney asked. When there weren't, George stepped back. 'Thanks for your insight. What else do we know about the leader of this centre, Troy Randall?'

'The business is registered at Companies House as Wellness Spirit Centre Limited. It's been in existence for ten years, and judging by the financial records, they're not short of money,' Ellie said. 'They own outright the actual centre, as it was donated to Troy Randall in the will of a Martha Brigstock. The will was contested by her family, but they didn't succeed.'

'If I knew being in the health and wellness business could lead to being left a mansion, I'd have gone into it,' Frank said.

'Not at your age, Frank,' Doug said to the older detective.

'I could start a fish, chips, and beer cult. That would go down well,' Frank said.

'I'm sure it would,' Whitney said. 'Now, let's get on. Going back over our three victims, they all had personality changes. That goes along with what George said. They'd also stopped seeing their families and had become withdrawn from their friends. In the case of victim one, Nicola Hurst, we know from her neighbour that she had a new friend she was spending a lot of time with. We can assume this person was someone from the centre.'

'If it's a limited company, who are the shareholders, Ellie?' George asked.

'Fifty-five per cent of the shares are in the name of Troy Randall, and forty-five per cent in the name of

Stewart Cross, who's the company accountant,' the young officer replied.

'Any joy with finding out about other people who work there?' Whitney asked.

'No,' Ellie said.

'Matt and I will be visiting the Centre tomorrow, after which we'll have more information.'

'We don't know yet whether they genuinely are a cult,' Sue said.

'You make a valid point,' George replied.

'We'll know more once we've been there, but the indications are that it is,' Whitney said.

Her phone rang, and she glanced at the screen. It was Claire.

'Walker,' she answered.

'I thought you'd like to know there are needle marks on both of the other bodies, which is consistent with them having been sedated. In my professional opinion, these are definitely murders.'

'So why were they sedated by injection and Hayley wasn't?' Whitney asked.

'That's your job to find out. Not mine,' Claire said.

'Any trace evidence?' Whitney asked.

'No. If they were sedated first, then there wouldn't have been a struggle. We can't identify the sedatives used on Nicola Hurst and Samantha Lyman because of the lapse in time since it happened.'

'If there were no signs of a struggle, it's likely they knew their killer, and presumably they would have let them into their house,' Whitney said.

'Again, that's your area of expertise. I just wanted to let you know,' Claire said.

'Thanks. We'll be in touch.'

The pathologist ended the call without even saying goodbye, but Whitney was well used to that.

'Anything of use?' George asked.

'Confirmation that they'd all been sedated. Listen up, everyone. We now know for sure these deaths weren't suicide. The victims were sedated before being hanged. Nicola and Samantha by injection, and Hayley in her drink. I think we need to assume they knew their killer, as there was no struggle. Frank, have you come across any cars that have been in all three areas around the times of the murders?'

'Nothing yet. But they're not easy places to check, as I mentioned. Also, we don't have a timeframe to work from,' Frank said.

'Well, keep looking.'

'What we need is the motive,' George said.

'True. We've got nothing that stands out other than it could be someone who has something against cults.'

'But why choose these three women? What is it about them that made them victims? It's frustrating that I can't go with you to the centre,' George said.

'I'm sure we'll be there more than once. You can come with us another time.'

Whitney's phone rang. 'What now?' she said. 'Walker.'

'I need you in my office,' Jamieson said.

'Yes, sir. I'll be up there shortly.' She ended the call. 'Jamieson wants me. I'll be back soon.'

She left the incident room and made her way upstairs. She hoped being summoned wasn't going to be a regular occurrence now she'd agreed to help. She didn't want to be spending more time with him than she had to. She approached his office. The door was open, and she walked in. For a change he wasn't on the phone. He was standing at the window staring out.

'You wanted to see me, sir,' she said.

'Yes, Walker. Further to our conversation on Saturday, I'd like you to take a look at the budget projections for staffing and recruitment for the next five years.'

'Budgets and maths aren't my strong point,' she said.

'You don't need to be good at maths. Just take a look at what's been sent through and prepare some comments. I'm sure you'll be fine. I'd like your responses by this time tomorrow. I'll email everything to you.'

'Yes, sir.' She could hardly say no as she'd already agreed to help. 'How's it all going at home?'

'I'm leaving shortly as my daughter has an appointment with a counsellor. She doesn't want to go, but I'm insisting.'

He let out a long sigh. Whitney felt sorry for him. She knew a thing or two about dealing with emotional teenager daughters.

'We need a press conference regarding the three suicides, which we now know are murders. Would you like me to sort that out?' Whitney said.

'Yes, that's an excellent idea. What do we have at this stage?'

'We've no idea of motive, but there's certainly a link between the victims, as they all had a connection to the Wellness Spirit Centre. Dr Cavendish believes it might be a cult.'

'Do they all live together?'

'No, not a cult in that respect. Although there may be people living there full time, we won't know until we visit tomorrow after they reopen. Many cults have their members living off site.'

'If Dr Cavendish is convinced by the cult theory, then we should go along with her view.'

Whitney tensed. Jamieson had George on a pedestal

because she'd studied at Oxford and had a PhD. Whenever George was in his company he acted differently, as if she was somehow more special than the rest of them because of her academic achievements. Not that she begrudged or denied George's expertise, because that's why they had her working with them.

'Yes, sir. If that's all, I really need to get back to my office. I'll start on the budgets once you've sent them.'

She turned and left, unable to trust herself to not say anything she'd later regret.

Chapter Thirteen

The manor house belonging to the Wellness Spirit Centre was large and imposing. She wished George had been with them as her insight would've been invaluable.

'Look at the size of it. And it was left to him in a will. Why can't I find somebody that generous?' she said, turning to Matt and grinning.

'What would you do in a place like this?' he said. 'There are far too many rooms to keep clean, and I know what you think of housework and anything domesticated.'

'You have a point. Then again, if I could afford something like this, I could afford a cleaner and a cook. I wouldn't have to do anything myself.'

'I wonder how old it is? Some of the windows look Gothic, don't you agree?' Matt mused.

'It's no good asking me, I'm not George. Let's go and find this Troy Randall.'

They headed around the building to the front and walked in through the entrance door, which took them into a large hall with a high ceiling and huge, stained-glass arched windows. Ornate wooden panelling ran alongside the walls, with paintings above it, and in the centre of the far wall was a large, stone fireplace.

They walked through the hall and down a long corridor. It was eerily silent, apart from their footsteps, until they reached a point where voices could be heard. They headed in their direction, stopping when they came to an open door and could see three people talking. Two women and one man.

'Good morning,' she said.

They turned to her. 'I'm sorry, we're not open today, as we've only just come back from our annual retreat,' one of the women said. She was a tall, athletic-looking, attractive woman in her late thirties, with blonde hair scraped back into a ponytail, and dressed in sports gear.

Whitney held out her warrant card. 'I'm DCI Walker and this is DS Price. We're here to speak to Troy Randall.'

'I'm afraid he hasn't appeared yet,' the woman said.

'And you are?' Whitney asked.

'Shelley Bates.'

'Do you work here?'

'Yes, I'm the manager.'

'You said he hasn't appeared yet. Does he live on the premises?'

'Yes. He'd normally be here by this time, but we got home late last night, and by the time we'd sorted everything out, it was gone eleven.'

'Do you live here, too?' Whitney asked.

'We all do.' Shelley gestured to the others who were with her.

Whitney would be interviewing them, but first she wanted to speak to the man in charge.

'Point me in the direction of his room and we'll go and see him.'

'But—'

'This isn't up for discussion.' Whitney cut her off in a cool voice. 'Where is he?'

'He lives in Camellia Cottage, in the grounds. Go back the way you came, out of the front door, and turn left. You'll see it about two hundred yards in front of you. I'll let him know you're coming. Can I tell him what it's about?'

'We'll explain when we see him. We'll be wanting to speak to all of you later, and anybody else who lives here. Which is how many?'

'Fifty-five recruits live here permanently and we also have people living-in if they're attending one of our programmes.'

'Do you have any running at the moment?' Whitney asked.

'We have a meditation retreat starting tomorrow.'

'What about staff? Cooks, cleaners, the people who run the retreats. Do they all live-in?' Whitney asked, trying to get a handle on how the place operated.

'Everything is taken care of by our recruits. The programmes we offer are tutored by our seniors.'

'So, everyone lives in and you don't hire people from outside?' Whitney asked, to confirm.

'We do have recruits living off-site, but they're more junior.'

She would need to look into that in greater detail.

'That's all for now. We'll catch-up with you later.'

They followed the instructions Shelley had given them and in the distance saw a small, grey stone cottage. Well, small compared with the main house, but not in relation to Whitney's semi-detached. Within a couple of minutes, they were at the door and she was about to knock when it opened. Standing in front of her was a very tall, slightly built man in his early fifties. His hair was blond and his face tanned. He was wearing a navy tracksuit with a Wellness Spirit Centre badge embroidered on it. He smiled and revealed a set of perfectly straight white teeth.

'You must be DCI Walker and DS Price. I'm Troy Randall. Please come in.' He held open the door and they walked into the hall. It had a light-wood floor with magnolia walls.

'Is there somewhere we can sit down to talk, Mr Randall?' Whitney asked.

'Call me Troy. Yes, follow me.' He led them into a small sitting room, with floor to ceiling floral curtains and a rust coloured carpet. On the walls were photos of Troy with groups of people, mainly women. Were they cult members?

He sat down on one of the upright chairs, and they sat on a small two-seater pale-lilac sofa.

'We'd like to know about the centre,' Whitney said.

'I opened it ten years ago, and our ethos is spiritual enlightenment. We believe if you heal the spirit then the body will follow.' He sounded like he was reading off a set of cue cards.

'I really don't understand what you mean,' she said.

'We help people go deep within themselves, so they can lead a better, and more fulfilling, life.' He leaned forward and smiled at her. It was quite disarming. There was definitely something mesmerising about him.

'How do you do that exactly?'

'We develop individual programmes for every one of our recruits.'

'I've seen your brochures. Do you design individual retreats for every person who signs up?' It made no sense to her. How on earth could they do that?

'When people come to us it's usually for something specific, like wanting to stop smoking, or to lose weight, or to join our yoga and meditation classes. That's just the first step. Once they've completed their initial programme, we look at each of them individually and work something out specifically for them.'

'So, once people have completed their course or retreat, you *suggest* they carry on doing something else, for which they pay you.'

'It's not quite like that. Why are you here? What is it you want to know?' His tone altered slightly. Was she rattling him?

'We're here to ask you about three of your past clients: Nicola Hurst, Samantha Lyman, and Hayley Tennant. Do you remember them?'

He looked thoughtful for a moment and then nodded. 'Of course. Why?'

'All three of these women have died.'

Troy's jaw dropped. 'All of them? How?'

Where was George when you needed her? His reaction seemed genuine enough, but was he just a good actor? George would have been able to scrutinise him in a way that Whitney couldn't.

'When the bodies were first discovered it appeared they had all committed suicide.'

'*Appeared to be suicide.* So, that means …' Troy said, leaving his words hanging.

'Our investigation has led us to believe their deaths are likely to have been murder'

'Murdered. How does that relate to me?'

'I thought that would have been obvious. All of them spent time here. And all of them, according to their friends and family, had changed a great deal.'

'If I remember rightly, they were all engaged in different activities when they first arrived.'

'But, as you've already explained to us, once people

have gone through their initial programme, they will do something else. Were they friends?'

'I'm not sure.' He shrugged.

'What did they all do after their initial programmes? What were their individually designed activities? Did they spend a lot of time together?'

'You need to speak to Shelley, my second in command. She designs the programmes for people. I'm sure they would have known each other, as we do a lot of group activities.'

He was being evasive.

'What sort of activities?' she pushed.

'Meditation. Yoga. Tai Chi. A variety of things. We also have twenty-four-hours of silence days, to enable contemplation.'

'And where do these activities take place?'

'Depending on numbers, we'll use different areas. The house is vast and can accommodate us all. During our days of silence, there might be two or three people to a room. No conversation is allowed. They also undergo a twenty-four-hour fast.'

'Can you think of any reason why three members of your centre would have been murdered?'

His captivating blue eyes drilled into her. 'No. I'm sure it's not connected. It's got to be a coincidence.'

She averted her gaze to break the spell. 'That doesn't seem likely. Is there anyone who has a grudge against you?'

Troy was silent for a while. 'Not a grudge exactly, but I was threatened by the boyfriend of one of our recruits.'

'I've noticed you call everyone here a recruit. It makes them sound like they're in the army. Why don't you call them members, or participants?' Whitney asked.

Was it a cult term?

'Because we're fighting a war against the lack of spirituality in everyday living,' Troy responded, his face hardening slightly.

'And what happened after this person threatened you?'

'I went to the police and reported it. They warned him to stay away.'

'Was he prosecuted?' Matt asked.

'I didn't want any charges laid against him. I just wanted him to leave me, and his girlfriend, alone.'

'And did he?' Matt said.

'Yes. It helped that she now lives here and works full-time in the centre. As far as I'm aware, she hasn't seen or heard from him since.'

'People who knew the victims claimed they'd become more withdrawn and didn't want to take part in their usual family, social, or work activities. Can you explain these changes?' Whitney asked.

'It's all part of their spiritual enlightenment. They're withdrawing because they're spending time inside their own heads in an attempt to achieve greater spirituality. Families, friends, and colleagues don't understand, and interpret it in the wrong way. What they don't realise is these are steps in the process of becoming more self-aware.'

It sounded a right load of nonsense to her.

'So, you don't want them to communicate with anybody outside of the centre, if at all possible. Is that correct?'

She caught Matt's eye, and he arched an eyebrow.

'No, it's not like that at all. It's their decision, but many people find being around those who lack spirituality, or the desire to find it, drains their energy.'

'We understand you have fifty-five recruits living on site,' Whitney said, clarifying what Shelley had told them.

'I believe so, plus me and my accountant, who lives in one of the other cottages in the grounds.'

'We will be speaking to all of them, to find out what they know about our three victims.'

'I understand.'

'Did Nicola, Samantha, and Hayley come to the centre regularly?'

He paused for a moment, glancing upwards. 'Hayley would come from Saturday morning through to Sunday evening. We have a lot of activities during the weekend because many of our recruits who don't live here work full-time. Samantha was the same, and she'd also try to get here some evenings in the week. During school holidays she'd spend a lot more time here. Nicola was also here fairly regularly. She had actually applied to live-in. She'd begun to spend a lot of time with one of our other, more senior, recruits and we were working towards her moving in.' He let out a sigh. 'I can't believe they're all dead. You have to understand I don't know anything about this. I don't see how it could be related to what happens here. We're a peaceful organisation. How can being spiritually aware lead to someone being murdered?'

For the first time he sounded genuine.

'That's what we're here to investigate. The only link we have between the three women is your centre. And that's where we're focusing much of our investigation.'

'How did they die? You said it initially looked like suicide.'

'They were all found hanging in their rooms.'

Troy's hand shot up to his neck. 'That's terrible. I will give you all the help you need, even if it's just to confirm their connection to the centre is a *coincidence*.'

It was the second time he'd mentioned the 'c' word.

George wouldn't have a bar of it. She believed there was no such thing.

'Is it likely they would have met up outside of the centre?'

'I don't know. They may have done … We encourage recruits to keep together so they don't get pulled back into their previous existence. It helps maintain their progress from where they were when they first came to the centre in their search for full spiritual enlightenment.'

'What happens to those who don't make this "spiritual enlightenment"?' Whitney asked, making quote marks with her fingers.

'With our guidance they will make it. They just have to learn to trust.'

Was he being authentic? He seemed so, but after what George had said about cults, she was unsure how to take him. He had to be persuasive to get people to join. She wasn't going to be fooled by a charismatic smile and genuine sounding words.

'Thank you for your help. We're going back to speak to your staff.'

'Is this going to take much time? We have a very busy day ahead of us preparing for the programmes starting this week.'

'It will take as long as it takes. We're dealing with three murders. I would've thought you'd want solving them to take precedence over everything else.'

'Of course, I'm sorry. I know you need to do your job, but it's not related to the centre. There's no reason for anyone to have taken the lives of my family.'

'Family?'

'Not in the blood relative sense. We're all family here.'

Yet, wouldn't his response to their deaths be more pronounced if he truly believed them to be his family?

'What were you doing on the twenty-seventh of August, and the fourth and eleventh of September?' she asked.

'Why do you want to know?'

'They were the dates of the murders.'

'You can't possibly think it was me.'

'We ask everyone we speak to so they can be ruled out of our enquiries. If you could answer the question.'

He walked over to the side and picked up his mobile. 'I'll check.' After a few moments he looked up at Whitney. 'On the twenty-seventh I was here at the centre all day, as we had a programme on. On the fourth I was doing a twenty-four-hour silent meditation in my studio in the main house.'

'Was anyone else with you?'

'No. I was on my own.'

'What about last Wednesday, the eleventh?'

'It was the day before our annual retreat. I spent my day packing and also went into town to get a few bits and pieces.'

'Can anyone vouch for you?'

'No, I was alone.'

'You seem to spend a lot of time on your own,' Whitney observed.

'That doesn't make me a murderer.'

Chapter Fourteen

Whitney and Matt left Troy Randall and headed back to the main house.

'What did you make of him?' Whitney asked, wanting to get Matt's opinion as a man, considering Randall had hardly looked in his direction.

'I think he's full of shit. All this talk of spiritual enlightenment. He's just as Dr Cavendish said.'

'But he seemed genuinely disturbed by the murders,' she said, unsure why she felt the need to stick up for him. Matt was usually measured in his responses. If he got that vibe from Randall, then she should listen to him.

'He was hardly going to act like it's an everyday occurrence. He would have to appear shocked.'

'Let's go and see what the recruits have to say.'

'Are you going to get a search warrant?' Matt asked.

'Not at the moment, and I doubt we'd be issued one. We need to have something a lot more concrete than *they all went to yoga classes here*. It's not like they were living-in. They only came here at certain times, and we have no idea whether they were friends or not. I'm hoping we'll get more information from the other recruits, especially the second-in-command, as I suspect she has more to do with them than our Mr Troy Randall, who doesn't seem to get involved at a grassroots level, but likes to lord it over everything.'

'A bit like those tele-evangelists they have in America,' Matt said.

'Yes, exactly that.'

They went back into the building and headed to the office they were in earlier. Shelley Bates was peering into a filing cabinet. She looked up.

'We've spoken to your boss and would now like to interview you. Is there somewhere private we can go?' Whitney asked.

Shelley looked at the others in the office who were sitting at desks. 'Please could you leave us?'

They left and closed the door behind them.

'You want to talk to me about Hayley, Nicola, and Samantha,' Shelley said.

'Yes. How do you know?'

'Troy phoned after you left. He's devastated. I don't understand who would want to kill them. Do you seriously believe it's connected to the centre?'

'We're investigating several avenues. What can you tell me about the three of them? Were they friends?'

'I wouldn't say *friends*, as we don't encourage friend-ships here.'

That seemed to go against what Randall had just said.

'But I thought you wanted all your recruits to stick together, so they didn't fall back into their old ways.'

'There's a difference between supporting each other and being close friends. You can't achieve spiritual enlight-enment if you're subject to the way another person's mind works, if you understand what I mean.'

Whitney let out a sigh. All this *spiritual enlightenment* talk was making her uneasy. She didn't get it.

'No, I don't. Explain it to me.'

'To achieve full spiritual enlightenment, you've got to be at one with yourself, and not influenced by others. This is why we spend a lot of time alone.'

'So, let me get this straight. People come onto a programme or retreat, whether it's to stop smoking, improve their lifestyle, or participate in yoga and meditation, and during that time you talk to them about their spiritual enlightenment and encourage them to come back to the centre and follow their own individualised programmes.'

'Yes, that's about it. We also allocate a mentor to each new person.'

'Who mentored Nicola, Hayley and Samantha?'

'I did.'

'How can you mentor all three of them? Doesn't that take up too much of your time?'

'I try to mentor all of the new recruits for the first six months they're here. After that, I place them with one of the others. Someone who's been with us for over twelve months and is well on the path to their own spiritual enlightenment.'

Did the woman really believe all this? It sounded so far away from reality that it wasn't funny.

'Did you contact any of the victims when they didn't show up at the centre?'

She averted her eyes, a guilty expression crossing her face. 'I'd intended to contact Samantha after the annual retreat, as we hadn't seen her for over two weeks. Although we don't condone it, it's not unusual for our recruits to occasionally miss weekends. They have their lives outside of the centre.'

It was all too convenient. And why didn't she say Nicola, who would've been missing longer than Samantha? What about the girl Dorothy Fletcher had seen at Nicola Hurst's flat?

'But in Nicola's case, you must have known she'd died, as her new friend found her. I'm assuming this friend was one of your recruits?'

Shelley coloured. 'Yes, I was told that Nicola had committed suicide. After discussing it with Troy, we decided not to mention it. We felt it best the others didn't know in case it put them out of balance.'

Whatever the hell that meant.

'So, Troy kept it quiet?' Whitney confirmed.

Not only did he not acknowledge he knew about Nicola, he neglected to tell them he'd kept it a secret. Which put doubt on everything else he'd said. What else did he know?

'Yes.' Shelley nodded.

'What's the name of the woman who found Nicola? We'd like to speak to her.'

'Kelly Yeoman.'

'Does she live at the centre?'

'No, she doesn't. We're expecting her at the weekend.'

'What did she tell you about Nicola's death?'

'She was distraught at being the person who found the body. We had no idea Nicola wanted to take her own life … Everything seemed to be going well for her. She'd successfully moved from one level to the next and was embracing her journey. Troy was especially pleased with her progress. That's why it was such a shock. It took Troy several hours of intensive counselling to bring Kelly back to where she used to be, and now she wants to join us full-time.'

'And is she going to?'

'She has one more hurdle to get over, and after that, yes, we will take her.'

'And what is this *hurdle*?'

'When recruits move in here permanently, they have to divorce themselves from all other aspects of their life so they can commit totally to the centre.'

'And is Kelly not ready to do that yet?'

'She's working on it at the moment.'

'Is it the case that anyone who lives and works here full-time, and you said that's fifty-five people, has no contact with the outside world whatsoever?'

'No, it's not like that. We go out shopping, we go for walks. But we don't see our old friends and family because they can pollute our spiritual enlightenment.'

'You seem to use those two words an awful lot,' Whitney said, unable to keep the sarcastic tone from her voice.

'That's because our whole life is based on it.' Shelley frowned.

'Regarding the mentoring, does Troy ever get involved?'

'Sometimes he takes recruits under his wing to develop their potential.'

'What about Nicola, Samantha, and Hayley?'

'He did work with them on occasion.'

'Recently?'

'No. Several months ago, we ran a few sessions involving a select number of recruits, which Troy super-vised. He wanted to try out some group meditative techniques.'

'How long did that last for?'

'Three consecutive weekends in May.'

'Can you tell me what you were doing on the twenty-seventh of August, and the fourth and eleventh of September?'

'I was here at the centre on all three days,' Shelley said, as if she'd prepared her answer in advance. Under Troy Randall's instructions, no doubt.

'And you didn't leave at all, even to go shopping?'

'It was a busy two weeks, as we had programmes to deliver and there was the preparation for our annual retreat.'

'Tell me more about this annual retreat. How many people went?'

'All the full-time recruits went, plus Troy and Stewart, our accountant, although he was only there for the first two days.'

'Why?'

'Because his role is more administrative, and in the first two days we were talking about the centre's goals and direction. The last three days were more about meditation and enlightenment.'

'So, Stewart isn't into all the enlightenment stuff then?'

That seemed strange. How could he live onsite and be the accountant, yet not adhere to the principles?

'Stewart is perfectly in tune with the ethos of the centre, but he doesn't involve himself in what we do on a day-to-day basis.'

That still seemed strange to Whitney.

'How did he become involved in the centre in the first place?'

'He's known Troy for many years. They opened the centre together. At first, all they offered were yoga classes and retreats. It wasn't anything like it is now. Thanks to the work Troy has done, our programmes have been attended by thousands of people from all over the country. The world, in fact.'

'And generated an awful lot of money, no doubt,' Whitney said.

'The money we make goes towards the upkeep of the centre. We're not interested in profit.'

'Are you a registered charity?' Whitney asked.

'You need to speak to Stewart about anything regarding finances.'

'That's a good idea, I think we'll go now. Will we find him in his cottage?'

'No. He's in his office, which is on the first floor. I'll take you.'

'Thank you. Perhaps you could give us a tour of the centre on the way,' Whitney said.

They walked with Shelley and she showed them the rooms on the ground floor. There was a dining room with four long tables that each seated around thirty. From there they went into the large kitchen, where five people were preparing food. Then they popped their heads into several studios.

'This is our largest yoga studio,' Shelley said as they walked into the fourth.

'Does everyone do yoga?' Whitney asked.

'Yes. The basis of everything we do is yoga and meditation. Whatever programme people come on, they are an integral part. That's why we have plenty of studios.'

'How many programmes do you have running at any one time?'

'Yoga retreats and classes run all the time. The retreats are usually every two weeks. We also have daily yoga classes, which are particularly busy at the weekends.'

'What about the stop smoking programme?' she asked, remembering that George was interested in that.

'We run those three times a year, sometimes more, depending on demand. The same with our weight loss and lifestyle programme. We can be flexible. If we have a lot of enquiries, we'll put on an additional course.'

Also on the ground floor were two sitting rooms with several large sofas and white boards. There were no TVs anywhere.

They went up the large dog-leg wooden staircase to the first floor.

'All the offices are up here. I have one, and both Troy and Stewart do, too.'

'What about the office you were in downstairs?'

'I use that for when I want to keep an eye on the recruits.'

They stopped at the third door along the corridor. Shelley knocked and opened it. 'Hi, Stewart. I've got the Lenchester police with me. They'd like a word.' She stepped to the side and they walked in.

Sitting behind an antique desk was an overweight, bald man who looked to be in his sixties.

He stood up and walked over to them with his hand held out. 'Hello. I'm Stewart Cross.'

Whitney shook his hand and then held out her warrant card. 'DCI Walker and DS Price.'

'I'll leave you to it,' Shelley said.

'Please sit down.' Cross gestured to two chairs facing his desk. He then returned to his chair. 'How can I help you?' He gave a broad smile.

He had none of the pretentious airs of Troy Randall.

'We're investigating the deaths of three of your recruits,' Whitney said.

He paled and clenched his fists tightly on the desk. The friendly smile on his face had disappeared and in its place was one of shock. 'Three of our guys are dead? This is the first I've heard of it. It was tragic enough to learn that Nicola Hurst had recently committed suicide. Now you're saying that three more have died. How? What happened?'

Interesting that Troy hadn't phoned to let him know about the two latest deaths.

'The three include Nicola. There were two further deaths which also appeared to be suicide, but now we're not sure.'

'Meaning?'

'We're treating them as suspicious.'

'How can I help? I don't really have much to do with the running of the centre. Who were the others?'

'Samantha Lyman and Hayley Tennant. Did you know them?' Whitney asked.

'Yes. I know all of our recruits, as I'm the one who deals with their payments.' He paused. 'When I say *know them*, I mean as names on paper. I don't engage in conversation with all of them.'

'Who do you speak to?'

'Mainly those who've been with us a long time. I don't get involved in any of the courses, or the yoga. I'm hardly a good advert for being fit and healthy.' He gave a wan smile.

'You and Troy appear very different from each other. How did you become business partners?' Whitney asked.

'We've known each other since school. We were friends and have remained so. Back then we weren't so different.'

'You were at school together?' she said, unable to hide the surprise in her voice.

'I might look at least ten years older than him, but this is all natural.' He patted his stomach.

'What did you mean by you not being different at school?'

'We were both overweight and subjected to bullying. We ended up hanging out together.'

'I'm sorry to hear that,' Whitney said. She loathed any sort of bullying.

'We got over it, in different ways. Troy went down the spiritual, improve your body route, and I focused on business. I studied to be a chartered accountant, while Troy studied all this woo-woo stuff.'

'Yet, you remained friends.'

'Yes, we did. When Troy had the idea of setting up yoga retreats in conjunction with his classes, he came to me for business advice.'

'Have you always held your classes here?'

'No. Initially we rented some rooms and studio space in Lenchester, but at the time when we were outgrowing the premises, we were fortunate enough to be given this beautiful home.'

'We understand it was left in someone's will.'

'She was one of Troy's very first students. She was impressed with what we did and wanted to make a difference.'

'Was she an older woman?' Matt asked.

'Yes,' Stewart said.

'There don't seem to be many older people around here. All the recruits we've seen look as if they're in their twenties and thirties. More female than male,' Whitney said.

'That's our current demographic, and it's always been the case. Women outnumber the men by ten to one. Women seem to be more concerned with their *spiritual enlightenment*.'

Did he actually believe in what was being undertaken at the centre? The way he spoke implied otherwise.

'What can you tell me about Nicola, Samantha, and Hayley?' she asked.

'None of them lived here full-time, so not much other

than processing payments for their classes. I would sometimes see them, if I happened to be wandering around. But we didn't speak.'

'We understand Troy had included them in some extra meditation classes he was trying out some months ago.'

'I don't know anything about that. Troy often runs extra classes, for his meditation experiments, as he calls them. I keep telling him he's hardly being scientific, and that to call them experiments is a misnomer.'

'How does he respond to your criticism?'

'In his usual Troy way. He just glosses over it.'

'Does this cause friction between you?'

'Absolutely not. As I've already told you, we've been friends since school. We know what we're like and totally accept one another. He's my best friend, and I like to think I'm his. Just because we have differing ideas, doesn't mean we can't get along.'

She could relate to that.

'Do you live at the centre alone?'

A shadow crossed his face. 'I do now. My wife died three years ago of cancer. We tried all sorts of treatments, but nothing could save her.'

'I'm sorry,' Whitney said.

'I couldn't have coped without Troy's support.'

'Thank you for your help. Here's my card if you do think of anything that might help us in our enquiries.' Whitney handed it to him.

'Thank you.'

'Before we go, please could you tell me what you were doing on the twenty-seventh of August, and the fourth and eleventh of September. We're taking details of everyone's whereabouts at the times of the deaths, to eliminate them from our enquiries.'

He picked up his desk diary and peered at it. 'On each

of those days I was here at the centre, either in my office or at home. I didn't go anywhere.'

'Can anyone vouch for you?'

'I don't know. It depends on who was on duty. Some of the time yes, but at other times, no. Sorry I can't be more helpful.'

'We'll be in touch if we need to speak to you again. Thank you for your time,' Whitney said as they left his office.

'Where to, now?' Matt asked.

'We'll find some of the recruits to interview and see what they have to say. I can't put my finger on it, but something doesn't seem right.'

Chapter Fifteen

George had managed to leave work earlier than she'd anticipated, so she called into the station to see how they were getting on. She was fascinated by the centre and keen to learn more about it. She pushed open the door to the incident room. Whitney was by the board, talking with Matt.

'How did you get on at the Wellness Spirit Centre?' she asked when she reached them.

'It's a very interesting set up. I'm sure you'll be intrigued, from a psychological perspective,' Whitney said.

'Tell me more.'

'Troy Randall was charming. In fact, overly charming. I'd even go as far as to say slightly creepy. He was almost a caricature of what you'd imagine someone in his position to be. He'd clearly had work done on his face, as we met his accountant and partner, Stewart Cross, who went to school with him and who looked at least ten years older. Stewart was very down-to-earth but wasn't much help as he didn't have much to do with the day-to-day activities of the centre. He keeps in the background looking after the administrative side.'

'And Troy Randall, how involved was he in the routine work?' George asked.

'We didn't see him with any of the recruits, but I imagine he floats around and considers himself more like a superstar.'

'Recruits?'

'Yes, that's how they refer to people who are part of the centre. The ones who have done more than just the retreats or programmes. They are the ones recruited into this spiritual enlightenment way of thinking.'

'Very interesting use of the army metaphor, because in the army discipline is paramount. Recruits do as they're told without question. Is that what happens at the centre?' George asked.

'We didn't see enough of it in action, but I imagine the people who live-in full-time and the ones who have gone through the initial programmes do as they're instructed.'

'Who else did you speak to?'

'After we interviewed Randall, Cross, and Shelley Bates, Randall's second-in-command, we spoke to six of the female recruits and one male. And, by the way, there are hardly any males. One in ten.'

'Hmmm. Interesting. Tell me, do the recruits look similar to one another?'

Whitney appeared surprised by George's question.

'I suppose they do. In their twenties and thirties, attractive and slim. I hadn't thought about it until you mentioned it.'

'Why?' Matt asked.

'Because either they're groomed into looking a certain way, or they target people with similar characteristics,' George said.

The more she heard, the more she was convinced her prediction of it being a cult was correct.

'But, again, why?' Matt asked, frowning.

'Cult leaders often like to see people in their own image. From what I gather, Troy Randall is concerned with his appearance and likes to be surrounded by beautiful things.'

'Apart from his friend Stewart,' Whitney said.

'There are always exceptions. Anyway, it's just a theory; we don't have sufficient information at this stage to back it up,' George said. 'Tell me about his second-in-command. Was she protective of Troy?'

'Yes. Why?' Whitney asked.

'I just wondered if there was any sort of sexual component in their relationship.'

'Impossible to tell, but she clearly idolises him. Then again, so do all the people we interviewed, apart from Stewart. But you could tell he was very fond of Troy. There's no animosity between the two of them.'

'Do they encourage relationships between female and male recruits?'

'They didn't say, but I doubt it, when you consider close friendships aren't condoned. According to Shelley, it's because they believe they'll interfere with people finding their true spiritual enlightenment. In order for that to occur, they have to be on their own and not influenced by anybody else.'

'The characteristics fall within the parameters of a cult,' George said. 'By keeping the recruits focused on Troy and his trusted leaders, it's easier to maintain conformity. The old *divide and rule* adage. We need to investigate further. I'm not saying it's necessarily bad. People are entitled to their own opinions and their own views. But cults can be extremely dangerous, especially if they strip people of their personalities.'

'Ellie's been working hard on investigating both Troy and Stewart's backgrounds, as they've been friends for a long time. I was about to ask her for an update.'

George went with Whitney and Matt to Ellie's desk, where the detective was peering at her computer screen.

'Guv, I have something for you. Troy Randall isn't his proper name. He changed it by deed poll twelve years ago. He was previously known as Albert Smith.'

'I'm not surprised he changed it, as it doesn't quite have the evangelical ring that Troy Randall does. Any convictions against him?' Whitney asked.

'No, but last year he did make a complaint against a Joshua Trent, who had threatened him.'

'He mentioned that to me. He's the boyfriend of one of the recruits. Randall said he went to the police, but no charges were laid.'

'Do you want me to look into it further?' Ellie asked.

'Yes, see what else you can dig up. What about Stewart Cross? Is that his real name?'

'Yes. He comes from Dorset, the same as Randall.'

'We know they went to school together. Any convictions against him?'

'No, nothing.'

'Where does Joshua Trent live?'

'Lenchester. I'll forward you the details.'

'Thanks. We'll visit him now. Let's go, George.'

As she followed Whitney back to her office to collect her handbag, George glanced at her watch. It was already five, and she'd made arrangements to meet Ross later. 'Do you know how long this will take?'

'Why? Have you got a hot date with the sculptor?' Whitney replied, grinning.

'We've got dinner reservations for seven-thirty.' She'd planned on using the time to give Ross a run down on her brother and his fiancée. Her brother was like her father, although not quite as bad, and she didn't want Ross to be upset by him.

'Don't worry, we'll be back in plenty of time. It shouldn't take too long. I'm also going out tonight.'

'Okay,' George said as they headed out of the station.

Whitney walked towards George's car. 'We'll go in yours, if that's okay.'

'I don't know why you bother asking, as we seem to have got into the routine of using mine.'

'Aren't you going to ask me?' Whitney said after they were five minutes into the journey.

'Ask you what?' George frowned, unsure of what Whitney was talking about.

'Where I'm going tonight.'

'You could've volunteered the information. Why didn't you?'

'Because I was waiting to see if you were curious enough to ask, but I got fed up of waiting.'

'Do you want to tell me?'

Whitney let out an exasperated sigh. 'Of course I want to tell you. Do you want to know?'

'Only if you want to tell me.'

'You're impossible, you know that, don't you?'

'I'm not you, Whitney. If you don't tell me something, I won't ask. You should know that by now.' She tossed a glance in the detective's direction and was greeted with a smirk.

'I'm going out tonight with the guy I met at choir rehearsal. Craig.'

'That's nice.'

'Is that all you've got to say? Don't you want to know where we're going?'

George let out a groan. 'For goodness' sake, Whitney. You know what I'm like. Don't expect me to want to know the ins and outs of everything. I'm happy, if you're happy, that you have a date.'

'Point taken. We've arranged to go out for a meal tonight. Questions?'

'None.'

'Really? Not one? Surely you can think of something.'

George hated small talk, even with Whitney. Though she wasn't sure this counted as small talk. 'Okay. Where are you going for your meal tonight?'

'The Black Swan. You and I went there once, remember?'

Of course, she remembered. It was there she saw her ex-live-in boyfriend, Stephen, with the woman he'd been seeing on the side. She hadn't been back since.

'Yes. It's nice there.'

'That's what I thought. I'm thinking of turning off my phone.'

George laughed. 'Even I know that's not going to happen.'

'You're right. I just have to hope we're not disturbed.'

'By another murder, you mean.'

'How many times have I told you about jinxing? You don't say things like that, because you know it will happen.'

'And you know my view on jinxing. It's a load of nonsense. You're going to have a nice evening out with your new man, and nothing is going to get in the way.'

'If you're wrong, then you're in trouble because …' She paused. 'Turn right here. We're looking for number sixty-eight.'

George turned into Gibson Street and looked at the

numbers. When they got to sixty-eight, she parked, and they walked up to the 1930s semi-detached house.

Whitney knocked on the door. It was opened by a pregnant woman in her late twenties.

'We'd like to speak to Joshua Trent,' Whitney said, holding out her warrant card.

'Can you tell me what it's about? I'm his wife, Rochelle.'

'We need to speak to him.'

'Come in. He's just got in from work and is changing.' She opened the door and they stepped inside. 'You can wait in the lounge.'

She ushered them in, and they sat on the cream sofa.

'They're going to regret this when they have a young child in the house,' Whitney said, running her hand along the arm of the sofa.

The rest of the room was modern and tastefully decorated. A glass coffee table stood in the centre, and there were several large vases filled with tall grasses in the corners of the room.

'They'll probably need to rethink the whole place,' George agreed.

After a couple of minutes, a tall, attractive, dark haired man walked in, followed by his wife.

'I'm Joshua Trent,' he said.

He sat down on the arm of the easy chair facing them.

'We'd like to speak to you about an altercation you had with Troy Randall,' Whitney said.

A worried expression crossed his face.

'Who's Troy Randall?' Rochelle asked.

'Someone from a long time ago.' His worry deepened. 'Please could you put on the kettle,' he said to his wife. 'Would you like coffee?'

Whitney and George both said yes.

Once Rochelle had left the room, Joshua closed the door.

'Rochelle doesn't know anything about what happened, and I'd rather keep it that way.'

'When did you last see Mr Randall?' Whitney asked.

'I haven't seen him since the incident.' His hands were clenched together in his lap, and he leaned forward.

'Could you talk us through it?' Whitney said.

'Why do you need to know? It's all a matter of record,' Joshua said quietly.

'We'd like to hear your side of the story,' Whitney replied.

'But it was over a year ago. Why are you suddenly asking now?'

'Please answer the question,' Whitney said.

'Before Rochelle, I was in a relationship for six years with Jessie. We'd made plans for our future. We were going to move to Canada, where she has family, get married, and have children.' He stood up and began pacing the room.

'What happened?' Whitney probed.

'I'd been nagging her to give up smoking and found a course run by that bastard Troy Randall. The testimonials said the results were excellent, quick, and effective. So, I booked a place as a surprise for her birthday.'

'How did she feel about that?' George asked.

'At first, she didn't want to go, but I persuaded her. The biggest mistake I ever made.'

'Why?' Whitney asked.

'When she came back, she'd stopped smoking, which was amazing, and she had no desire to start again. So, in that sense it was a success. She'd also taken up yoga and meditation. She continued attending the centre at the weekends to go to yoga classes, telling me it was to help her keep off the cigarettes. At first, I was fine about it, but she started to change.'

'In what way?' Whitney asked.

'She was quoting all this spiritual stuff and talking about how bad our world is at the moment. She'd never done that before. She also tried to persuade me to go along with her to classes, but I wouldn't. I play sport on a Saturday. And then …' He paused.

George could see he was wrestling with whatever it was he wanted to tell them.

'Keep going,' Whitney said gently.

'One day, when she was in the bath, I looked through her phone and found texts from Randall.'

'What did they say?' Whitney asked.

'How much he valued her, how she was special, and that he wanted her to live with him at the centre.'

'Was anything sexual in these texts?' Whitney asked.

'What do you think *live with* means? It was clear to me something must've been going on.'

'What did you do?' Whitney asked.

'When she came downstairs, I challenged her about it. She told me she wanted to be with him. I left the house and drove straight to the centre to confront the bastard.'

'When you say *confront* what did you do exactly?' Whitney asked.

'I accused him of having an affair with Jessie, and he denied it. I didn't believe him; it was written all over his face. I punched him and, judging by the crack, broke his nose.'

'Then what happened?' Whitney asked.

'I stormed off and went home. When I got back, Jessie had taken her clothes and left. The next day the police came around and arrested me.'

'But you weren't charged.'

'No. Randall decided not to press charges. Probably out of guilt.'

'Have you seen Jessie since?' Whitney asked.

'No. She texted and asked that I forward all her mail onto her parents, which I did.'

'And you haven't had any contact with her since?'

'No.'

'You've since married Rochelle. That was quick,' Whitney said.

'Yes, she was a friend of my brother's wife, and we'd known each other for years. She was there when I needed her, and we're now expecting a baby. She knows about Jessie but doesn't know what happened with Randall. I'm not proud of my behaviour, but that place, and that man, shouldn't be allowed.'

'What were you doing during the days of the twenty-seventh of August, and the fourth and eleventh of September?' Whitney asked.

'Why do you want to know?' he asked.

'We're investigating some suspicious deaths linked to the centre.'

'How can you think I had anything to do with them? I haven't been anywhere near the place since the fight.'

'Please answer our question, and then we can eliminate you from our enquiries,' Whitney said.

'I was at work on all of those days.'

'Where do you work?'

'Hunter Associates. They're architects.'

'Can anyone vouch for you?' Whitney asked.

'The people I work with, but they don't know anything about what happened between me and Randall. Do you have to tell them?'

'We can be very discreet,' Whitney said.

'What about if I show you my work diary? You'll be

able to see the meetings I had during the day. Would that help, rather than you having to interview people?'

'Yes, looking at your diary will certainly assist us, in the first instance,' Whitney said.

He picked up his tablet from the coffee table and sat next to Whitney on the sofa.

'On the twenty-seventh I had three meetings. Ten o'clock, one o'clock, and three o'clock.' He held out the tablet so they both could see the diary entries. 'On the fourth I was with a client in the office for the morning, and then I had a meeting in the afternoon. And on the eleventh, I had a managers' meeting first thing, which went on until lunchtime, and then I was with a client from two in the afternoon.'

Whitney pulled out a notebook from her pocket and made some notes. 'Thank you for your help, this should suffice for now.' She stood, and George followed.

'I'll see you both out,' Joshua said.

They left the house and went to George's car.

'I think we can exclude him from our enquiries. Shame we missed out on the coffee. If it was taking that long it must have been the good stuff,' Whitney said once George had started to drive away. 'We didn't really learn much, and I don't think he has anything to do with it.'

'I wouldn't say we didn't learn much,' George said. 'I think we got to know a lot more about Troy Randall. He's a man who shouldn't be underestimated.'

Chapter Sixteen

I didn't want to kill those women. I'm not a psychopathic serial killer like the ones you read about who get a kick from killing other people. I'm perfectly sane and always have been. I've always done what's right, worked hard, and never been in trouble. But sometimes things don't go as planned, and everything you've been preparing for gets kicked back in your face.

Some people are liars and cheats, and yet nothing bad ever happens to them. Whereas other people have done nothing wrong and end up being faced with something life destroying.

Up until recently, the thought of taking another person's life had never even entered my head. But that was before the bitches threatened my whole existence. They brought it on themselves. What is it with some women that they can't keep their noses out of things which don't concern them?

I can't believe the police managed to work out it wasn't suicide and then linked them together. I thought I'd nailed it. But that won't stop me continuing.

More women have to die.

Not men. Because they know how to mind their own business and not get involved in something that's nothing to do with them. If those women had been more like the men I know, they would still be alive. They have no one to blame but themselves.

Do I feel guilty?

I didn't enjoy it, even though it got easier by the time I got to number three. The way I view it is, it's one of those things you have to get on and do.

Now I have to sort out how I'm going to pursue the next woman on my list. My list isn't never-ending, and once it's all over, when I've made sure no one else can destroy me, everything will go back to how it was before.

I'll be happy to get back to normal.

Happy is a relative concept, though. As in some ways I'll never be truly happy again.

But I will be able to get on with my life.

Chapter Seventeen

Whitney caught sight of George coming in through the back door of the station and waited. She hadn't seen her for a couple of days and had missed her input.

'Hi,' she said once George had reached her. 'How's it going?'

'Yesterday was a nightmare. One of the Masters students had been falsifying her research findings, and I had meetings all day with both departmental and university research ethics committees. And you know how long meetings with academics can take.'

'Actually, no. I don't.' Whitney's eyes narrowed.

'Given the opportunity, they'd prevaricate over how many angels you can get on a pin head. It's exhausting.'

'Listen to you making jokes about your work.'

'What joke?' George frowned.

'The angels and the pin head.' Whitney shook her head. 'Never mind.'

'I had another meeting scheduled for today but cancelled it. I wanted to be here.'

'As long as you won't get into trouble,' Whitney said.

'I'll be fine. It was only one meeting, which wasn't overly important.'

'Did you have a good date with Ross the other night?'

'Yes, thank you. And now you want me to ask about yours.'

Whitney smiled. 'At last, you're finally learning. For an academic you can be a bit on the slow side, at times.'

'I've learned to go by how you are towards me, and then I can emulate.'

'Emulate away. In answer to your question, yes, we had a very nice uninterrupted meal. He's exceptionally good company, and what goes in his favour is he doesn't keep asking about my job and making remarks about the police.'

'Have you arranged to go out with him again?' George asked.

'You really are taking this to the next level, aren't you,' Whitney said, grinning. 'Well, nothing has been arranged but we'll be seeing each other at choir rehearsals and I'm sure we'll go out again, once I've got time. At the moment I have to devote my energies to this murder case. Do you think we should expect more deaths?'

'It's difficult to predict as we don't know the motive behind them, and we need more information about the Wellness Spirit Centre,' George said.

They walked into the incident room. 'Good morning, everyone. I want a rundown on where we all are with the suicide murders. Ellie?'

'I've nothing more to report on Troy Randall or Stewart Cross, guv. But I have been investigating more deeply into the three victims, to see if there's any connection between them other than the wellness centre. I've checked their schooling. Their employment. Their social lives prior to visiting the centre. Even the doctors and dentists they were registered with. And every time I've come up with nothing. The centre really is the only common factor.'

'Does it give us enough to get a search warrant?' George asked.

'I'll go and see Jamieson and see what he says, but I suspect we'll need something more concrete before we can go barging in there all guns blazing. If any of them had lived on site, it would've been easier. CCTV footage, Frank?'

'Nothing more to report, guv,' the older officer said.

'This is ridiculous. There must be something. The murderer couldn't have visited under an invisibility cloak. There must—'

The incident room phone rang before she could continue. Matt, who was standing closest to the table, picked it up.

'DS Price.' He paused for a moment. 'Okay, we'll be there straight away.' He ended the call.

'What is it?' Whitney asked.

'Another suicide has been reported. Uniform are there but didn't want to take it further in case it's the same as the others. I said we'd go and check.'

'Text me the details. George and I will go. Matt, get in touch with pathology and make sure they send Claire. After the fiasco with the first two murders, we can't risk any more mistakes.'

Whitney and George left the incident room.

'Before you ask, yes we can go in my car,' George said as they hurried to the rear entrance of the station.

'Soon we won't even need to talk because you're learning to read me so well,' Whitney replied, laughing. Her phone pinged. 'This looks like the details coming through.' She opened the message and let out a groan.

'What is it?' George asked.

'The supposed suicide is a woman called Kelly Yeoman.'

'Who's she?'

'The friend of Nicola Hurst who found her and disappeared before the ambulance or police arrived. She's also a member of the centre and was very shortly going to be moving in there permanently.'

'Did you meet her?'

'No. She was on the list of people we wanted to talk to. She was due at the centre this weekend. I'd planned to go over on Saturday. Damn. Why didn't we check her out yesterday? We might have prevented this from happening.'

'We don't know that. You can't blame yourself,' George said.

'We'll never know. She lives at 16 Manor Street in Shillingworth, which is fifteen miles out of town towards Rugby.'

They drove in relative silence to Kelly's house as Whitney found herself wrapped up in her own thoughts. Could she have done more? Could the young woman's life have been saved? She sighed. It was pointless going down that path because it would get her nowhere, other than cloud her judgment. Plus, they had no idea yet whether she'd been murdered. This could genuinely be a suicide. But, who was she kidding?

Within twenty minutes they were at the house. A familiar blue sports car was parked outside. Claire was on call. If it was a suicide, they'd soon know.

'Whose car is that?' George asked as they stepped onto the pavement.

'Claire's. Haven't you seen it before?'

George made a beeline towards it, unusually eager. 'No. You do know how rare it is, don't you?' She bent down to inspect it.

'It's an MG, and as even I know that, it means it isn't rare,' Whitney said.

'No. It's an MG*C*. See that power bulge in the bonnet?' George pointed to a small bump.

'Yes. It looks weird.'

'It's there because there wasn't enough space under the bonnet to fit the carburettors. And look at those wired wheels. It's a classic.' She peered in through the window. 'It's an automatic transmission as well. That makes it even rarer. It's beautiful.'

Whitney didn't get it. A car, was a car, was a car. Some were new and expensive looking, like George's, and some were old and past it like hers. And that was as far as her car appreciation went.

'I'll take your word for it. Let's go inside and see what's going on.'

'Of course.' George tore her gaze away from the car, almost looking guilty that she'd allowed herself to be distracted.

A uniformed officer was waiting by the door.

'Hello, Jade. Were you the first officer attending?'

'Yes, guv. With, Phil. Constable Brooker. Once we'd ascertained the victim was dead, we left the body exactly as we found it, believing it could be linked to the murders.'

'Good, that was the right thing to do,' Whitney said.

'Everything else is in order. The pathologist arrived a few moments ago, and I've got the crime scene log.'

'Who phoned the death in?'

'The victim's sister. She has a key, and when she went into the house this morning, she found the body upstairs.'

'Is the sister still here?'

'Yes, guv. She's with Constable Brooker in the lounge.'

'Thanks. We'll go upstairs and see Dr Dexter first.'

They both signed in and went into the small nine-teenth-century terraced house and up the narrow staircase.

There was a noise coming from one of the rooms. The door was open slightly.

'Claire, is that you?' Whitney called out, knowing better than to walk right in, especially as they didn't know where the body was hanging.

'Yes. Stay where you are,' the pathologist barked.

'When can we come in?' she asked.

'When I say. Give me a couple more minutes to finish photographing.'

True to her word, after two minutes Claire opened the door and they walked in. The body was still hanging from the window latch.

'Shit,' Whitney muttered as she stared at the lifeless body in front of her. 'Murder?'

'I can't confirm anything until I get the body back to the lab, but it seems likely. It has all the hallmarks of the last one, even down to the rubbish bin being left on its side to make it look like the victim kicked it away herself.'

'Can we look around the room?' Whitney asked, pulling out two pairs of disposable gloves and handing a pair to George.

'As long as you don't get in my way,' Claire said.

'Look at this,' Whitney said as she walked towards the table against the far wall.

There was a laptop, a notebook, and a familiar book —*Enlighten Your Spirit*.

'Well, that's hardly surprising seeing as we already know she's a member of the centre and was planning to move in permanently,' George said.

'I know that. But look at the book next to it,' Whitney replied.

George joined her. She picked up the book. *How I Escaped the Cult.* 'Now that is interesting.'

'What do you think it means?' Whitney asked.

'A variety of things. Do we know where she worked?'

'No. But she might have done shift work, as she hung out with Nicola Hurst at all times of day.'

'She was a student,' Claire said.

'How do you know?' Whitney asked.

'Because I've just found an ID card in her pocket. She goes to the university and studies philosophy.' She handed Whitney the card.

'The card won't tell you that,' George said.

'No, but the timetable taped to the wall just above where you're looking will. Not to mention the copy of Wittgenstein's *Culture and Value* on the bedside table. I'd say she was a post-grad. Call yourselves detectives.' Claire shook her head and returned to putting her equipment back into her bag.

Whitney and George exchanged glances. 'Thanks for pointing them out, Claire. We would've found them; we'd only just started looking,' she said, rolling her eyes. Though as Claire had her back to them it didn't have any effect. She put the laptop, notebook, and books into evidence bags.

'My pleasure. Now, if you've finished in here, I need to arrange for the body to be moved, and it would be easier with you two out of the way.'

'Can you give us an approximate time of death?' Whitney said before going to leave.

'As the body has reached the ambient temperature and rigor has set in, it would appear she's been dead for at least twelve hours. I'll be able to give a more precise time once I've done a full post mortem.'

'So, we're looking at around ten last night,' Whitney said.

'And this is why I don't like to give out information in advance. You've totally misinterpreted what I said,' Claire snapped, glaring at her.

'You said she's been dead for at least twelve hours,' Whitney said.

'Note the words *at least*,' Claire said.

'Sorry, Claire. We'll go and speak to the sister, see what she can tell us,' Whitney said, realising they'd more than outstayed their welcome.

'Maybe she'd had a change of heart about moving into the centre after reading the book,' George said.

'Let's go and find out.'

They left Claire in the bedroom and went down to the lounge. Sitting in an old armchair was a woman in her thirties, her face white and her eyes red from crying.

'Guv, this is Maria Denver. She's Kelly's sister,' the constable said.

'I'm DCI Walker and this is Dr Cavendish. We're very sorry for your loss. Do you feel up to answering a few questions?'

'Yes,' Maria said, nodding.

'I understand you called to see Kelly this morning. Was that planned?' Whitney asked.

'No. She was meant to come around for dinner last night with my family, but she didn't turn up. I tried calling her mobile, and texting, but there was no answer.'

'Was it unusual for her to do that?'

'She did occasionally miss coming to see us, so I wasn't too worried. But when she still wasn't answering her phone today, I decided to come and check.'

'Do you know she was considering going to live permanently at the Wellness Spirit Centre?' Whitney said.

'Yes, but not for the reasons you think.'

'Please could you be more explicit? What do you know about the centre?' Whitney asked.

'Kelly swore me to secrecy.'

'You can tell us.'

'She was pretending to be part of them. She was undertaking research into the centre and its beliefs. She thought it was a cult.'

'We understand she was a student at Lenchester University,' Whitney said.

'Yes, she was studying for her PhD and—' Maria's voice broke, and she began to sob. 'I can't believe she'd take her own life. Everything was going well for her. She was immersed in her research and had been planning to experience the cult from the inside. She'd also been in talks with a publisher in London. They were keen to see her thesis, once it was finished, with a view to publishing it as a book.'

'We don't think Kelly took her own life,' Whitney said. 'There have been several other deaths recently, made to look like suicides, which we now believe are murders.'

'You think she was murdered? Why? Who would do something like that?' Maria said.

'That's what we're investigating. Did she ever mention Nicola Hurst?'

'There was one girl from the centre she saw often, but I don't know her name.'

'Did she tell this girl what she was doing?' Whitney asked.

Maria frowned. 'I doubt it, since no one else knew apart from her supervisor at university and me.'

'Do you know the name of her supervisor?' George asked.

'I think it might have been a Carol someone, but I can't be sure.'

'When was the last time you spoke to Kelly?' Whitney asked.

'Two days ago when we organised last night's dinner.'

'Where was she then?'

'She was on her way to do one of the yoga classes, so it would've been late Tuesday afternoon.'

'Does Kelly live here on her own?'

'Yes, she began renting it last year. She wanted to live alone to ensure no one would know what she was doing. I didn't want her to do this research. You hear all sorts of things about cults, and I worried they'd do something to her. But …' A sob escaped her lips. 'Sorry.'

'Before moving in, where did she live?' Whitney asked.

'She shared a student flat with three others.'

'Did Kelly do all her studying at Lenchester?' George asked.

'Yes, she did her degree, then stayed on and did her Masters and then her PhD. She also tutored undergraduates to earn some extra money.'

'Do you come from this area?' Whitney asked.

'Yes, we were both born here. Our parents died ten years ago in a car accident, and since then it's just been the two of us. I'm seven years older than Kelly. We were very close.'

'Is there anyone we can call to be with you?' Whitney asked gently.

'My husband's at home looking after the children.'

'Would you like us to contact him?' Whitney asked.

'No, I can do it. He needs to know what's happened, as he'll be wondering where I've got to.'

'I can arrange for someone to give you a lift home and one of the other officers will take your car, if you like?'

'Thank you,' Maria said, sniffing. 'I'm not sure I could face the drive home on my own.'

Whitney left the room with George and asked Jade to phone Maria's husband and arrange her a lift.

'Let's go,' she said to George. 'I'm bringing Troy Randall in for questioning, a-sap.'

Chapter Eighteen

While waiting for Troy Randall to come to the station, George got on the phone to the administrator of the Philosophy Department. She wanted to find out more about Kelly Yeoman and who her tutor was. She knew a few people in that department, so it wasn't going to be a problem.

'Hello, Jane, it's Dr Cavendish. I'm enquiring about one of your students, Kelly Yeoman. I'd like to know who her supervisor is.'

'I know Kelly. She's a great girl and has been with us for about six years now.'

Should she tell her about her death? Whitney hadn't said not to.

'I'm very sorry to tell you, and please don't share this because it's not yet been announced, but unfortunately Kelly has died.' Had she worded it correctly? She wasn't used to delivering news about deaths.

'Died? What happened?'

'The police are investigating it as a suspicious death.'

The woman gasped. 'You mean she was murdered?'

'We can't assume that at the moment,' George said, thinking that was a ridiculous thing to say, because if it was suspicious, then what else could it be?

'Does anyone know? What about her family?'

'Her sister knows, as she was the one who found Kelly's body. Please keep this confidential. Who was her PhD supervisor?'

'Carol Anderson.'

'Is she in today?'

'I saw her earlier when she came in to do some photocopying.'

'Okay, thanks. The police will want to speak to her.'

'I can't believe it,' the administrator said. 'That poor girl and her family.'

'Yes, I know it's shocking. But, like I said, please don't say anything until it's been publicly announced. The family would be extremely grateful for your cooperation.'

Would the woman be able to keep it to herself? With hindsight, she suspected not.

After ending the call, she went to Whitney's office.

Whitney glanced up. 'This bloody report I have to do for Jamieson is doing my head in.' The phone rang on her desk and she picked it up. 'Walker.' She paused. 'Thanks, we'll be there shortly.' She replaced the phone. 'Troy Randall's here.'

'What's the plan?'

'I'm going to interview him with Matt, and I want you outside watching.'

Whitney pulled out two earpieces and mics from her drawer, handed one to George, and kept one for herself.

They returned to the incident room and went over to Matt's desk.

'I want you with me for Randall's interview,' Whitney said.

'Mr Sleaze, you mean,' Matt said.

'You didn't tell me you thought he was sleazy,' Whitney said.

'Maybe sleazy isn't the right word. Mr Slick is probably better.'

'George will be watching from the other room, so she can give her opinion.'

'After the interview, shall we go and speak to Kelly's PhD supervisor?' George asked. 'She's at work at the moment.'

'Do you know her?'

'Only by sight. We haven't worked together or been on any committees.'

'Okay, that can be our next port of call.'

They arrived at the interview room, and George went into the room next door. She peered through the one-way mirror at Troy Randall, scrutinising him. His hair was clearly coloured, and his tanned face, especially across his forehead, looked tight and smooth. Botox. There was no indication of any concern. He looked calm and serene, sitting upright in the chair with his hands resting loosely in his lap. It was almost like he was meditating, although his eyes were open and he was staring straight ahead.

When Whitney and Matt walked in, he acknowledged them with a nod.

'Good morning, Mr Randall. Thank you for coming in to see us,' Whitney said.

'Please, call me Troy.' He flashed a bright white smile.

And veneers on his teeth, she noted.

'I hope you don't mind if we record this, as it saves taking notes,' Whitney said.

'Not at all. Anything I can do to help,' he said.

Whitney turned on the recording equipment.

'DCI Whitney Walker with DS Price and Mr Troy

Randall. Mr Randall, please could you confirm for the recording that you are here voluntarily to help us with our investigation?'

'I confirm that's correct,' Randall said.

'Mr Randall. Troy. As you know, we're looking into the deaths of three women who were part of your Wellness Spirit Centre.'

'Yes, and I assume that's why you want to speak to me again.'

'There has been a fourth death, which we are linking to the others.'

'Another?' he said.

'We have some rapid blinking,' George said to Whitney. 'It could be shock, or he could be trying to brace himself for what comes next.'

'Yes. Kelly Yeoman.'

He visibly paled. It appeared to be genuine shock, but it was difficult to say.

'Kelly? What happened?'

'She was found hanging in her room.'

'Suicide?'

'It was made to look so, but we suspect murder, as it was very similar to the deaths of the other girls.'

'And you think it's something to do with the centre?'

'Do you believe it's a coincidence that they were all recruits?' Whitney asked.

'I don't know. I just don't know. I can't believe Kelly has gone.' He averted his gaze and unconsciously touched his mouth. A possible courtship?

'Ask about his relationship with Kelly,' George said to Whitney.

'How well did you know Kelly?' Whitney asked.

'I mentored her.'

'Did you spend more time with Kelly than some of the other recruits?'

'She was going to join us full-time, so yes, I did. She's a very interesting girl, and many of her beliefs philosophically complemented mine.'

'Perhaps you can be a bit more explicit?' Whitney asked. 'Try plain English.'

George laughed out loud, having been the butt of Whitney's annoyance when words were used that she hadn't understood.

'We would have discussions about spiritual enlightenment, and she would always bring in a philosophical angle.'

'Do you know what she did for work outside of the centre?'

'Yes. She was a nanny for her sister's children. That was why she hadn't joined us yet on a full-time basis. She was waiting for a suitable replacement to be found.'

'Actually, she was a student at Lenchester university, studying for her PhD,' Whitney said.

'What?' His jaw went slack. This was definitely a surprise to him.

'Don't mention the research. Let's find out more about him and Kelly,' George said to Whitney.

'Yes. And she hadn't told you?'

'No. Maybe she worked for her sister as well to supplement her studies.' He frowned, tapping his fingers against the table. He didn't seem as calm and collected as he had earlier in the interview.

'Can you account for your movements yesterday?'

'I was at the centre.'

'What were you doing there?'

'My work.'

'Please be more specific.'

'I was meditating on my own for a time, and I was writing. I'm planning to bring out a new book next year.'

'We've seen your book *Enlighten Your Spirit*. What's this new one about?'

'It focuses on the journey and on advanced strategies to deal with obstacles that threaten progression. It further develops the ideas I explored in book one.'

'Can anyone vouch for you?'

'I saw various people when I was walking around, but most of the time I was alone. Even if people didn't see me, they would have seen my car because it didn't leave the spot where I'd parked it, along the side of the building, after I came home from having gone out first thing in the morning.'

'Where did you go?'

'I had an appointment with my doctor.' He bowed his head slightly.

'Pursue this; there's something he doesn't want you to know,' George said.

'What did you go for, and who is your doctor?'

'I didn't see a general practitioner. I visited a doctor who does cosmetic work,' he admitted, his eyes focused on the far wall.

'Ask him if he went for Botox injections,' she said.

'For Botox?' Whitney asked.

'Yes, but it's not something other people know.'

'If you can please give us the name of your doctor, we will confirm that's where you were.'

'Why are you convinced these deaths are something to do with me?'

'We've got to investigate all avenues. What can you tell me about Kelly?'

'No more than I've already told you. She was an intelligent woman who seemed very in tune with my spiritual enlightenment ethos. I had high hopes for her and believed she was going to rise through the ranks quickly.'

'Ask him how his second-in-command felt about this. It might have put her nose out of joint,' George said.

'What were Shelley's views on Kelly?'

'The same as mine. She felt she'd be a valuable asset to the centre.'

'Did you find Kelly attractive?' Whitney asked.

'I don't know what you mean.' He frowned.

'Yes, he does,' George said. 'I think you've hit on something here.'

'Was there anything sexual between you? Something more than being just her mentor.'

'I'm not denying that Kelly was an extremely attractive young woman, but our connection wasn't superficial. This was a meeting of minds, not bodies, and I resent your implication that it could be anything else.' He tapped his fingers again before seeming to realise what he was doing. He quickly put his hands back in his lap.

'Yes, you're definitely onto something … He's losing his cool,' George said, while scrutinising the way the charismatic leader's body had tensed and lost its fluidity.

'As I've already explained, we do have to cover all angles, and we'd like to know Kelly's exact position in the centre. What can you tell us about her friendship with Nicola Hurst?'

'I didn't know there was a friendship between them.'

'They used to see each other outside of the centre. Shelley Bates knew. Are you saying you didn't?'

'Well … maybe I did, but it didn't mean anything.'

'What about the other victims? Was Kelly friends with Samantha and Hayley, too? Did the four girls hang out together?'

'We don't *hang out together* at the centre. Achieving spiritual enlightenment is something that has to be done alone.'

'Are you saying that social engagement is prohibited?'

'No. Of course the recruits spend time together, but they don't form deep friendships in case it interferes with their spiritual enlightenment.'

'Typical divide and conquer, as I predicted,' George said.

'When we spoke last time, you said you encouraged the recruits to stick together. Doesn't that imply friendship?'

'No. There's a difference.'

'Well, discounting the fact that they weren't best friends, can you tell me whether Kelly, Nicola, Hayley, and Samantha spent any time together while they were in the centre?'

He stared ahead for a few moments. 'They could have been in the same group meditations and yoga classes. They might have worked together in the kitchen or the garden.'

'Any other time?'

'Sometimes the more experienced recruits spend time with groups of new ones to help them discover themselves.'

'Was Kelly considered one of the older recruits, even though she didn't live-in?'

'Yes. I made an exception with her because she was in tune with our way of thinking. She could have been in a study group which included the three other girls.'

'But you don't know for definite?' Whitney said.

'No. Shelley would be the one to help you with that because she sees to the day-to-day running of the centre.'

'Ask him what happens to people who want to leave the centre, especially those living-in,' George said.

'Troy, if somebody wants to leave the centre, how do they go about it?'

'Recruits can leave whenever they want. We don't force them to remain.'

'Physically no, but emotionally is another question,' George said.

'Do you use emotional blackmail to make them stay?'

'Why would we do that? People are there because they want to be.'

'But if you control their thought process, and their minds, then maybe they wouldn't be capable of leaving, even if they wanted to.'

'I think you're mistaking us for some sort of prison. People come to the centre because they want spiritual enlightenment and to be the best person they possibly can. We help them do that. I'm truly sorry about the deaths of Hayley, Nicola, Samantha, and Kelly, but it's really a coincidence and nothing to do with me or the centre. It's not as if any of them were living-in.'

'Coincidence, my arse,' George said. 'There's no such thing.'

Whitney coughed, clearly hiding a laugh. 'How do you explain the fact they were all part of the centre?' she said after a few seconds.

'I don't know. Maybe someone followed them.'

'Could it be someone who has a vendetta against you?'

He bowed his head. 'I don't know. But if that's the case, why not target me? Or the people actually living at the centre?'

'Wouldn't it be hard to get those people alone?'

'I suppose you're right. I can't help you. I've told you everything I know. If that's all, I've got to get back. I've got things to do, to prepare myself for classes.'

'Why did you change your name from Albert Smith to Troy Randall?' Whitney asked.

He paled. 'How do you know that?'

'We make it our business to know. Please answer the question.'

'My new name reflects the changes I've made in life now I'm on my developmental path.'

'Not to mention Troy Randall has a much better ring to it when you're trying to lure people in.'

'It's not illegal to change one's name.' He folded his arms. 'May I go now?'

'Yes. We will be speaking to Shelley Bates again. Please don't leave the area without first contacting us, because we will definitely want a further interview with you.'

They all stood. 'DS Price will show you out.'

The door opened and Whitney came into the room from where George had been observing.

'What did you think?' Whitney asked her.

'You certainly got under his skin,' George said.

'Yes. Especially when I mentioned his real name.'

'He does seem the archetypal, charismatic, evangelical leader,' George said.

'He looks the part, too, with his dyed hair and tanned skin. He's also very good-looking. Perfect for luring impressionable people into his cult,' Whitney said.

'But irrespective of that, those characteristics don't make him a murderer, and he did seem genuinely shocked when you mentioned Kelly. When you discussed the sexual component, it was obvious he'd been attracted to her. Was he attracted to any of the others? When we interview his second-in-command, we should see what she has to say about it.'

'What about Kelly's research? Does he know about it? Did he think all our victims were involved?'

'We'll know more after we've read Kelly's notes and spoken to her supervisor,' George said.

'Which is exactly where we're heading next. Let's hope her research holds some clues for us. We need to solve this before our killer strikes again.'

Chapter Nineteen

The philosophy department was housed in a building similar to the one George worked in. They made their way straight to the administration office on the ground floor next to one of the staff rooms.

George knocked on the admin office door and opened it. Jane wasn't there, but another woman was sitting at one of the desks.

'Where would I find Carol Anderson's office?' she asked.

'She's in G24, down the corridor on the right,' the woman answered.

The place was deserted, as many of the staff worked from home during the holidays. In other words, having extra time off but not taking paid leave. It was accepted, as long as they made themselves available for meetings.

When they got to G24, the door was open and Carol was seated at her desk. George tapped and walked in with Whitney behind her.

Carol was a small, slight woman with short blonde hair, and she wore tortoiseshell glasses. She'd been working at a computer but glanced up and gave a wry smile as they walked in.

'Hello, Dr Cavendish. Jane explained you'd want to speak to me. Such dreadful news about Kelly.' She took off her glasses, pulled out a tissue from her sleeve, and wiped her eyes. 'I was only with her a few days ago. And to think she's been murdered. I can't believe it.'

'I did actually ask for the information not to be spread around, as it's confidential,' George said, not even attempting to hide the icy tone in her voice.

'Jane was devastated, she came to speak to me as she knew I'd worked closely with Kelly. I can assure you we've been very discreet.'

'Good,' George said. 'This is DCI Walker from Lenchester CID. We'd like to ask you some questions about Kelly.'

'Yes, of course. What would you like to know?'

'What can you tell us about the research Kelly was undertaking into the Wellness Spirit Centre?' Whitney asked as they sat on the chairs opposite Carol's desk.

'Kelly decided she wanted to investigate the centre after one of her relations, a cousin, I believe, moved in there and changed dramatically. She believed that under the guise of a health and wellness centre it was a cult, and that they operated under the same principles as many cults do.'

'Could you explain further?' Whitney asked.

'Yes, they ensure people lose their sense of identity and take on the values and beliefs of the cult and the leader. In this case, Troy Randall. Do you know him?'

'Yes,' Whitney replied.

'From what I've read, and discussed with Kelly, he is quite a charismatic personality.'

'Kelly was undertaking covert research; did you go

through the REC protocols?' George asked. 'I don't remember anything coming through since I've been on the Research Ethics Committee.' A breach of ethics might be secondary to Kelly's death, but if Carol had been involved in such a breach, there would be consequences.

'We made the application to do the research eighteenth months ago and received approval.'

'How long had Kelly been attending the centre?' Whitney asked.

'She joined twelve months ago after signing up to a wellness retreat. The same one her cousin had attended.'

'Is her cousin still there?' Whitney asked.

'Yes, I believe she is. She's very high up in the organisation, now.'

'Do you know her name?' Whitney asked.

'Shelley. I'm not sure of her last name.'

George glanced at Whitney, whose eyes were wide. How come they hadn't known Shelley and Kelly were related?

'Did this cousin know what Kelly was doing? Was she an inside informant?' Whitney asked.

'As far as I'm aware, Kelly hadn't discussed it with her because she didn't believe she could be trusted. I know they had a private conversation. Kelly sensed her cousin had a few reservations about certain aspects of the management, although nothing was actually said.'

'Was the cousin thinking of leaving?' George asked.

'Not that I'm aware of. She seemed fully engaged in the lifestyle and ethos.'

Could Shelley have found out about the research and, believing Kelly had been discussing it with the other women, felt convinced her cousin might try to do something to damage the cult? If so, then Shelley was the person they needed to speak to, as she had the biggest motive to stop the women going public.

'Thank you for your help,' Whitney said. 'If you can think of anything that might assist in our enquiries please let us know.'

Outside, George turned to Whitney. 'Do you mind if we pop into my office to collect a few things I need to take home with me? I've got back-to-back meetings all day tomorrow and won't be able to see you.'

'Be my guest,' Whitney said.

They walked across the grass and went into the psychology building. George's office was on the ground floor. It was large and square, with a bay window over-looking the grounds.

'Very impressive,' Whitney said.

'Thank you, I like it. I enjoy working here; it's quiet and I don't get bothered by too many people.'

'Unlike at the station where the hustle and bustle is constant and often you can't hear yourself think. Then again, I don't think I could have it any other way.'

'We all like different things. What's your view regarding the relationship between Shelley and Kelly?' George asked. 'If she'd found out about the research, it could be a motive.'

'Exactly. I want to know why Shelley hadn't mentioned they were related. We need to interview her straight away. I'd already planned on seeing her again, but we'll bring it forward. I'll give Matt a ring and ask him to arrange it.'

While Whitney was phoning the station, George picked up the reports she needed to go through before her meetings the following day. She also intended to go into the database to have a look at the Research Ethics Committee minutes from before she was on there, to see what was noted regarding Kelly's research.

'Are you ready?' Whitney said as she placed her mobile in her pocket.

'Yes,' George said.

'We'll head back to the station now and interview Shelley Bates, providing Matt can track her down and get her to the station. I wondered if you fancied going out for a drink later to go over everything, especially as you won't be here tomorrow. Or are you seeing Ross?'

'No, I'm not seeing him as he's busy with his latest commission. A drink later would be good. Why don't we go out for an early dinner, as that will save cooking, and I'll be able to get stuck into my reading as soon as I'm home?'

'Sounds like a plan,' Whitney said as her phone pinged. She studied the screen and then looked up. 'Time to go. Shelley Bates is on her way.'

Chapter Twenty

George stood by the two-way mirror and positioned herself to get the best possible view of Shelley Bates. She was eager to ascertain how much the woman was under the influence of Troy Randall. Shelley's face was calm, but she was moving around in her seat, unable to sit still. Very different from the way Troy Randall had acted when in the same position.

Whitney and Matt sat opposite her.

'Thank you for coming in to see us, Shelley. We have some follow-up questions from our last chat. Did Troy Randall inform you about Kelly Yeoman?'

'Yes. Yes, he did.' Her voice was unsteady. 'I couldn't believe it when he told me. It was such a shock.'

'More than Nicola, Samantha, and Hayley?' Whitney asked.

'What? No. Of course not.'

'We're treating this death as suspicious, like the others.'

The woman let out a sigh. 'I can't believe this has happened to Kelly. Everything was going well for her. Why do you think she was targeted?'

'That's what we want to ask you,' Whitney said.

'How am I meant to know?' Her shoulders stiffened.

'Mention the fact that they're related,' George said.

'I understand you and Kelly were cousins,' Whitney said.

Shelley's head shot up and she stared at Whitney, her eyes wide.

'How do you know?'

'Don't mention anything about the research yet. We need to investigate it further,' George said.

Whitney gave an almost imperceptible nod as assurance she'd got the message.

'It's our job to know. Why didn't you mention this when we last spoke?'

'It wasn't relevant. I hadn't seen Kelly for many years before she joined the centre. I didn't want our being connected getting in the way of her spiritual journey. I treated her in exactly the same way as the others at the centre.'

'Did you tell Troy you were related?'

'No. He didn't need to know. As far as he's concerned, we are all individuals and any connections we have with others away from the centre is immaterial.'

'Does anyone else know about you and Kelly?'

'Not from me,' Shelley said.

'Do you think Kelly would have told anyone? What about Nicola Hurst? They spent quite a lot of time together.'

'I don't know whether Kelly mentioned it or not. I did instruct her to keep it quiet because we didn't want to affect the other recruits' progression, which it might have done if they'd known.'

'Not to mention how it might have damaged her position there with Troy,' George said.

'What would Troy say if he found out you'd lied to him?' Whitney asked.

'He's not going to find out. Unless you tell him,' Shelley said defiantly.

'Keep going, she's rattled,' George said.

'You haven't answered my question,' Whitney said.

'I don't know what he'd say.'

'Would you be in danger of losing your position as second-in-command?' Whitney said.

'I don't know.'

'When Kelly first arrived at the centre, what did you do?' Whitney asked.

'She came on one of our lifestyle retreats. Once I realised it was her, I took her to one side and we discussed it.'

'What did she say?' Whitney said.

'It didn't seem to matter to her, and after that first meeting, we didn't mention it again.'

'Is this why you were anxious for her to live full-time at the centre and for her to be pushed up the ranks quickly?' Whitney asked. 'A touch of nepotism.'

'That was nothing to do with it. Kelly had come a long way, very quickly.'

'And Troy had taken a shine to her,' Whitney said.

'I wouldn't use those words. I think he realised, in the same way I had, that she was a special recruit, destined for great things.'

'Were you jealous that Troy was singling her out for special attention?'

'Good call,' George said. 'I was about to ask you to mention it.'

Shelley coloured slightly. 'No.'

'She clearly idolises Troy Randall. Keep going in that direction,' George said.

'Do you like being second-in-command?' Whitney asked.

'It's my destiny, and if I can help Troy put across his message to the rest of the world, it's what I want to do.'

'Are you in love with him?' Whitney asked.

'That's a ridiculous question to ask. I'm there to help with the centre and to mentor other people towards finding their spiritual enlightenment.'

'She sounds like she's reading from a set of notes,' George said.

'You haven't answered my question,' Whitney said.

'I've already told you, I have a purpose for being there.'

'Yes, to help Troy Randall. But you still haven't answered my question.'

'Because there's nothing to answer and it's not connected to spiritual enlightenment.'

'Have you reached it, yet?' Whitney asked.

'I'm on the path, the same as everyone else at the centre.'

'What about Troy Randall himself. Has he?'

'It's a long process, but he's closer than anyone else. It's not something you achieve easily. You have to work at it on a daily basis,' Shelley said.

'Can you think of anyone who would wish to end the lives of Hayley, Nicola, Samantha, and Kelly?' Whitney asked.

'No.'

'Do you think it's someone with a vendetta against Troy?' Matt asked.

George glanced at the detective. It was the first question he'd asked. Why? He was fully aware of the rules of questioning according to Whitney. As in, she does it all.

'That can't be possible. He doesn't have any enemies,' Shelley said.

'How do you think the families of your recruits feel? You take away their loved ones. Do you think they'd be full of praise for Troy?' Matt continued.

'The families should accept it,' Shelley said.

'Is that what your family did?' Whitney asked.

'I haven't spoken to my family since I moved there. I have no idea how they feel, but I'm sure they understand.'

'Where are they now?'

'I believe they're still in Rugby.'

'How did you feel when Kelly first arrived and you got to see a member of your family again?' Whitney asked.

'It did remind me of them, but it didn't make me want to leave and visit.'

'Why not?'

'Because if I did it might put me back. I can't allow other people to get in the way of my progress.'

'Suggest to her that the centre's a cult,' George said, curious as to how the woman would react.

'People have said the centre should be classified as a cult. How would you respond to that?' Whitney asked.

'I have no response … It's just a word. People can call us whatever they like. We know the difference. We're a centre designed to help people become the best they possibly can be, by furthering their spiritual enlightenment. It doesn't matter what you call us, we know what we are.'

'Ask more about the links between the four girls,' George said.

'Going back to Hayley, Samantha, Nicola, and Kelly. We know that Kelly and Nicola saw each other away from the centre, and we understand from Troy they were all in a study group together, which would have made them closer. Can you confirm this?'

Shelley cleared her throat. 'Our study groups usually

contain people of different levels and theirs was no exception. It was a coincidence they were all put together.'

'Why didn't you mention this before?' Whitney asked.

'I didn't think it was relevant.'

'How can it not be relevant when several members of a study group are dead? Are there others in the group?'

'Yes, there are four more.'

'Do they live in or out of the centre?'

'They all live-in.'

George sighed. At last, they were getting somewhere.

'We'll need to speak to them.'

'Okay.'

'Write their names down for me.' Whitney slid her notebook and pen across the table.

Once she'd finished, Shelley passed it back. 'Here you are,' she said.

'As you mentor this particular study group, does that mean you attend all their meetings?' Whitney asked, glancing at their names before returning the notebook to her pocket.

'Most of them.'

'And what goes on in these meetings?'

'We talk about our own individual journeys and offer help to those who need it,' Shelley said.

'Do you know whether they meet away from the centre?' Whitney asked.

'We don't encourage people to meet outside because we have no input.'

'That's not what I asked. Do you know whether they did actually meet?'

Shelley averted her gaze. 'I did overhear a conversation between those who didn't live-in about meeting up, so I assume they did.'

'Did you confront them about it?' Whitney asked.

'No. Confrontation isn't the way we operate, but when we were having our one-to-one mentoring discussions, I gave them the opportunity to tell me what they'd done and whether they'd been speaking to other people.'

'Did any of them admit to it?' Whitney asked.

'No, they didn't.'

'Isn't meeting away from the centre, and keeping it from you, being deceitful and disrespectful? Doesn't it go against the centre's ethos?' Whitney asked.

'As I've mentioned, it's all a learning process. We're all on our own individual journey. They didn't tell me, and I didn't question them. It didn't matter.'

'She's going around in circles here. Be more direct,' George said, recognising the verbosity of someone trying to steer the conversation in a certain direction.

'Did you think they'd been conspiring against the centre and were planning to do something to discredit it?' Whitney asked.

'That's a big leap to make. I don't know whether they met up or not. But even if they did, it doesn't mean they were plotting against us.'

'Did it cross your mind they might be doing something underhand?'

'The thought may have entered my head, but I dismissed it straight away because thoughts like that have a low energy, which is detrimental to my own path. Plus, I couldn't see what they could do to cause us damage.'

'Did you tell Troy they were getting together?' Whitney asked.

'I can't remember,' Shelley said, a little too quickly.

'She's lying,' George said.

'As head of the centre, shouldn't he have been informed?' Whitney pressed.

'Not necessarily.'

'Maybe you just casually mentioned it to him,' Whitney said.

'I can't remember if I told him. It's really not important, because nothing they did could have damaged the centre. We're too well established and recognised for that to happen.' She sat back in her chair and folded her arms across her chest.

Defiant? Protective?

'What can you tell me about people who have left the centre?' Whitney asked.

'I don't understand what you mean,' Shelley said, frowning.

'Over the past two years, how many recruits have left?'

'Do you mean people who started yoga classes, and attended courses and retreats? Because if that's the case, we have a continual stream of people. Especially the yoga classes, where they might attend for a while and then drop out.'

'Do you get in touch with them to try to persuade them to return?' Whitney asked.

'We keep in contact with everybody through our regular newsletter. We do email people to find out if there's a reason why they haven't been to classes.'

'Do many respond?'

'Some do, and if so, we encourage them to give the classes another try.'

'What about recruits who live-in? How many have left?'

'Over the past two years, three have left for various reasons.'

'What reasons, exactly?' Whitney asked.

Shelley paused and looked upwards.

'She's debating whether or not to tell you something. Keep going on this,' George said.

'Surely you can remember,' Whitney pushed.

'One of our recruits left, or rather, she was forced to leave. We didn't realise at the time, but her family had sent people to infiltrate our yoga classes. The recruit didn't recognise them, or I'm sure she would have said. After one of the classes, before anyone knew what had happened, they escorted her off the premises and drove away. We didn't hear from her again.'

'Did you report her disappearance to the police?'

'No, we didn't want to.'

'Did you investigate, yourselves? Maybe go to her house?' Whitney asked.

'Troy did visit the address we had for her parents, but they had moved.'

'So, you have no idea where she is now, or how she is?'

'If she wants to return, she'll find her way back. They can't keep an eye on her all the time.'

'When did this happen?' Whitney asked.

'About twelve months ago.'

'What's her name and where did the parents live?'

They'd ask Ellie to check, but it seemed unlikely she was connected to the murders after all that time.

'Sadie Letts, and she came from Desborough,' Shelley said.

'What did you do with her possessions?'

'They were collected by someone.'

'And you just let this person take them?'

'Like I said, we can't force people to be at the centre, and we're not going to get involved in any confrontation.'

'Was it you who dealt with the person who came?'

'Yes.'

'And you were convinced the recruit was fine?' Whitney said.

'Why would they lie to me? They'd got what they

wanted by taking her from us. They'll regret it in the long run because you can't contain people who don't want to be contained.'

'Is that how you feel about the centre? Recruits can come and go as they please and leave if they want to?'

'If anyone wants to leave, all they have to do is say. We don't keep them there against their will.' Her arms were still folded. Definitely defiance.

'I'm sure they don't make it easy for them to leave,' George said. 'Find out what happens.'

'Do they have to go through a process if they want to leave?' Whitney asked.

'If anybody wishes to take such a drastic measure, we require them to spend time alone thinking through their decision.'

'How long?'

'Seven days, at least.'

'So, they're left on their own for a week. Are they locked in a room? Are they fed and allowed to sleep?' Whitney asked.

'No, they're not locked in and of course they're allowed to eat and sleep. I fail to see how this is relevant. I having nothing further to say.' Shelley bristled.

'She's putting up a barrier. We've pushed as far as we can,' George said.

'That's all for now, but we may need to interview you again. We'll be coming out to speak to the others in the study group. When do you next meet?' Whitney asked.

'We're having a session tomorrow, after they've finished work.'

'What time?'

'Six,' Shelley said.

Shelley was shown out by Matt. Whitney picked up her folders.

'Looks like now we're getting somewhere,' Whitney said when she came into the observation room.

'Yes. We certainly need to look at this study group and the other people in it,' George said.

'Before we leave, I'll take Ellie the names of these other women, so she can start researching. Their lives could well be at risk.'

Chapter Twenty-One

George had suggested they go to the St Augustus pub. The food was good and the atmosphere congenial. They also served excellent beer, which she was more than happy about. She could murder a pint.

After ordering their meal and drinks, they found a table in the garden, as it was such a lovely day and the sun was still shining. It was a typical beer garden with wooden picnic tables and umbrellas. In one corner stood some play equipment, although luckily there were no children playing and making a noise.

'It's a shame you can't come with us tomorrow,' Whitney said. 'I'm going to see Jamieson first thing for the search warrant. I also want to interview the four other people in the study group.'

'There's no way I can be there, but I'm sure you can catch me up on what you discover.'

'What did you make of the enforced seven-day thinking period for those people who want to leave?' Whitney asked.

'I suspect they do it to deprive them of the comradeship of the cult and make them believe they couldn't manage without the centre. We don't know the exact circumstances. Seven day's isolation can feel like months. At the end of the period they might be so relieved to be back with the rest of the recruits that they change their mind about leaving. It would be interesting to know more about the process. Whether anyone does speak to them. Maybe it's something we should pursue, although I suspect all it will do is confirm to us that the centre is a cult.'

'And that's not going to help us solve the murders, so for now we don't have the time,' Whitney said.

'What's more important is to find out what it is about that particular study group that led four of them to be murdered,' George said.

'Maybe someone found out about Kelly's research and that those in the study group had helped her. If this person felt threatened by it, they might have wanted to destroy all the evidence, including the people.'

'It would have to be something really bad for it to warrant killing everyone who knew,' George said.

'That's what we need to find out.'

'Is Kelly's laptop back from forensics? We need to look at her research, in particular her notes, to see if she discovered anything untoward.'

'I'll check. If it's not, I'll hurry them up. If she is the reason behind them all being killed, we need to see what she unearthed,' Whitney said.

'If it's Shelley who found out, she'd be one of our prime suspects, especially if it turns out the findings are detrimental to her idol, Troy.'

'That's assuming the research is the reason behind their deaths. We ought to consider the sequence of the murders. Why would Kelly be number four? Why wasn't she the first, if she was the cause?' Whitney said.

'Unless it was a question of convenience. Maybe the murderer couldn't get to Kelly straight away.' George picked up her pint and took a sip. She really should come to this pub more often.

'She lived on her own. It should've been easier to get to her rather than Samantha Lyman, who was living with her parents,' Whitney said.

'True.'

'The same goes for Nicola Hurst. She would have been an easier target because she, too, was on her own,' Whitney said.

'Yes, it's definitely something we need to look into and —' George paused, as she could see Whitney's attention had been diverted. She frowned. 'What is it?'

'Nothing,' Whitney said, her cheeks flushing slightly.

'I think it's more than nothing. You're blushing.' George turned to have a second look. Two men were engrossed in conversation at one table, and a couple sitting at another. 'Who are you looking at?'

Whitney's colour increased. 'See the two men over there? The one on the left is Craig, the guy I met at choir and went out with the other night.'

'Do you want us to join them?' George asked.

'No. He doesn't even know I'm here. I didn't expect to see him in this pub. He doesn't even live close by.'

'Why don't you go over?' George asked.

'Because I don't want to interrupt their conversation. He might be talking business. He's dressed like he's in a business meeting.'

'I'm sure he won't mind you saying hello.'

'Look, I'm not going to do anything … Oh crap.'

'What?' George said.

'He's just seen me. Now he's saying something to the

guy he's with. Who's also looking at us. Craig's getting up and coming over here. Just act natural.'

'Natural? Of course I'm going to act natural. I don't understand what you mean.' George frowned.

'Act like you're surprised to see him.'

'How can I be surprised to see someone I don't even know? That's ridiculous.'

'Don't say anything and let me do the talking.'

'Okay, now I get it.'

When Craig arrived at their table, George stared at the man who'd made Whitney blush. He was much as Whitney had described.

'Hello, Whitney. I didn't expect to see you here,' he said.

'Likewise. This is George. She's a forensic psychologist who works with us on certain cases.'

'Pleased to meet you, George.' Craig held out his hand and she shook it. 'Would you like to join us? I'm with a friend.'

'What do you think?' Whitney turned to her, eyes bright.

What George thought didn't really come into it, because clearly Whitney wanted to spend some time with this Craig. 'Entirely up to you.'

'Why don't you come over here? Our table is bigger. Have you ordered your food?' Whitney asked.

'Yes, but we can get it sent over here. I'll go and get Steve.' He walked away.

'You don't mind, do you?' Whitney asked, eyes still gleaming.

'It's fine with me if you want to spend some time with him, but I can't stay very long. I'll have to go once we've eaten.'

'This isn't because of Craig, is it?'

George shook her head. 'You know I'm busy and have to work once I'm home. I just meant that if you wanted to stay with Craig, maybe he could give you a lift home, rather than you leaving when I do.'

'Let's play it by ear,' Whitney said.

The two men came over carrying their drinks.

'I'm afraid it's just going to be me,' Craig said. 'Steve's had a call from his wife. His son fell over during a football match and they think he might have broken his arm. He needs to get back.'

'Good to meet you, ladies,' Steve said. 'Sorry I can't stay, but I'll leave you in Craig's capable hands.' He smiled and walked away.

Craig slid along the bench next to Whitney, and opposite George. This gave her the chance to scrutinise him properly while he was talking to Whitney. He seemed friendly enough, maybe a little too friendly. But she wasn't there to judge. If Whitney liked him, that was good enough.

'So, what's it like being a forensic psychologist, George?' Craig asked, cutting across her thoughts.

'Fascinating. I enjoy analysing people's behaviour.'

'Is that what you're doing now? Do you know things about me I wouldn't want others to find out? Can you tell what I'm thinking?'

'I'm not a mind reader. There's no such thing. I analyse behaviour and can tell a lot from people's body language and posturing. Often more than their words tell me.'

'So, I'd better be careful,' Craig said.

'Do you have anything to be careful about?' she asked, frowning.

'It's just a figure of speech, George,' Whitney said, laughing.

'I know that. I was just playing along,' George said,

fully aware of the discrepancy between her profession and the fact that some social cues totally missed her. But that didn't stop her from doing a good job.

'Of course you were,' Whitney said.

'Whitney tells me you sell upmarket supplements. Is it a lucrative business?' George asked, thinking that Whitney would be pleased for her to change the subject.

'That's a rather direct question,' Craig said.

'George is direct. Don't feel you have to answer,' Whitney said, flashing her a warning glance.

George frowned. 'I was only asking whether it's a good business.'

'I'm happy to answer,' Craig said. 'Yes, it is a lucrative business, and in the last few years I've done very well.'

'You sing in the choir,' George said, deciding she'd change the subject again following the glare from Whitney.

'Yes, I enjoy being in the choir, it's a great place to meet people.' He looked at Whitney and winked.

'It is. I only wish I didn't have to miss so many rehearsals,' Whitney said.

'What case are you working on at the moment?' Craig asked.

'You know I can't discuss my work. It's confidential,' Whitney said.

It was Whitney's standard response to anything that hadn't been reported in the press.

'I totally understand,' Craig replied, smiling.

Except his smile didn't reach his eyes, which were narrowed, as if calculating the situation. A definite disconnect. As to what that meant, she'd need to observe him longer before reaching a conclusion.

She was distracted from her thoughts by their food being delivered, closely followed by Craig's.

They ate in virtual silence. Whitney occasionally spoke,

as did Craig, but mainly they were quiet. George ate quickly so she could leave. She wasn't enjoying herself and she wanted to get on with her work.

'I'm leaving now,' George said as she took her last mouthful and finished her beer.

'I'm ready, too,' Whitney said.

'I can give you a lift if you like?' Craig said.

'Thanks for the offer, but it's fine,' Whitney said.

'It's no trouble.'

'I'm not going straight home. My car's at the police station, which is in the centre of Lenchester.'

'It's up to you. The offer's there, if you like.'

Whitney looked at George. 'Thanks, but I'll go back with George, as we still have a few more things to discuss.'

They left and headed for George's car.

'What do you think?' Whitney asked as they drove out of the car park.

'What about?'

'Craig. Did you like him?'

'I've only just met him. If you like him, why didn't you stay and get a lift?'

'Because if he took me back to the station, I'd have to then invite him home, and the house is a mess, as usual. I also want to take Rob to see Mum for a quick visit. The longer this case goes on the less time I'm going to have to visit them. Is that okay?'

'Of course, it's okay. You don't have to answer to me. I just thought you'd like to spend more time with him,' George said.

'I don't want to come across as too keen.'

'Are you keen?'

'It's early days. I do like him, but I'm not sure I have the space to fit in a relationship. I have very little time as it is, especially as I'm having to do Jamieson's work. Adding something else might be pushing it a bit too far. But I'll see how it goes. I'm sure I can manage the occasional date. What about you and Ross? You haven't spoken about him much recently. How are you doing?'

'Everything's going well. We're both busy. We see each other when we can.'

'Is it serious?'

'It's comfortable. I don't want anything serious. I'm happy for it to stay as it is for now. I enjoy living on my own, and I also enjoy seeing him.'

'I'm happy for you.'

'Thanks, I am for you, too. We deserve it.' She quickly glanced at Whitney, who was glaring at her. 'What?'

'How many times do I have to tell you? Stop with the jinxing.'

Chapter Twenty-Two

'Walker,' Jamieson said, as she walked into his office. 'I was just about to ask you to come up to see me. How fortuitous.'

'Good morning, sir,' Whitney said, groaning inwardly as she wondered how much of his work he wanted to pass on this time.

She was seriously regretting ever agreeing to help him out. No matter how often she told herself it was for the long-term good, it didn't help when, instead of giving the murder investigation her full attention, she found herself thinking of budgets and policy.

'How are you fixed for standing in for me at a drinks reception lunchtime today?'

'We're very busy with the murder investigation, which is why I came to see you,' she said, hoping he'd retract his request.

'I'm sure you can delegate to one of your team. I've got a counselling appointment with my daughter I want to attend. It's only for an hour.'

'Yes, sir. I'll make sure to go along,' she said, not having the time to debate the issue with him, especially as he'd already made his decision.

'I'll get the details sent to you. What do you want to see me about?' he asked.

'As you know, we've got four bodies and we've linked them to the Wellness Spirit Centre, just outside of Lenchester. Although none of the victims were live-in recruits, we have discovered Kelly Yeoman was actually an undercover researcher and she had met up with the other victims away from the centre. There's a possibility she'd been found out, and that was the motive for the murders. She was also related to the second-in-command at the centre. I'd like to request a search warrant so when we go out to interview them again, we can also complete a search of the place. I'll need a large team, as the grounds and manor house are extensive.'

'Do you have a suspect?'

'We'll be interviewing Troy Randall, the owner, again, although we have already spoken to him twice. The women murdered were part of a study group run by the second-in-command. There are four others in the group who live at the centre, unlike our victims. We'll be interviewing them to find out if they knew anything of the research Kelly was undertaking.'

'Are they in danger? If so, we need to get them away from there,' Jamieson said.

'We're unsure, but as all four murders took place away from the centre, we suspect it's unlikely, but it's not something we'll be taking for granted. During their interviews, we'll impress on them the need to be vigilant and suggest they don't spend time alone. We also need to consider that one of them could be the killer.'

'Is that likely?'

She refrained from giving an exasperated sigh. Wasn't it obvious?

'It needs to be borne in mind.'

'What about the press conference you were arranging?' Jamieson asked.

'I'd decided to put it on hold to give us time to investigate, as they'd been reported as suicides. Now we've confirmed they're murders, and linked them to the Wellness Spirit Centre, it's time to go ahead.'

'Leave it with me, and I'll get in touch with Melissa to organise it for this afternoon at three. We should both be back by then.'

'And the search warrant?'

'I'll get onto it straight away. It should have come through by the time I'm back from my appointment.'

'Thank you, sir.'

He picked up the phone to make a call, and Whitney took that as a signal to leave. She went back to the incident room. The team was waiting for her to begin the briefing.

'Listen up, everyone. The Super's sorting out the search warrant, which we should get this afternoon. Matt, get on to SOCO, I want them to come with us. We're going to interview everyone there. We'll go after the press conference, which takes place at three, so we'll be leaving around three-thirty. I don't want to be any later. Our priority is to interview the four remaining in the study group.'

'I can't be late tonight, guv,' Frank said.

'Why not? What is it this time?' Whitney asked.

'The wife wants to go to the cinema to see the new Colin Firth film.'

'Well, you'll have to phone her and tell her you might not make it.'

'Easy for you to say,' he muttered.

'I'll ignore that comment,' she said. 'Plan for when we

get there. Assuming there are classes going on, Matt take Frank and two uniformed officers and do a sweep of all the studios. Direct everyone you find to the dining room. Same in the kitchen and any toilets you pass. Let me know if you come across Shelley Bates or Troy Randall, as they're to be kept separate.'

'Yes, guv,' Matt said.

'Where are the studios?' Frank asked.

'Matt knows. I'll go to the administration offices with Sue. Doug, I want you to take uniform and search the cottages in the grounds.'

'Yes, guv.'

'Ellie, I'll leave you here answering the phone with some extra bodies from uniform. After the press conference, we should have people coming forward with information.'

'Yes, guv.'

'Do you have anything more for us on Kelly Yeoman?' Whitney asked.

'She was much the same as the others. She had a strong social media presence up until a year ago. After that everything stopped,' Ellie said.

'That was because of her research. She wanted to fit in with the ethos of the centre. Apart from her sister, as far as we're aware, the only person who knew about her being undercover was her supervisor. Although when we question the others in the study group, we might discover they knew.' She walked over to the board, and beneath the names of the four victims and their photos, she wrote "study group", with arrows from all the photos pointing to it.

~

Whitney and Jamieson followed Melissa out of the press conference, and they walked down the corridor. Once the PR officer had gone towards her own department, Whitney stopped and turned to Jamieson.

'How did the counselling session go?'

'We're getting there slowly. Thank you for asking. The drinks?'

'As predicted. Boring.'

'The search warrant has come through, as I'm sure you're already aware. Keep me informed.'

'Will do, sir.'

They walked together down the corridor until reaching the stairs, and then they parted company. She made her way back to the incident room.

'Right. Is everyone ready?' She glanced at the team, who were all nodding. 'We'll meet outside the centre's main building. I want one hundred percent focus. If there's anything incriminating there, we're going to find it.'

Chapter Twenty-Three

SOCO were waiting outside the main entrance when Whitney and the team arrived.

'Wait until you hear from me. I'm going to Shelley Bates's office to let her know what's happening.'

She walked through the main door and headed to the office. Just before she got there, Shelley came towards her from the opposite direction.

Whitney held out the piece of paper in her hand. 'I have a search warrant and my officers are waiting to start.'

'You can't do that. We're in the middle of classes.'

'Actually, we can. Where's Troy Randall?'

'He's in one of the meditation rooms,' Shelley said.

'You can take me to him. I also want to speak to the four remaining recruits from Kelly's study group. Where are they?'

'Two of them are in the yoga class, and two are in the kitchen on catering duty.'

'All classes will be ended, and no one allowed to leave, until we say so. My officers will be speaking to everyone. How many classes are in progress?' Whitney asked.

'We have a yoga class and the start of a meditation retreat, with five people participating. Troy's currently doing the introductory session,' Shelley said, a belligerent tone in her voice.

Whitney pulled out her radio. 'Start the search now. Make sure everyone is taken to the dining room.'

'Why there?' Shelley asked.

'So they can be interviewed.'

'Troy won't like this. Isn't there another way?' Shelley asked.

Whitney let out a frustrated sigh. 'We're investigating four murders. We can't just wait until you decide the time is right for us to come and talk to your people. It's got to be done now. Take me to Troy.'

Shelley took her to one of the classrooms, knocking on the door and gently opening it. Whitney could hear Troy talking. He stopped mid-sentence.

'Sorry to interrupt, Troy. We need to speak to you out here,' Shelley said.

'Can't it wait?' Troy said, a slight edge to his voice.

'No. We need you now.'

'I won't be long,' Whitney heard him say.

He walked out of the door and his eyes widened when he saw her.

'We have a search warrant for the centre, which my officers are executing, and we will be interviewing everybody who's here,' Whitney said.

'You do realise I'm in the middle of an introductory session for the meditation retreat I'm running?' He shook his head.

'And you *do* realise we are investigating four murders?' Whitney retaliated.

'I'm very sorry about the murders. But I fail to see why you have to search the centre.'

Was he really that dense, or just being provocative?

'The victims may not have lived onsite, but they all spent a great deal of time here. In particular, they were in a study group together.'

'Do you need me with you when you're searching?' Randall asked, a resigned tone to his voice.

'I want you to wait in your office. One of my officers will escort you.' She pulled out her radio. 'Matt, send an officer to the meditation rooms to take Mr Randall to his office on the first floor, and to stay with him.'

'Yes, guv.'

She turned to Troy. 'We need complete access. Is anywhere locked?'

'We operate an open-door policy. Everywhere is accessible, except my cottage. I'm assuming you won't need to go through there.'

'You assume wrong. We will be searching through your cottage and the others on the grounds. Do you have the key to yours?'

He reached into the pocket of his tracksuit bottoms and pulled it out. 'Here you are,' he said, handing it to her.

'The meditation students are to wait in the room until my officers arrive. They will be escorted to the dining area,' Whitney said.

'This is a brand-new course, and the people on it haven't been here before,' Randall said.

'Then it won't take long to interview them. Let them know and come back here.' He opened his mouth as if to speak, then closed it. He walked back into the room, returning after a few seconds. An officer had already arrived and he escorted Randall from there.

'I need a room to interview the four women from Kelly Yeoman's study group,' she said turning to Shelley, who'd been standing there in silence.

'You can use one of our smaller meeting rooms. I'll show you.'

They walked further along the corridor, and Shelley stopped outside another room and opened the door. 'Here it is.'

'I want you to go straight to your office and stay there until you've been interviewed.'

'Again? I can't tell you any more than I have already,' Shelley said.

'Please do as I ask.'

Shelley took off down the corridor, and Whitney radioed Matt to arrange for an officer to go to the woman's office. She didn't want her conferring with Randall. She also instructed him to identify the four women from the study group and ask one of the uniformed officers to bring them to her.

She went into the meeting room and brought four chairs out into the corridor.

After a few minutes, one of the PCs arrived. 'Guv, the women you asked to see,' he said.

Whitney pulled out her notebook. 'Who's Leah?' she asked gently.

'I am,' the youngest looking one said.

'Tamara?'

'That's me,' replied the one with curly auburn hair.

'Jenny?'

'Me,' said the older of the four.

'And you must be Abi.' She nodded in the direction of the remaining girl.

'Yes.'

The women were pale and uncertain. 'Please sit down. I'm DCI Whitney Walker. We're investigating the deaths of Nicola Hurst, Samantha Lyman, Hayley Tennant, and Kelly Yeoman. We'd like to ask you some questions, as you were all in the same study group.'

'T-they're all dead?' Abi said, her eyes wide.

'We thought they'd decided to leave,' Jenny said.

'Why did you think that?'

'When they didn't turn up for a few weeks, we assumed they'd gone.'

'Jenny, if you could come with me, I'll interview you first.' Already Whitney could see she'd be the best person to start with, as she was the most vocal and the others were sitting there looking bewildered.

'Okay.' Jenny followed Whitney into the small room.

'How close were the members of the study group?' Whitney asked once they were seated.

'Fairly,' Jenny said.

'Didn't you think it strange when so many members of the group stopped attending?'

'No. It happens sometimes, especially when people don't live-in and are unable to embrace our style of living.'

She was acting very calm, as if the deaths weren't a surprise. According to George, it's the guilty people who can try very hard to show their shock and disbelief, so they're not suspected.

'When you moved in here, did you leave your job, or do you still work outside of the centre?'

'I left my job as a corporate lawyer.'

Whitney did a double take. A lawyer and now a recruit? Then again, remembering what George had said, it was very easy to pull in intelligent people.

'Didn't you enjoy the law?'

'It was too superficial. I'm happier here. It's where I belong.'

'Do you leave the centre often?'

'There's hardly any need to. We grow much of our

own food and anything else is ordered in or Shelley will collect it,' Jenny said.

'What about doctor or dental appointments?'

'Yes, we leave to go there, if necessary. We're not held captive. It's our choice.'

Was it?

'Returning to the four victims, can you think of any reason why someone would want to end their lives?' Whitney asked.

'I can't. It seems inconceivable.' Jenny shook her head.

'What about one of the recruit's families? There must be some angry people out there, if they lost their loved ones to the centre. What did your family think when you left your job and moved in?' Whitney asked.

'My family emigrated several years ago. We've lost contact.' Jenny shrugged.

'Was this after you came in here?'

'My parents divorced when I was young, and they both have new partners. They know where I live but neither wanted to find out about it. They're too busy with their lives.'

'How did you become involved in the centre?'

'I took a meditation course after my GP recommended I do something to reduce the stress I was under. It was the best thing I'd ever done.'

'How long was it between taking the course and you moving in as a full-time recruit?' Whitney asked.

'Eighteen months. It was a gradual process. I began to spend more and more time at the centre. The further along the path I went, the more I realised what I'd been doing up to then was playing at life. I wasn't developing myself at all. It was all work, work, work, without paying attention to what it was doing to me.'

'You must miss the money you were earning?' Whitney said.

'Money means nothing. It doesn't help true spiritual enlightenment. I'd take that over money any day of the week.'

'Did you know the others in the study group before joining?' Whitney asked.

'No.'

'Did the eight of you spend time with each other outside of the study group?' Whitney asked.

'Sometimes, when we were doing the garden,' Jenny said.

'Does everyone work in the garden?'

Yes. Troy believes that being at one with nature will help us develop more,' Jenny said.

'What about members who don't live-in, like Kelly, Hayley, Samantha, and Nicola?' Whitney asked.

'Everyone helps in the garden if they're here on a regular basis and attend more than just a single yoga class. It's all part of the programme. Along with our one-to-one sessions with Troy and Shelley.'

'How much time do you spend in the garden?'

She had a gut feeling the gardening had something to do with the case.

'We usually do a couple of hours at a time, sometimes more, sometimes less, but we don't spend that time talking. If we do, someone will come up and ask us to stop,' Jenny said.

'So, you're instructed not to talk, but you do?'

'It just depends on whereabouts we are. There's always someone around if we are in the main grounds, and we get on quietly. So, we can be mindful of what we're doing. That's the whole point of it. It's a mindfulness exercise. You can't be mindful if you're talking.'

'Where are the quieter areas where you do talk?' Whitney prodded.

'The three cottages. They're out of the way.'

'Do you do those gardens in pairs?' Whitney asked.

'Usually two or three of us will go.'

'Were you ever alone with Kelly?'

'Occasionally we would do the weeding together,' Jenny said.

'Did you talk during these times?'

'A little. Mainly about the centre and how well we were doing,' Jenny said.

'Did Kelly ask you about your life before moving in here?'

'We're not meant to talk about it because it gets in the way of our progress.'

'That's not what I asked. Did you speak about it at all?' Whitney pushed.

'We might have talked about it a little.' Jenny glanced at her feet, appearing a little awkward.

'Did Kelly ask you probing questions?'

Jenny frowned. 'Yes, she did. How do you know? I thought it was because she hadn't moved in permanently and wanted reassurance.'

'Did you answer her questions honestly?' Whitney said.

'Of course.'

'What were you doing on the twenty-seventh of August, and the fourth, eleventh, and eighteenth of September?'

'I was here. The only time I've left the centre over the last few months was when we went on our annual retreat. Everyone here can vouch for me.'

'Is there anything else you can think of that might help us?' Whitney asked.

'No.'

'You can go back outside. Please send Leah in.' Having interviewed the eldest, she'd next try the youngest.

Leah walked in with a scared expression on her face. 'Y-you want to see me next?'

'Yes, come and sit down,' Whitney said.

'I can't believe they're all dead.' Tears rolled down her cheeks and she brushed them away with the back of her hand.

Whitney reached into her bag and pulled out a tissue. 'Take this,' she said.

'Thanks.' Leah wiped her eyes and sniffed.

'I'd like to ask you about when you go gardening,' Whitney said when the girl seemed more in control.

'Yes?'

'Did you garden at the cottages with Kelly recently?'

'Yes, I did.'

'What sort of things did you talk about while you were there?'

'Our backgrounds, where we came from and how long we've been here, and how much we enjoy it.'

'Didn't you think it odd that she was asking you all these questions?' Whitney asked.

'Not really. She hadn't moved in and it's a big step to take. Even though for all of us it was a natural progression, it's still hard because there are things you miss,' Leah replied.

'What do you miss most from your previous life?' Whitney asked.

The girl averted her gaze and coloured slightly. 'Chocolate.'

That took Whitney by surprise. She'd been expecting her to say family or work or friends.

'You don't eat chocolate when you're here?'

'We don't have anything with sugar as it's addictive. We

have to keep ourselves pure, otherwise we won't be able to reach our spiritual enlightenment. We can't consume anything that will affect our brains.'

'Does that include alcohol?' Whitney asked, remembering that Hayley was found with some in her body.

'Yes.'

'We do know that Hayley had been drinking prior to her death.'

'The rules are only enforced once we move in here permanently. We're encouraged to resist beforehand, but it's not always easy.'

'Apart from chocolate, is there anything else you miss?' Whitney asked.

'By the time I moved in, everything I wanted was here,' Leah said.

'What about your family? How did they feel about you being here?' Whitney asked.

'They didn't understand, but they have their own journeys to make. I can't be responsible for them,' Leah said, full of the centre's rhetoric.

Did she genuinely believe it?

'Tell me about Nicola, Hayley, and Samantha. Did they spend time alone with Kelly?'

'Samantha and Hayley worked with me and Kelly on Stewart's garden. We all spent time talking about being at the centre then,' Leah said.

'And how long ago was this?' Whitney asked.

'We started a few months ago. We've been spending quite a lot of time there because it's being turned into a Buddhist garden.'

'What does that involve?' Whitney asked, certain that George would know straight away.

'It's simple and goes by the Buddhist principles of peace, serenity, goodness, and respect for all living things.

We put in Buddha statues and a pond with lotus blooms floating in it. We've also placed lanterns in there. It's beautiful.'

'Why Stewart's garden and not Troy's?' Whitney asked.

'I believe Troy's is going to be done next. He wanted us to tackle Stewart's first, to iron out any issues,' Leah said.

George had said he was a narcissist. This seemed to confirm it.

'How did you get selected for doing Stewart's garden, instead of doing the ordinary upkeep of the grounds?'

'Because we're all in Shelley's study group. She allocated us the task.'

Why would she just use them and not the others? What was she up to?

'Would you say you're Shelley's favourite study group?'

'She doesn't have favourites. That's not in line with the ethos of the centre,' Leah said.

'So why were you chosen?'

'Shelley looks at the groups' strengths when deciding how to allocate tasks, and for us it was the redesigning of the gardens,' Leah replied.

'What about Nicola? Did she ever work on the garden?'

'Yes. But not often.'

'Were you happy to do it, or was it a chore? How did you all feel about it?' Whitney asked.

'It isn't a case of being happy or unhappy about doing a designated task. We do whatever we're asked because we know it will help us on our individual journey,' Leah said.

'But do you enjoy doing it?' Whitney pushed.

'It's very satisfying work,' Leah said.

Clearly, she wasn't going to get anything else out of her. She'd been so indoctrinated into the centre's way of thinking it was like talking to a puppet. But at least she had a better idea of what questions Kelly had been asking.

'Thank you for your help. That's all I need at the moment. I may come back to you at a later date. Before you leave, did you report to anyone that Kelly had been asking you questions?'

'When Shelley asked me how the garden was going, I mentioned Kelly had been asking what it was like when we moved into the centre,' Leah said.

'And what was her response?'

'She didn't say anything. She just listened.'

'Thank you,' Whitney said.

Now they were getting somewhere.

Chapter Twenty-Four

'Did you find anything of interest in the search?' George asked Whitney when she arrived at the station first thing on Monday morning. 'I wish I'd been with you; I'm sure it was fascinating.' Although she hadn't been able to go with them to the centre, she had found time to check the Minutes archive of the Research Ethics Committee, and Kelly's application and approval. Everything had seemed in order.

'We discovered how Kelly had been undertaking her research. She'd definitely been using her study group. Not as informants, because they didn't know why she was asking questions. I interviewed all of them individually, and their answers were all similar.'

'How did she manage to do that without people realising what she was doing?' George asked.

'The study group was tasked with redesigning the accountant's garden, and they were alone for most of the time. Kelly took advantage of that.'

'Did they think it strange she was questioning them?' George asked.

'They just thought it was because she wanted to know how it was before she made her final decision about joining them permanently.'

'Did anyone else know what she was doing?' George asked.

'Shelley Bates was told by one of them.'

'Did you speak to Shelley about it afterwards?'

'Yes, and she said although it wasn't condoned, she understood why Kelly had done it.'

'Very non-committal.'

'Exactly. Oh, by the way, Claire's report came in earlier. Kelly had traces of the same drug in her blood stream that was used on Hayley. No injection site. It was administered orally. Not through alcohol, but most likely apple juice. Also, there was no evidence of a struggle.'

'Indicating she knew her killer,' George said.

'Yes.'

'Did you chase up Kelly's laptop?'

'Yes. They promised it would be here this morning. Let's see if Ellie's heard back.' They headed over to the officer's desk. 'Any progress on Kelly Yeoman's laptop?' Whitney asked.

'Yes, guv. They emailed me the files a while ago. I've been going through them.'

'What have you got on her research?' George asked.

'There's a sub-folder called PhD in a larger research folder. It has lots of documents in it. I'll email you the entire thing.'

'Thanks,' George said. 'I'll look through and see if there's anything that might help us.'

She went over to the desk she often used when she was at the station and turned on the computer. The research folder was already in her inbox. A lot of it was theoretical. There was an itemised literature review, showing Kelly had been examining other studies into cults and their behaviour. She'd also included Troy Randall's book *Enlighten Your Spirit*, which she'd criticised for being a one-sided rhetoric, and for not taking a more unified approach.

Next, she got onto Kelly's notes from her time at the centre. They were in diary format and discussed the rules and regulations. She'd concluded they were cleverly enforced and weren't implemented in a strict, dictatorial way, but appealed to the emotional and more easily manipulated parts of the human psyche. She'd referred to it as brainwashing. George quickly flicked back to the literature review and confirmed she'd included texts relating to the successful brainwashing of people. George would have happily supervised such a promising student. There was also a folder containing Kelly's discussions with the recruits. Again, her notes were in diary format. She came to the entry regarding Nicola's suicide.

'Found anything?'

She jumped at Whitney's words and dragged her focus away from the files.

'Kelly's research is very interesting and once published would definitely have made a difference to the centre. She believed the way it operated was very much like other documented cults, and that the people in there are brainwashed and manipulated in discreet ways, through conversation and policy. I've just opened the folder on her interviews and started to read about Nicola.'

'What does it say?' Whitney asked as she pulled out the chair next to George and sat down.

'She was distraught about the death, especially as she'd been the one to find the body. She blamed herself for not noticing Nicola was suicidal.'

'Does she mention anything about Samantha and Hayley?'

'Not so far. Let me look.' She scanned the pages in front of her. 'Here's something. Kelly met with them both and told them about Nicola. She swore them to secrecy because Shelley had told her they weren't going to tell others at the centre. She also noted that the two women didn't attend classes for the next two weeks. She assumed it was because they were upset about Nicola. Her last entry was that she intended to contact them if they didn't appear the following week. But by then she was dead.'

'If someone had found out about Kelly's research, they would definitely have wanted to put an end to it,' Whitney said.

'Agreed.'

'That points the finger at Shelley Bates. Maybe she'd found out about the research. We know she'd been told about Kelly asking questions, and she knew it was only the study group Kelly had been talking to. She might have also worked out that the rest of Kelly's research was being undertaken through her being undercover and that she wasn't interested in becoming a recruit.'

'It's what we call *covert participant observation*,' George said.

'What I still don't understand is, why murder Nicola, Samantha, and Hayley first, and not Kelly?'

'Logistics?' George suggested.

'Also, why leave the other four recruits?'

'Because they didn't meet with Kelly away from the centre to discuss their experiences. It could be that Kelly confided in the other three victims about her research.'

'Why would she do that?'

'She was an inexperienced researcher. She might have believed she could trust them. She told them about Nicola, so she may have thought of them as her friends. She wouldn't be the first to let down her guard in that way,' George said.

'Another thing to consider is that although there were eight of them in the study group, the victims were different from the other four recruits because they *chose* not to live onsite.'

'The one flaw in that argument is, although I can see Samantha and, to a point, Hayley not wanting to live there full-time, why wouldn't Nicola? She didn't have a job or any life away from the centre,' George said.

'Perhaps none of them had been asked. From what I gather, it's not easy to get into the centre full-time. They have to be selected, and their progress is monitored. Like Kelly's was,' Whitney said.

'Alternatively, they wanted to live-in, but they hadn't been allowed and were unhappy about it. It would make them more inclined to help Kelly when she questioned them.'

'But if they were unhappy with what was going on, they could have just left,' Whitney said.

'It wouldn't be easy to leave. They wanted to be a part of the centre because they adhered to the beliefs and values and had been indoctrinated. Not being allowed to live-in meant they were trapped, not knowing what to do. They'd also distanced themselves from their other lives and would be feeling in limbo,' George said.

'From what we've discovered, the motivating factor for the four deaths appears to be Kelly's research. But we need to know more about what goes on at the centre.'

'Ideally we need someone undercover.'

'It's definitely worth considering,' Whitney said. 'And—'

'Guv,' Frank called out, interrupting them.

'Yes?'

'The Super wants you in his office immediately.'

'What the hell does he want this time?' Whitney said, sighing heavily. 'I won't be long.'

Whitney left, and George brought up the centre's website to study. She clicked on the list of programmes on offer and discovered there was another stop smoking one starting at the end of the week. Four days' duration, from Friday through to Monday. She pulled out her phone and checked her diary to see if she was available. She was.

'Why not,' she muttered to herself. 'Kill two birds with one stone. I get to quit smoking and find out more about the place.'

It was one of Whitney's win-win situations. She found the phone number on the webpage, annoyed she couldn't sign-up online.

She keyed in the number.

'Wellness Spirit Centre, Dana speaking.'

'I've just been on your website and see that you have a stop smoking course this weekend. Are there any spaces available?' George asked.

'I'll just check for you. I think it's full, though,' Dana said.

'Damn,' she muttered while listening to the crashing waves hold music.

'Hello,' Dana said, coming back to her after a few moments. 'We do actually have a space; I just need some details.'

George was about to give her full name when she realised they might know about her relationship with the police. She decided to use her mother's maiden name. 'Georgina Pilkington.'

She then gave her mobile number. She'd have to change her voice message and set up an email address. She should've thought of all this before calling them.

'The cost is seven-hundred and fifty pounds. We take payment by credit card or Internet banking.'

She couldn't give her card details, as it had her real surname. 'That's lovely. I'll pay online.'

It'd better be worth it for that money.

'Please could you let me have your email address. I'll send your receipt once the money has gone through, together with the details. The programme lasts for four days. We expect you here by eight-thirty on Friday morning and the course will end at five o'clock on Monday afternoon,' Dana said.

'I'm having trouble with my email and I'm looking to change it. I'll get that sorted out today and let you know what it is later.'

She ended the call and then hurriedly set herself up a new account in the name of Georgina Pilkington. She was just about to phone the centre to pass on her details, when Whitney strode over.

'Bloody Jamieson has given me another report to look through. Have you found something?' she asked, nodding at the screen, which still had the website up on it.

'I've signed up for a stop smoking programme this weekend,' George said.

'W-what?' Whitney spluttered.

'We need someone undercover, and I want to quit smoking. When I saw they had a course this weekend, I signed up.'

'You've got to be kidding me. Jamieson's going to go ballistic. You can't go undercover, you're not a police officer.'

'I want to stop smoking and this seemed a perfect opportunity. I'm not doing anything dangerous. Nobody knows who I am, as I signed up under a different name. It's not going to cause any problems.'

'Easy for you to say. You don't have to deal with him.' Whitney glared at her. 'Think of all the trouble we went through just to get you on the train with us during the Carriage Murders.'

'Don't tell him. What I choose to do in my own time is my business. I'm not contracted to the police. I'm perfectly entitled to take a course if I wish.'

'I'll pretend you didn't say that because this isn't the George I know. Tell me more about the course.'

'It starts on Friday and finishes on Monday. I've got the time free, so it's perfect.'

'Why are you adamant about wanting to stop smoking? Is it because of Ross?'

'It's good for my health to stop. I have mentioned wanting to stop before.'

'Yes, but you didn't seem serious about it. I thought you were paying it lip service.'

George leaned back in her chair and folded her arms. 'I'm serious about it now. Plus, it will save me money. Well, it better, the amount the course costs.'

'How much?'

'Seven-hundred and fifty pounds.'

'Bloody hell. I could lock you up in a room for four days and keep you away from cigarettes for half that amount. Are you sure you want to do this? It's very expensive and we don't even know if it's going to work. And I doubt we'd be able to claim the cost back on expenses.' She paused for a moment. 'Then again, we could always try.'

'I don't want to claim it back on expenses. I'm sure it will be more involved than just locking me in a room on my own for four days.'

'How many do you smoke a day?'

'Depends on what I'm doing. Since I've been working

with you, I'm smoking more, because we get ourselves into some very awkward situations. I've been smoking ten a day and I hate it.'

'There must be cheaper ways of quitting. But now you've signed up I suppose it'll be useful to have you on the inside, even if it's only for a few days. We'll work out a strategy for keeping in touch.'

'That should be easy enough.' She paused. 'Damn.'

'What?' Whitney asked.

'I've just remembered, I'd arranged for Ross and I to meet up for lunch with my brother and his fiancée on Saturday.'

'Can you cancel?'

'I'll have to, because this is far more important. We might learn something we wouldn't have from other avenues. And, even if I don't find anything of use to the investigation, if I stop smoking it's a win.'

'You're right. We just have to hope Jamieson sees it the same way.'

Chapter Twenty-Five

Whitney headed into Jamieson's office, holding her report on the initiative to tackle serious violent crime that he'd wanted her to look at. It might put him in a better frame of mind when she told him about George. As she walked down the corridor, she bumped into his assistant.

'Is he in?'

'Yes, but he's not in a very good mood.'

Whitney debated whether to turn back and return later. But she couldn't risk it in case he ended up leaving early for the day. She needed to get the George business sorted, pronto.

'Thanks for letting me know. Unfortunately, this can't wait.'

She carried on to his office and knocked on the closed door.

'Come in,' Jamieson called.

'I brought my comments back for you on the violent crime initiative. I thought you'd want them straight away.'

'Thank you, Walker. Is there anything of note?'

'I did agree with the suggestion to fund a special task-force to tackle the problem, and also to involve community groups. But it also contained a lot of bureaucratic waffle.'

'I hope you didn't put that in your comments. I need to present it to the Chief Constable later.' He arched an eyebrow.

'No, sir. All you have is my objective assessment.'

'Why didn't you email it to me?' he asked, strumming his fingers on the desk impatiently. 'It would've been quicker. I've got a lot on and have to leave shortly.'

'I did email it to you but, as I needed to discuss something else, I thought I'd bring a paper copy, in case you wanted to go through it with a pen before making any changes.'

'That's not the way I operate, Walker. I work directly onto the computer and don't feel the need to handwrite anything. That's so last century.'

Of course it was. What was she thinking? Him and his bloody twenty-first century policing he threw in her face at every opportunity.

'Well, I still need to speak to you about another matter,' she said, choosing to ignore his remark and not let him see it riled her.

'Make it quick. I don't have much time.'

She inwardly seethed. If she didn't need to get permission for George, she would've cheerfully told him where to stuff it, but she couldn't do that because she was a grown up. But that didn't stop her from thinking it.

'As you know, we're investigating the Wellness Spirit Centre, and nothing turned up from the search. We've discovered one of the victims was an undercover researcher from the university and that she'd spoken to the other three victims about their time there. Although we're not sure if they actually knew she was researching the place.'

'Do you believe the offender is someone who found out about her research and thought it would harm the centre?'

'That's one avenue we're investigating. But what we are going to do is have someone actually attend a course at the centre. Then we can get an insider's view of how they operate.'

'You mean you want someone undercover. Which officer did you have in mind?'

Whitney sucked in a breath. 'We're not planning on putting an officer in there. Dr Cavendish has signed herself up for the quit smoking course, starting this Friday for four days.'

'What?' he yelled, putting both hands on his desk and leaning forward, staring directly at her. If it was possible for smoke to come out of his ears, she suspected it would have.

'George has been talking for some time about wanting to give up smoking. It was her idea to register.'

'Are you sure you didn't encourage her so we could use her as an undercover informant?'

'George only does what *she* wants to. I certainly didn't encourage her. I wasn't even there when she did it. I know it's not ideal, but—'

'There are no buts about it. What happens if they find out Dr Cavendish works with the police? We already have four bodies; we don't want her to be the fifth.'

'I think you're overreacting. For a start, nobody at the centre has seen George. Also, she enrolled under a different name. They won't be able to connect her back to us. And, lastly, we'll be in contact with her all the time. She'll be perfectly safe.'

Whitney was tempted to cross her fingers behind her back because she still had her doubts.

'I cannot believe that, after what happened when she

was attacked on the train a few months ago, she is prepared to put herself in this position, and you're willing to go along with it.'

'I understand, but I think this is our best chance of finding out what's going on. George wants to quit smoking, so she has a genuine reason for being there. She could have gone on the course anyway, irrespective of our investigation.'

Jamieson stared at her, the expression on his face not giving anything away. Finally, after what seemed like thirty minutes, but was probably only one, he spoke.

'I will sanction this, but just know I'm not happy about it. If anything happens to Dr Cavendish, I will hold you personally responsible.'

'Yes, sir. Thank you. I understand that. Believe me, if anything does happen to Dr Cavendish, which it won't, I will feel more than *personally responsible*.'

A part of her had hoped Jamieson would say no. Especially after he'd mentioned the train attack. Then again, they did need George there.

'I want a daily report from you on how it's going. You can go now.' He dismissed her with a flick of his hand, and she left his office.

Whitney knocked on the door, holding a bottle of wine in her hand. She hoped it would meet with George's approval, as she was such a wine buff. It was a New Zealand Sauvignon Blanc, and she'd seen a similar bottle in George's fridge on a previous occasion.

George opened the door dressed casually in jeans and a T-shirt.

'I brought this for us,' Whitney said, holding up the

bottle and handing it to her. 'To drink while we're getting you prepared for the weekend.'

'Good choice,' George said as they headed to the kitchen. 'I'll put this in to chill first.'

'Isn't it cold enough? It's only been out of the fridge for fifteen minutes.'

'It could do with a bit longer.' George rubbed her hand along the bottle before opening the fridge and resting it on the top shelf.

'I went to see Jamieson and, as predicted, he went off on one.'

'What did he say?'

'He wasn't happy about you going, and he brought up you being attacked by the Carriage Killer.'

'Did he say I couldn't go?' George asked.

'No, he didn't. He said if anything happened to you, then it's going to be on my head. Which is what I expected.'

'You could have said it wasn't up to him whether I went. It was my decision and I'm not employed by the police. I do want to quit smoking.'

'That's exactly what I did say. Anyway, he's given us his permission, which means if you do collect any evidence, we can use it, and some crafty barrister won't be able to get it thrown out of court.'

'Good.'

'Now we have to devise a strategy for what's going to happen while you're there. We need to decide the times we're going to be in contact for your feedback. We also need to have a code word if I phone, or you phone, and there's an issue.'

'Agreed. I'm actually looking forward to going. Not just to stop smoking, but it will be fascinating to get an insider's view of how a place like that operates.'

'Make sure you don't ask too many questions; we don't want to raise any suspicions. What job are you going to say you do?' Whitney asked.

'I was going to tell the truth. A university lecturer.'

'What happens if they check you out? Members of staff at the university are very easy to track down because of the extensive website. Not only that, what about all the publicity you've had from your research into working with the police? A Google search is bound to bring that up. Perhaps you should think of something else that would make it impossible for them to discover it's not true.'

'I'll say I'm a medical researcher and work at the hospital. They'll never be able to find me there,' George said.

'Great. I'm assuming you know something about medical research and could answer any questions.'

'Yes, I can bluff my way around that.'

'Is the wine ready yet?' Whitney asked, trying to stop herself from going over all the things that could possibly go wrong.

George took the bottle from the fridge, opened it, and poured them both a glass. Then she sniffed and finally took a sip.

'Excellent. You're definitely learning more about wine.'

'No. I'm just a good detective. I spotted something similar in your fridge a while ago and bought a bottle. I kept it at home until such time as I might need it.' Whitney laughed and took a sip of her own drink.

'Okay, good detective work. You mentioned having a strategy for being in contact with each other. It might be hard initially, as I don't know the itinerary. Whether they're going to keep us busy during the day only, or whether we have activities going on right through until we go to bed at night. The best thing is for me to text once I've seen the programme, which I'm assuming they'll give to us on the first day. After that we can plan times to keep in contact.'

'That would work. I want to speak to you every day, or every evening, so you can pass on anything you've found out,' Whitney said.

'That shouldn't be an issue. We're bound to have some time to ourselves. It's not a prison, and I'm assuming it's only going to be normal people like me on the course.'

'From what I gather, people attend courses and from there are encouraged to join the yoga or meditation classes and go on a regular basis. It's a gradual enticement to join the centre.'

'There's clearly going to be something going on during the course, because we know from our victims that they changed immediately after attending,' George said.

'Brainwashing right from the start?'

'It's a possibility. It really depends on the structure of the course and how much time we're being instructed. If it's four days of intensive tuition, then yes that could quite easily happen.'

'What if you end up being brainwashed?' Whitney asked.

'I'm aware of the possibility so won't allow it to happen.'

'But didn't you say cults are able to indoctrinate highly intelligent people easily?'

'It's true they are more susceptible, but I'm going in having the knowledge about cults and how they operate. I'm not going to engage in dialogue and argument, because that's how they manage to persuade people of their views. I'm going to make sure I participate, but at the same time, I will observe,' George said.

'And, because you're talking to me every day, I'll be able to bring you back to reality.'

'That will help, but I'm sure it won't be necessary. Kelly managed not to become indoctrinated. I will be the same.'

Whitney looked closely at George and began doubting if they were doing the right thing. 'You know it's not too late to back out. I don't want you to find yourself in some sort of trouble.'

'Whitney, you're talking nonsense. It's only a four-day course. Nothing's going to happen, except I might finally stop smoking.'

Chapter Twenty-Six

George was up at five, packed and ready to go by six. She didn't have to be at the centre until eight-thirty and, even allowing for traffic, she didn't need to leave until seven-thirty at the earliest. She'd only packed casual clothes as she didn't imagine there would be a need for anything else. She'd also included some gym gear, as in the confirmation letter it stated to bring comfortable clothes for the activities they'd be doing, one of which she assumed was yoga.

She made herself some coffee and stared longingly at the packet of cigarettes and lighter on the side. She'd contemplated throwing them away but changed her mind. When she got back on Monday evening, whether she could resist smoking one, would be a test of how successful the programme had been. In the meantime, she'd have one last cigarette before she left for the centre, to help quell her nerves.

By seven-twenty she'd decided to leave. She was fed up with pacing around the house. The journey was easy along the country roads, and she'd made it to the centre before eight. She drove up the main drive until the house was in front of her. It was a fine example of a nineteenth century manor house. The grounds were equally as beautiful. She was looking forward to having a look around as she could already see the care and attention taken with them.

She drove around the left-hand side of the house into a car park. The sky was already bright blue, and the sun was shining. September was always a bit hit and miss, but today it was perfect. Their instructions were to walk around to the front of the house and into the main entrance, where there would be signs for registration.

There was one other car in the car park. She wondered if they were also there for the course. A man in his fifties, slightly overweight with short grey hair, got out of his car and looked around, appearing unsure of where to go next. Normally, George wouldn't make the first move and talk to someone she didn't know. She much preferred to stay in the background if it was non-work related. But this was different. She got out of her car and walked over.

'Are you here for the quit smoking programme?' she asked.

'Yes, I am, and I'm dying for a cigarette. What about you?'

'Ditto. Although I did have one just before I left home,' she admitted.

'Me too. My wife gave me the course as a present for my birthday. She'd been nagging me to give up smoking for a long time because of my health. I get asthma.'

'Maybe it is a good idea to give up, if it's affecting your health,' George said.

'What's your reason for wanting to quit?'

'Because it's antisocial. It's expensive, and my boyfriend doesn't smoke.'

What made her say that? Especially to a stranger.

'They sound good enough reasons. My name's Ian Spark.'

'Georgina Pilkington,' she said, holding out her hand and shaking his. 'But most people call me George.'

'Good to meet you. Now I'll have someone to complain to when I'm desperate for a smoke. Did you bring any with you?'

'No, of course not. Why would I do that?' She frowned.

'I've got some in the car, in case I feel the need to sneak out.' He gave a wry smile.

'They'll smell it on you.'

'I brought breath mints, too.'

'Are you sure this is what you really want to do? Because bringing cigarettes with you probably isn't the best of ideas,' George said.

'To be honest, no it isn't. But I've promised the wife to give it a try.'

'Even if you have brought some as back-up.' She shook her head. 'Maybe you should give me the cigarettes and I'll look after them for you. That way you won't find it easy to sneak out for one.'

And now she was suggesting she helped him. What was coming over her? It wasn't even as if she had a hangover and wasn't thinking clearly. Last night she'd gone to bed early, after a quick phone conversation with Ross who, like Whitney, wanted her to keep in touch and let him know how it was going. He didn't know the other reason for her being there, though.

'Thanks for the offer, but no thanks. If you have them, it will be too much of a temptation for you.'

'It won't be.'

'What about if I feel tempted, before actually coming

out to have a cigarette, I find you, so you can talk me down?'

'Deal,' George said.

She was pleased to be going in knowing someone, albeit very briefly, and he did seem like a nice guy. She wouldn't look obvious when looking around if she had someone with her. He could be of assistance.

'Shall we walk around and register?' Ian said.

'Okay. As we're early, we'll have time to explore and see more of the house. It is beautiful, don't you think?' George said.

'Yes. Also, being early means we'll appear keen, and they'll think we're going to be top of the class.'

'Arrival time doesn't correlate with how well a person's going to do on the programme.'

He looked at her and frowned. Had she misinterpreted his comment?

'Come on, let's go,' Ian said.

They walked around the building until they got to the front of the house.

'What an impressive hall,' Ian said as they walked inside.

'It's breathtaking,' George replied. 'It's a fine example of neo-gothic architecture and the portraits on the wall look like the work of Gainsborough, as do the landscapes.'

'You know all about art and architecture?' Ian said.

'I'm not an expert, but I do enjoy it.'

'Not me. I'm a philistine when it comes to anything to do with art. What do you do for a job?'

'I'm a medical researcher,' she said, just managing in time to stop herself from saying she was a forensic psychologist.

'You must be clever. I left school at sixteen with hardly

any qualifications. I trained as a builder and now own a building company.'

'Sounds very interesting,' she said.

'I'm not sure interesting is the word, but it certainly gives us a good living.'

They followed the signs until they came to a room with a 'stop smoking programme' notice on the door. They walked in. At the front, behind a desk, George recognised Shelley Bates. She'd seen her from the interview room where she'd been hidden on the other side of the glass.

'Good morning,' Shelley said. 'You're nice and early.'

'Yes,' George said.

'I'm Shelley Bates and I'll be leading the programme. Please sign in here.' She pointed to a piece of paper on the desk. 'Take your name badge and a course itinerary. Feel free to sit anywhere you like.'

George took hers and counted nine others. Only ten of them on the course. That would give her plenty of opportunity to get to know everyone. Centre staff included. The tables were set out in a horseshoe style. She went to the back and sat in the middle as it gave her a good view. She wasn't sure whether all the training would be undertaken by Shelley or if there would be others, as the itinerary didn't give the names of the instructors. Maybe even Troy himself would do a session. She'd like to hear him speak.

Ian sat next to her. 'We should have gone for an explore first,' he said.

'We have plenty of time. We'll have to go to our rooms to unpack. I imagine it will be first thing, or maybe at lunchtime.' She glanced at the itinerary. 'Actually, looking at this I think we'll be taken to our accommodation sooner rather than later as we have a yoga class this morning and people will want to get changed.'

'Yoga? I didn't sign-up for that,' Ian said, scowling.

'I'm sure there's a reason for why it's included. Did you bring something comfortable to wear as stated in the information sheet they sent us?'

'I think my wife put in a pair of shorts and T-shirt.'

They sat in relative silence until the other delegates arrived. Out of the ten of them, there were four men and six women, including her. They were a variety of ages, from what appeared to be late twenties to someone in their sixties.

'Welcome, everyone, to the Wellness Spirit Centre,' Shelley said. 'This is very different from any stop smoking programme you might have come across in the past. That's because we address more than wanting to quit smoking. We're going to work with you all, sometimes as a group, sometimes individually, to look at the deeper reasons behind why you smoke, and how beneficial it's going to be for you once you've given up. We're proponents of being mindful in all we do, and this will help you in giving up your addiction to cigarettes. If you've looked at the itinerary you've been given, you will see that it's going to be a very full on four days. We're going to start with a yoga class, followed by a meditation session. They should relax you so you're more receptive to the other sessions. We're going to have a discussion on smoking, during which I encourage you all to participate. After lunch we're going to engage in a group hypnotherapy session.'

Hypnotherapy? She hadn't realised that was included. Ellie had mentioned they offered it, but there was no mention on the course details she'd read. In the past, she'd undergone hours of hypnotherapy to help with her aversion to blood. It had worked well. But she wasn't sure a group session would work. She looked again at the itinerary. All it said after lunch was "group session".

Shelley then gave everyone a run-down of the health and safety regulations.

'Any questions?' Shelley asked.

'I'm not dressed for yoga,' a woman to the right of George said.

'We're going to take you to your accommodation shortly, then you'll have time to unpack your belongings and get ready for the first class. Any other questions?'

'When I phoned to explain my dietary requirements, I was told to mention it when I arrived,' another woman said. 'I can't eat gluten.'

'Let the server on duty know when you collect your lunch, and she'll point out which dishes are suitable. We have a vegan menu and offer gluten-free versions of everything.'

'Thank you,' the woman said.

'Before we go upstairs, I'd like to go around the group so you can say a bit about yourself and why you're here. We'll start over there,' she said, pointing to the first person on her right.

George listened intently to everyone's bio in case there was anything she needed to report to Whitney, but nothing stood out. When it was her turn, she introduced herself as a medical researcher and said she was there to give up smoking because of the expense and her boyfriend didn't smoke. Having said it once to Ian, and been convincing, she decided to repeat it.

'Now we know each other, grab your cases and I'll take you to your rooms,' Shelley said.

Chapter Twenty-Seven

George picked up her travel bag and, along with the others, followed Shelley out of the classroom and back down the corridor until they got to the main hall. They went up the big oak staircase to the second floor. There were no numbers on the doors; instead each door had the name of a flower or plant on it.

'These rooms are reserved for people on our programmes. You have the last five on either side. Pick a room; none of them are allocated,' Shelley said as they came to the end of a long corridor.

George waited while others chose theirs and then went to one named 'fuchsia'. She opened the door and was about to enter when she heard someone calling Shelley's name. She stopped to listen.

'There's no key,' a woman called Rita said.

'None of our bedrooms have keys. We don't think it's necessary.'

'What about all my valuables?' Rita said.

'What valuables do you have?'

'My laptop and my jewellery.'

'If you have any items you don't wish to leave in your room, give them to me and I will put them in the safe.'

'Thank you. Do we get any free time?' Rita asked.

'We finish for the day, after all activities, at around nine-thirty. We expect everyone to be in their rooms by ten. We encourage early nights, so you're fully receptive the following day,' Shelley said.

George continued into her room and took a look around. It was very basic, with a single bed adjacent to the wall, a white wardrobe with matching dressing table and chest of drawers, and a small bedside table. There was also an antique easy chair in the corner of the room with a floral textured print. She wasn't keen on there being no locks, and decided she'd put the chair in front of the door when she went to bed. If anyone tried to come in, she'd be alerted. There was an en suite bathroom, with a shower, toilet, and sink. Small, but adequate. That did have an internal lock on it.

She changed into her yoga clothes and returned to the corridor where Shelley was waiting. She was the first one ready, which gave her the opportunity to have a chat with the woman.

'It's a beautiful house,' George said.

'Yes, we're very lucky to have such a wonderful place to work, and it really helps in the development of a person's spirit to be surrounded by nature.'

'Have you been here long?' George asked.

'Six years. I first came on a yoga retreat and very quickly found myself embracing all of Troy's teachings. I joined the centre full-time eighteen months later.'

'What did you do before you came here?' George asked.

'I was a model.'

That didn't surprise George, as she was tall and attractive with a defined jaw line. She wasn't as thin as some models, but that didn't mean she hadn't been in the past.

'That must've been exciting work if you got to travel.'

'I did see various cities around the world, but the fashion industry is very superficial. It pays no attention to what's going on inside a person, it's only looks that matter. I discovered it wasn't enough. I wanted my life to mean something, and being here has meant I've achieved my dream.'

'Will we get to see Troy Randall?' George asked. 'I saw on your website that he'd written a book called *Enlighten Your Spirit,* and it looks fascinating. I'm going to read it.'

'I'm hoping Troy will introduce himself to you all, so you can meet him. As a rule, he doesn't take part in the programmes. At the moment he's engrossed in taking the centre more international.'

'In what way?' George asked.

'We do have people from overseas come onto our courses, and some of them are very high-profile. But we want to develop that side.'

'To what end?' George asked.

Before Shelley had time to answer, other doors began to open and, one by one, the rest of the delegates came out wearing a variety of casual outfits.

'Now you're all ready, I'll take you to the studio where you're going to have an hour and a half of yoga, followed by meditation. Then you'll have lunch. Any questions?'

'When are we going to do something directly related to smoking?' Ian asked.

'As I explained earlier, we want you relaxed and settled. This afternoon, we'll gently start to address your issues with tobacco.'

They went downstairs and Shelley took them into a large studio.

'I'll leave you with our instructor and will see you later,' Shelley said.

They all stood in silence in the middle of the room.

'Welcome everyone. I'm Dana and I'll be doing a beginner's class with you today. Has anyone done yoga before?'

George and three others put up their hands.

'Good. I'll give you some harder poses as we go through, but only do what you feel comfortable doing. The aim of today is to get you relaxed and ready to embrace the rest of the programme.'

The time passed quickly. George was able to clear her mind of all thoughts. Being relaxed reminded her how much she enjoyed yoga, and she decided she'd take classes more regularly.

After they'd finished, Dana went straight into meditation, teaching them breathing techniques before asking them to lie down and focus their thoughts. It lasted for an hour, and once they'd finished, she sent them back to their rooms to get showered and changed before lunch.

Walking into the dining room, Shelley was waiting for them.

'I hope you all benefited from this morning. In half an hour, I'd like to see you back in the classroom. Lunch is over there.' She pointed to the far end of the room, where it was all set up on a table. 'There is someone there to explain what everything is. Don't eat too much; we want you energetic and receptive for this afternoon's session.'

George helped herself to a plate of food and went to sit at one of the long tables beside Ian.

'I think I'm a convert,' he said, tucking into a mound of rice salad with lentil balls and hummus. 'I've never eaten vegan food before, but this is absolutely delicious.'

'Yes, it is very good,' George said, looking at the

amount on her plate compared with his. If he fell asleep during the afternoon, she wouldn't be surprised, especially as he was eating a vast amount of carbs.

On the other side of her was a woman called Felicity.

'What do you think of it so far?' she asked George.

'Too early to say. I enjoyed the yoga and meditation, and I'm looking forward to seeing how they're going to approach the quit smoking aspect.'

'Me too. But I have to say I'm gasping for a cigarette. Would anyone notice if I slipped outside and had one?' she said.

'I don't know, but wouldn't that defeat the object of coming on the course?'

Was she the only one not to bring a supply?

'I smoke thirty a day and going cold turkey for four days made me nervous, so I have some for emergencies. But I left them in my car in case they searched my bag, and thank goodness I did, seeing as there are no locks on the doors.'

'I doubt anyone will search your room. I think we're here on trust, as we're adults and have paid a lot of money to do the course,' George said.

'It was expensive.'

'Yet you're talking about going out for a cigarette already. That makes no sense.'

Felicity scowled. 'It's easy for you to say. You're clearly not as addicted as I am. I'm going to try my best, but it's going to be hard.'

Damn. As per usual she'd managed to put her foot in it.

'I'm sorry, I didn't mean to upset you. It will be hard, but we're here to help each other.'

Felicity's face relaxed, and she gave a dry smile. 'I'm

sorry, too. It's been over four hours since I last smoked and it's getting to me.'

'Did you find the yoga and the meditation helped?' George asked.

'Not really. My mind kept wandering back to wanting a smoke. I didn't think it would be like this. I thought it would be a boot camp where we're forced into a room and fed all the facts and figures about how damaging smoking can be to us. And that they'd keep an eye on us all of the time, so we didn't have a chance to go near a cigarette even if we wanted to.'

'You make it sound more like a prison.'

'Yes, that's exactly how I thought it would be.'

'But then as soon as you left here, you'd go back to your old ways. What they're planning to do here is more subtle. You have to want to change. Embrace the difference it's going to make. It can't be forced.'

'How do you know so much? Are you sure you're not here to check up on us?'

'Absolutely not. I've just been listening to what they said.' George flinched. She would have to be more careful.

Having finished her meal, she decided to go outside for some fresh air and text Whitney. She headed down the path and through the grassed area until she was out of sight behind a hedgerow.

She pulled out her phone.

Good start. Nothing to report. Spoke to Shelley Bates. Will phone you after nine-thirty.

Whitney instantly replied.

Okay, speak soon, W xxx

She turned off her mobile and returned it to her pocket. She didn't want any calls or messages to come through during the afternoon. As she walked back, a silver Lexus drove up the drive and stopped outside one of the cottages. Although it was a stylish car, she'd never fancied owning one. An older man got out and went inside. Was he the accountant Whitney had mentioned?

When she arrived at the classroom, six of them were already there, and the remaining three came in a couple of minutes after she did.

They were followed by Shelley and Troy Randall. He was wearing a Dhoti Kurta in cream and gave off such a charismatic air that everyone became alert, sitting upright in their chairs as soon as they saw him. It was almost like he'd floated in. The way he piously clasped his hands together added to his air of being on a higher plane.

'We're very lucky that Troy is here to talk to you today. He managed to take some time out of his busy day. He's going to lead the group hypnotherapy session, after which we will do some meditation and have an informal class discussion. Any questions before I handover to Troy?' Shelley asked.

There weren't. Everyone sat there in silence, staring at him. Despite herself, George's own curiosity was pricked. She leaned forward, waiting to see how the session was going to proceed.

Chapter Twenty-Eight

'Guv, I've got something for you,' Frank said as he replaced the phone on his desk.

Whitney walked over to him. 'What is it?' She was glad of the distraction, as she'd been nervously playing over in her mind all of the possible scenarios that might occur with George being undercover.

'I've got the details of a woman called Tracey Tate. She saw the press conference and came forward because she used to be part of the Wellness Centre until she managed to get out.'

'Great. Arrange for her to come in to see me straight away.'

'Ahead of you there, guv. She'll be here soon.'

'Thanks, Frank.'

She went back into her office as she had some work for Jamieson to get out of the way. All this help she was giving him better result in his promotion, or she wouldn't be happy.

She'd spoken to George last night. She'd had a good day and was impressed with the way it was all going.

They'd had a group hypnotherapy session, which Whitney voiced her concern about, but George said was fine. It was designed to get them in the right frame of mind for the rest of the programme. So far, they'd hardly mentioned smoking at all. George was going to be reporting in later, probably at the same time.

There was a knock on the door and Matt walked in. 'Tracey Tate has arrived to see you. Would you like me to come with?'

'Yes. This should be extremely useful.'

They went together to the interview room.

A slight woman in her late thirties was seated. She had light brown hair and wore no make-up. A scared expression was etched across her face.

'I'm DCI Walker and this is DS Price. Thank you for coming in to see us.'

'I didn't want to, but after hearing that the murdered women were connected to the centre, I knew I should tell you about my experience.' Tracey's voice was quiet, and Whitney had to strain to hear.

'Do you mind if we record our conversation? It saves taking notes.'

'You won't tell anyone I'm here though, will you? I don't want it to get back to the centre.'

What on earth had happened to her?

'No, of course not. This is confidential.' She pressed the record button on the equipment. 'Interview between DCI Walker, DS Price, and Tracey Tate. Saturday the twenty-sixth of September. I understand you used to be a member of the Wellness Spirit Centre.' Whitney wanted to spell it out in case it was going to be used as evidence.

'Yes.'

'When did you first get involved with them?'

'Four years ago, I went with a friend to a health retreat.

My boyfriend had just broken up with me. He said I was too fat. I thought the centre would change my life for the better and, at first, I loved it. I left the retreat feeling amazing about myself and my future, so I started attending the yoga and meditation classes to maintain my progress. I'd go every weekend and sometimes during the week.'

'That must have been expensive,' Whitney said.

'Part of my progression to living there full-time was that I had to give a portion of my wages to them and just keep enough money to live on during the month. My contribution covered all my classes.'

Whitney glanced at Matt. This confirmed their findings about people paying.

'How long before you moved in?'

'Eighteen months. I had to prove myself worthy through hours of self-meditation. Being willing to distance myself from the secular world, including family and friends.'

This was the brainwashing George had explained to them. Offering the reward of being part of the community while controlling their interaction with others.

'When you decided to live there, what did your family say?' Whitney asked.

'They tried to persuade me to stay where I was, and not give up my job, but I didn't listen to them. The centre was my future. It was all I wanted.'

'What was it like living there?'

'Initially it was great. I wanted to do well and please Troy. I worked hard towards my spiritual enlightenment.' She paused.

'And then what happened?'

'I started to put on the weight I'd lost, and they told me I wasn't going to achieve enlightenment if I didn't take myself in hand. They made me stay in a room on my own, meditating for hours, and I was only allowed to eat small portions. They decided exactly what I could eat and when.'

She was powerless and dependent, aka brainwashed.

'What can you tell me about Troy Randall?' Whitney asked, trying to move the conversation away from the most painful memories.

'I thought I was in love with him, as do all the women there, and some of the men. He's that type of person, and he encourages the adoration.'

'How?' Whitney asked.

'Troy has his *special* girls. The ones he takes a shine to. When you see the attention he gives them, it makes you want to be one of them.'

'This attention, is it sexual?' Whitney asked.

'Many of the women there wanted to sleep with him, and I'm certain some of them did.'

'Why certain?' Whitney asked.

'I was walking in the garden once and decided to go to his cottage and see if he was there. He has this way of making you desperate to impress him, and I think a part of me missed the one-to-one time we used to have. I caught a glimpse of him near one of his windows. He was naked, as was the recruit he was with.'

'Did you tell anyone?'

'No. I kept it to myself in case I got punished for prying.'

'But just because he had a relationship with that recruit doesn't mean he did with others,' Whitney said.

'Maybe not, but I think he did. Or why else would the pretty young girls be invited over to his cottage for their one-to-ones? He normally held those at the main house, but some, the special ones, I suppose, were invited to his cottage.'

'What kind of relationship does Shelley Bates have with him?'

'I think she's just as besotted with him as the rest are.'

'Is she having a sexual relationship with him?'

'I don't know. I think she might be too old. She's around forty, and he did seem to gravitate towards the younger women.'

'What about you?'

'No, but at the time I would have, had he asked. But, look at me. I'm not in the same league as many of the women there.'

Whitney's heart went out to the poor girl. There was nothing wrong with her, whatsoever.

'Why did you leave?'

'After I'd been there two years, an old friend, someone I'd known since school, came to one of the yoga classes. I hadn't seen her for ages. She was horrified at the way I looked, because by that time I'd lost a lot of weight. They were still monitoring my food intake because they didn't trust me not to put it on again. After the class, she followed me into the garden to talk. I tried to tell her to go away because we weren't meant to mix outside of the class, but she refused. She wanted me to leave, but I said no. She didn't understand. I didn't want to leave. I was scared to.'

'Why scared?'

'I knew I'd never survive away from the centre. As far as I was concerned, I wasn't strong enough to control my life in the 'real' world. In the past, I'd lived a train-wreck lifestyle, punishing my body and mind with the decisions I made. Troy and everyone there were the only family I'd known for two years; they'd convinced me my family didn't love me, as they'd let me destroy my life before. I was fat, I was unlovable, and I had very few friends. That all changed at the retreat, and the thought of leaving and going back to that life made my skin crawl. I wasn't prepared to feel how I did before I went there. I needed them to guide me.'

Control her, more like.

'But you did eventually leave. How?' Whitney asked.

'My friend kept coming to the classes and would walk behind me, whispering about what my family were up to. She'd got in touch with them and had all their news. I started to look forward to my friend's visits, and realised what I was missing out on. Eventually, she tried again to persuade me to leave. I came up with excuses not to until I discovered a cousin, who I was close with before, had had a baby and got married. It hurt that I hadn't been there for her like we'd always planned, and I knew I needed to go. My friend promised to help.'

'What sort of help did you need? Couldn't you just pack your bags and tell them you were going?'

'No.' She gave a hollow laugh. 'I'd seen what happened to people who said they wanted to leave.'

'What?'

'They were locked in a room until they were broken and begged to stay.'

'How did you manage to leave?'

'We came up with a plan. I made sure to be in the garden when my friend was leaving after class. I jumped into her car as she drove past. I left everything behind. But it didn't matter. I didn't have many belongings.'

'Then where did you go?'

'Back to my parents' house. My dad wanted me to phone the police, but what would I say? I voluntarily gave up my stressful lifestyle to live in a beautiful manor house rent-free, I haven't worked for two years, instead I've spent my days doing yoga and gardening … please will you arrest the people who made it possible?' She looked ashamed, but Whitney knew she was right. Before all this, even she would have assumed it was a prank call and put the phone down.

'Do you still live at home?'

'Yes. It's only been six months since I left, and I'm not ready to live on my own yet. It still haunts me. If I could go back in time and change everything, I would never have signed up for the yoga classes, because that was where it all started.'

'The girls who died—Nicola, Hayley, Samantha, and Kelly. Did you know them?'

'I don't remember them.'

'Can you think of any reason why they would be murdered?' Whitney asked.

'No, I'm sorry, I can't.'

'Thank you very much for coming in to see us. We appreciate your candour.'

Whitney walked Tracey out of the building. Now they had something else to consider. The fact Troy Randall most likely had sex with some of his recruits put a whole different complexion on things. Were the murdered girls part of his harem? Were their murders committed by someone jealous of them? Or did the victims know something they shouldn't?

She needed to speak to George this evening and ask her to find out more. Kelly's research might have nothing to do with the murders.

Whitney's phone rang at exactly nine-thirty. It was George.

'I'm glad you called; we've found out something I need you to investigate.'

'What?' George said.

'We've been informed that Troy Randall might have been having sex with some of the recruits. That could be the reason behind the killings, and not the research. I'm telling you, this place is a hotbed of secrets, and one of them is going to lead us to the killer. Mark my words.'

'I can look out for any signs of him with recruits, but I'm not sure I can ask outright questions about it.'

'I'm sure you'll find a way. Anything new to report from the inside?' Whitney asked.

'Not much. The second day has been exceptionally good. We've done a lot of meditating and thinking through our life choices, especially regarding smoking. They have a very good approach. They're not showing us awful pictures of our bodies to illustrate what smoking does to us, instead they're instructing us in fulfilling ourselves as human beings, so we can be the best person we possibly can. It truly is fascinating.'

'Are you saying you think what they do is good, and that you're happy with the way they operate?' Surely they couldn't be brainwashing George already.

'No, I'm not saying that exactly. But they are excellent in enabling us to understand the reasons behind our need to smoke. They're doing a good job.'

'Do you think you're going to give up smoking?' Whitney asked.

'Yes. And I'm also going to work more on developing myself. I'm going to continue with the yoga.'

'George, what's going on? This is only day two and you're waxing lyrical about how good they are. You're there for a purpose, remember? To help with the murder enquiry.'

'I haven't forgotten what I'm here for, but it doesn't mean I can't acknowledge their attributes. I have to go, as I want an early night. Tomorrow I have a one-to-one with

Troy. I've been lucky enough to be chosen to have my intensive session with him. Only two of us were picked.'

Whitney's stomach plummeted. George had been chosen. Did that mean he'd be making a pass at her? 'Just be careful.'

'Of course, I will. I'll be in touch tomorrow and report in.'

Chapter Twenty-Nine

There's one more to go and that's it. But it's not going to be easy. The stupid bitch is never in the right place for me to pounce. It nearly happened earlier. I was just about to lure her over to me when she got called away.

I will change my approach with her.

Suicide by hanging is too suspicious.

This time I'll make it look like an accident. That way, the police won't link her murder to the others.

I'd love to stop now. I'm not getting any pleasure from it. But I can't.

I couldn't allow the ones who discovered my secret to live. In case they decided to expose me.

She's one of them.

Enough said.

Mess with my business and pay the price.

The police have been hanging around, but they've found nothing. They won't. I'm too clever for that.

I read that more than a quarter of all murders are never solved, and mine will fall into that category.

They won't be able to pin anything on me because there's no evidence.

Chapter Thirty

George got up at five the next morning, excited at the thought of what was going to happen that day. She'd been sleeping better than she had done in years. It was hard to say if it was the yoga or the meditation, or a combination of both. But it had given her time to examine her relationship with her parents, and her relationships with Whitney and Ross. She realised that even though she was a loner, she could do more to make herself whole. And she hadn't even thought about smoking since she'd been there.

She didn't know how Ian was feeling, but he hadn't mentioned going out for a cigarette. Maybe it was working on him, too. It was incredible the way everyone was being helped. She was really looking forward to her intensive one-to-one session with Troy, as it would give her the chance to find out more about him. It could be they were wrong about the murders having anything to do with him and the centre.

Breakfast was a bowl of fruit with coconut yoghurt, which sat easier on her stomach than her usual toast. She'd start having that for breakfast in the future. She had herbal tea to drink; they weren't allowed any coffee or tea, as they were stimulants.

Maybe she'd recommend to Whitney that she should come here to quit her caffeine addiction.

'You're very lucky,' Felicity said, distracting her from her thoughts.

'Why?'

'Because you were chosen to have your one-to-one session with Troy, while most of us are with Shelley and Dana.'

'Shelley's good,' George said. She'd been very impressed with her.

'Yes, she is, but it's not like being with the man himself. Are you excited?'

'I am looking forward to it,' she acknowledged. 'But it's only for an hour, which isn't much time to talk about my growth.'

'What time is your appointment with him?'

'Nine,' George said.

They'd all been given appointment times. Apart from that, they were to be in one of the meditation rooms, in silence, contemplating their improved lives.

'I envy you,' Felicity said.

'How are you feeling about the course?' George asked. 'Have you thought about smoking?'

'Occasionally I've had the urge for one, but to be honest, not as much as I thought. I know we're only halfway through, but I've been surprised at how well it's going.'

'I'm glad it's working for you. I'm going to take a quick walk in the garden before my session with Troy.'

'To make yourself beautiful, you mean?'

'Not at all. I want to centre myself and make sure I get

as much out of our session together as I can. I don't know why you said that; it makes no sense.'

'I was only joking.'

'I didn't realise.' The woman seemed remarkably like Whitney in humour. Maybe she attracted people like that. Did she mind? Not really. It was just a bit strange, that's all.

She left the dining room and headed outside. The sun was shining, and the early morning dew was still on the grass. She walked along the path for a couple of hundred yards and then turned to face the house. What would it be like to live there all the time? Away from the hustle and bustle of city life. Where the only sounds were the birds singing. It was certainly tempting.

She shook herself. She was getting sucked into the place and hadn't even realised. Whitney had been right. Two days and she'd already changed. She hadn't believed it would be possible. But that didn't mean she was going to succumb to its lures and give everything up, even if she had learnt that going inside of oneself could be very thera-peutic. She was sure that, with this new calmness and restraint, she'd be better able to tackle life. At least, that was what she told herself.

Anyway, she had her appointment with Troy to look forward to. He was a riveting man and seeing him in his natural habitat, rather than the police station, was a revelation.

'Tell me, Georgina. Have you ever envisaged a life where you are the one to call all the shots?' Troy leaned forward in the easy chair he was sitting on and locked eyes with her.

They'd been together for almost an hour. Sometimes

agreeing, sometimes differing, on the philosophy of life. His views were challenging but, even so, had some merit.

'What do you mean?' she replied.

'Are there people in your life who try to dictate what you should be doing?'

Her mind immediately flashed to her parents and brother, and their demands.

'Yes.'

'Who?'

Should she tell him? Opening up hadn't been the plan, but his voice and the way he stared at her seemed to be drawing it out of her.

'My parents are very demanding, which is why I don't see them often.'

'But when you do,' he prompted.

'When I do, it's under their terms.'

'So, back to my original question. Have you ever imagined being able to call all the shots?'

'Not really. I accept the way things are.'

'But life has much more to offer if you travel your own path and become spiritually enlightened.'

'You make it sound idyllic, but it's simply rhetoric. It doesn't work in the real world, it—' The alarm on his watch interrupted her.

'You're an enigma, Georgina, and I'm sorry our session has come to an end. I've really enjoyed having a person of your intelligence to talk to, but now I have to meet with someone else. I hope you found our discussion stimulating.'

'Yes, I did. You've given me much to think about. I came here to stop smoking, but I've got more out of it than that. I believe there's a lot I can do to move myself forward.' George had been surprised at how easy he was to talk to.

'I can only work with what is presented to me, and you

are exceptional. I'd like to meet with you later. Perhaps we can go for a walk in the grounds?'

'What about our class?' she asked.

'No one will mind. Meet me at four and we can continue our work together.'

'Where will you be?' George asked.

'Come to my cottage, and I'll show you my garden. We'll go out from there.'

She left him, and before returning to the class, decided to go to her bedroom. She wanted time to consider her options.

She sat on the end of her bed. Whitney had warned her that Troy was known for being too close with his recruits, but was he coming on to her? He'd seemed genuine, and they'd had a really good session together. It wasn't like she'd take him up on the offer if he did make a pass. She would enjoy some extra time with him, to find out more about his views and beliefs.

Should she let Whitney know what had happened? At the moment there was nothing to tell her, so it was point-less. Whitney would only warn her to be careful, and she could manage that on her own, without being told.

George went to the meditation room and tried to settle, but she found it very difficult and was glad when it was finally lunchtime and she could sit with the others, and take her mind off Troy.

They had another group hypnotherapy session after lunch, during which time they focused on how they were no longer going to smoke, and they also did some work on spiritual enlightenment, and how smoking and other addictions could get in the way. They then had yoga, which she enjoyed and felt relaxed and refreshed after. By the time she'd gone back upstairs to change and shower after the class, it was almost time for her meeting with Troy.

She decided to take a wander around the grounds and then make her way to his cottage. She headed down the back stairs and out of the side door, as she didn't want to bump into anyone from the course, in case they asked where she was going. They'd all been interested in how her session with Troy had gone, but she'd been very limited in what she'd told them.

As she walked in the direction of his cottage, with a view to having a look at the grounds where he lived, she saw him standing by the gate leading to his front door. A man walked over to him, coming from the other direction. He wasn't very tall, with short dark hair and wide shoulders. Troy turned to meet him. There was something familiar about him. His voice carried as he greeted Troy, and George stiffened.

'What the hell?' she muttered to herself.

Troy was talking to Whitney's boyfriend Craig. She quickly moved before they could spot her. What was he doing there? She couldn't let him see her, as her cover would be blown. She ran back the way she'd come and went to her room. She picked up her mobile and called Whitney.

'What are you doing phoning at this time?' Whitney asked.

'I was just about to go to meet Troy and—'

'I thought your meeting was this morning,' Whitney interrupted.

'It was, but he wanted to meet me later at his cottage.'

'I warned you about him. He's coming on to you.'

'Whitney, will you just listen? That's not why I'm phoning. I was a little early for our meeting and I saw Craig with him.'

'Craig? What, my Craig?' Whitney's voice was tight.

'Yes, him. Why is he here? And what am I meant to

do? I can't let him see me … He knows who I am. Did you tell him I was here?'

'Of course I didn't, and I resent you implying that I'd confide in him about our operations.'

'Sorry. There's only one thing for it. I'll leave before anyone finds out,' George said.

'Do you think that's a good idea? He's meeting with Troy and he's not part of your course. How likely is it you'll see him?'

'I don't think we can risk it,' George said. 'I want to stay, but not under these circumstances, because it could all blow up in our faces.'

'I'll leave it up to you. Let me know what you decide.'

George ended the call and began packing her bags. She didn't want to leave, because she'd felt a connection with Troy and the centre, but her duty was to Whitney and the police. She couldn't risk it.

Whitney sat at her desk, staring at her phone. What was Craig doing at the centre? Was he connected to the murders? She picked up her phone.

'Matt, I'd like a word in my office,' she said to her sergeant. She'd tell him and not the others.

'Yes, guv?' he said as he walked into her office and closed the door behind him.

'This is to go no further, but recently I've been seeing someone I met at choir.'

'Good for you. It's about time. You work hard, and could do with a—' He paused. The look on her face must have told him this wasn't a heart to heart.

'That's not the issue, here. I've just spoken to George, and the man I've been seeing, Craig Robbie, has turned up at the centre and is meeting with Troy Randall. I need to know why. Craig imports nutritional supplements, so that's the most likely connection, but I'm not taking any chances. Dig around and see what you can find. Get back to me as soon as you have anything.'

'Yes, guv.'

Matt left the room and Whitney pulled out her phone to text George.

Keep out of the way until you hear from me.

Chapter Thirty-One

George had finished her packing when the text came in from Whitney. Should she now stay? She wanted to, but keeping out of the way meant staying in her room and, if she did that, it would be suspicious. She didn't have an option; she'd have to leave. She picked up her bag just as there was a knock on the door.

'Come in,' she called.

The door opened and Shelley stood there. 'Where are you going?' She nodded at George's bag.

'I decided the course wasn't for me and I'm leaving,' George said.

'Why? You were doing so well. We've all been pleased with your progress.'

'I've enjoyed it, and definitely won't smoke again. But I've got a lot on at work and I need to get back.'

'Think about it. We've only got the rest of today and tomorrow to go. If you don't complete the programme, it's a waste of your fees, plus we want you to come away with a positive experience and help you on your way to spiritual enlightenment. You're much further down the path than many on the course. It would be a shame to see you go. I really insist you stay. You had a very good session with Troy this morning, I understand.'

'Yes, I did,' George admitted.

'I've just seen him, and he was asking where you were. He wants to speak to you.'

Did that mean Craig had gone? It must do if Troy was looking for her. Perhaps she wouldn't leave.

'Okay, I'll stay. It has been a very good experience for me.'

'We'd like you to think about coming back after the course has finished.'

'To do what?' George asked.

'Yoga and meditation classes, and you might like to join the enlightenment programme we offer, specifically for people we think will benefit from it. Those who show a lot of promise.'

'I'll think about it.'

'Please do. We'd love you to be a part of our centre. You have a lot to offer.'

'Thank you. Where is Troy?'

'I left him in my office. He'd come in asking where you were, and I said I'd find you.'

When they reached Shelley's office, she opened the door. Troy was sitting at the desk. He got up when they entered.

'I'll leave you to it,' Shelley said.

'We were meant to meet this afternoon. Where were you?' Troy asked.

'I'd decided to leave. Shelley convinced me otherwise.'

He walked towards her until he was very close and put both of his arms around her waist.

'What are you doing?' she said.

'I'm drawing you towards me, in a spiritual way,' he said, his voice intoxicating.

She relaxed into his hold, enjoying the feeling of his arms around her. She felt protected. There was a knock on the door, which made her start. She jumped back. What the hell had been going on? How did he manage to affect her like that?

'Who is it?' Troy said.

The door opened and one of the recruits stood there. 'S-sorry, Troy, I was looking for Shelley. I'm sorry. I'll leave you,' she said stumbling over her words.

'I'll be going, too,' George said, relieved that they'd been interrupted.

She went to the class. Dana was talking when she entered the room.

'Sorry I'm late,' she said taking her seat beside Ian.

'Where have you been?' he whispered.

'I'll tell you later,' she said, fobbing him off. She had no intention of telling anyone how she'd almost succumbed to Troy's charms.

When Matt couldn't find a legitimate reason for Craig to be at the centre, Whitney took the decision that they should bring him in for questioning. She messaged George and told her he was at the station.

While Matt and Ellie interviewed Craig, Whitney stayed in the observation room. It felt strange being the one looking on; usually it was George feeding her information and talking about what the interviewee was doing and suggesting how she should progress.

She scrutinised Craig. He seemed relaxed and wasn't acting as if there was anything to be concerned about.

'Thank you for coming in to see us, Mr Robbie,' Matt said.

'I didn't have a choice. I would like to know what it's about,' Craig replied.

'We're investigating the Wellness Spirit Centre, and we understand you and Troy Randall are friends.'

'I'd hardly call us friends,' he responded.

'You were with him, today,' Matt said.

'How do you know that?'

'It doesn't matter how we know. Tell us about your relationship with him.'

'I sell supplements, and I want to sign him up as a customer.'

'And you went see him on a Sunday about business?' Matt said.

'I happened to be passing and decided to call in to find out what he thought of the samples I'd given him. If he does sign-up, he'll bring a lot of business. I'm counting on him recommending the supplements to all the people who come to his classes.'

'Why were you passing? It's not close to where you live,' Matt said.

'I went for a drive to Lenchester, and then decided to go further, to see Troy, as it was such a nice day.'

'Were you on your own all this time?'

'Yes. Why do you need to know my movements?' He folded his arms across his chest and stared at Matt.

'We're investigating the murders of four women. Where were you on the twenty-seventh of August, and the fourth, eleventh, and eighteenth of September?'

'You can't be suggesting I have something to do with them. I'm a friend of Detective Chief Inspector Walker, you know,' Craig challenged.

'Your friendship with DCI Walker has nothing to do with this. We would like an answer from you.'

'I'd need to consult my diary.'

'Please do,' Matt said.

He pulled out his phone. 'On the twenty-seventh of August I was at a conference in London, and I returned late the following day.'

'Can anyone vouch for you?' Matt asked.

'The conference organiser. The delegates. I was one of the speakers.'

'We'll need their details to confirm that. What about the other dates?' Matt asked.

'On the eleventh I was at choir rehearsal from five, and after that I was with your DCI. She can vouch for me.'

'Ask him a bit more about the centre,' Whitney said into the mic.

'What can you tell us about the Wellness Spirit Centre, and Troy Randall?'

'I've visited him several times. He seems a bit full of himself, to be perfectly honest. But that's to be expected, as everyone there adores him. They hang on to his every word.'

'What about you? What do you have to say about Randall's philosophy on life?' Matt asked.

'He talked to me about his spiritual enlightenment theory, and I found it thought-provoking, but it wasn't something I wanted to pursue further. My only aim in being there was to get myself a new client. I'm in business, and I meet a lot of people like him who exist on a more spiritual plane. Don't get me wrong, I'm not condemning them, but that approach doesn't work on me.'

'Before we let you go, please write down the name and contact number of the conference organiser, so we can confirm your attendance there,' Matt said.

He gave Craig a piece of paper and pen.

'Am I free to go?' Craig asked after he'd finished writing.

'Yes.'

'Is DCI Walker here?' he asked.

'Tell him no,' Whitney said.

'No, she's not on duty today. I'll let her know you were here.'

'Don't worry, I'll phone her.'

Whitney tensed. She didn't like being used like that. It didn't seem as if he was involved, but if he was, she'd have to deal with it. She waited until Craig had left the room with Ellie and then walked out into the corridor where Matt was waiting.

'It looked like a coincidence he was there,' Matt said.

'Agreed. But, as George would say, we don't deal in coincidences. What are the odds he'd appear at exactly the same time George was there? We need to check his alibi. I can confirm meeting him on the eleventh, but that wasn't until later in the day.'

'Do you think he singled you out deliberately to get close to the investigation?' Matt asked.

'I don't see how. He wasn't to know I'd be the officer called out for the third victim. I wasn't even on-call that night.'

'What do you want to do now?' Matt asked.

'We need to get back to the centre and speak to Troy Randall about his extra-curricular activities.'

Chapter Thirty-Two

George left the class with the rest of the attendees. She turned the corner into the hallway and came to a halt. Whitney and Matt were standing there.

What should she do? Acknowledge them? Pretend she didn't know them? She hadn't heard from Whitney since the text about Craig and didn't know how everything had gone with him at the station.

Had her cover been blown?

Whitney was staring directly at her and gave a slight shake of her head, which she took to mean act like we don't know each other. That she could do. She carried on into the dining room and got herself a mug of herbal tea and a slice of date cake. She was going to miss the food more than anything when the course was over.

Once she'd finished, George decided to go into the garden to keep out of the way. As she walked along the path, she saw Whitney and Matt standing on their own. She glanced over her shoulder and, after ascertaining no one was around, decided to go over to them.

'Why are you here?' she said as she approached.

'We're waiting to speak to Troy Randall. It seems he's otherwise occupied,' Whitney said. 'If he's not here in five minutes, we'll start looking in the rooms. I don't like being kept waiting.'

'Is he in his cottage?' George asked.

'According to Shelley Bates, he's doing a one-to-one session with someone from a course and can't be interrupted as it involves hypnotherapy.'

'It's no one from the quit smoking programme because I've just been with them for our afternoon break,' George said.

'Is there another course going on?'

'Not that I know of. Unless he's with one of the recruits, because he does work with them.'

'Or Craig has come to tell him what happened at the station,' Whitney said.

'Surely if Craig was involved, he'd keep well away after being questioned,' George said.

'True. But Troy's still only got five minutes before we start looking for him. I want to know about his sexual exploits with the women here. Have you noticed anything?' Whitney asked.

'He did put his arms around me earlier, when we were alone in Shelley's office.'

'And you didn't think to tell me?' Whitney said, an incredulous expression on her face.

'He said it was because he wanted to make us as one, spiritually. I'm not sure there was a sexual component.'

'Seriously, George? How naïve are you? Of course that counts as a sexual component, as you call it. He was coming on to you.'

'I'm perfectly able to look after myself.'

'Were you attracted to him?'

'I admit I did feel a connection. He's very overpowering, in a charismatic sort of way.'

'You're not to stay here any longer. I know I left the decision to you, but you have Ross to think about. I don't want you doing anything you'd regret.'

'I'd actually packed my bags to leave, but Shelley persuaded me to not to, as did Troy.'

'And I'm *persuading* you not to stay. Go get your bags and leave. I'll speak to you later and you can come into work tomorrow.'

George turned and left them. She was about to head inside when she bumped into Shelley.

'I saw you talking to the police,' she said.

'Yes.'

'You know them, don't you? I could tell.'

George debated telling her no, but as she was leaving it didn't matter. 'Yes, I do. We were just discussing what was happening at the centre. I'm leaving. I'm on my way to collect my bags.'

'Have you been reporting on us to the police?' Shelley demanded.

'It's not like that. I wanted to give up smoking and the programme seemed an ideal opportunity.'

'Are you a police officer?' Shelley asked.

'No, but I work with them sometimes.'

'So, you've been lying to us this whole time.'

'Not entirely,' George said. 'I've enjoyed my time here and learnt a lot. I'm going to make some changes in my life. I'd rather you didn't mention this to the others on the programme. I don't want them to feel I've been underhand,' George said.

She was amazed at how remarkably calm Shelley was being, but maybe it was all part of her *spiritual enlightenment.*

'I won't tell them, but I will mention it to Troy. The

fact we've been infiltrated is something we need to discuss further.'

'You haven't been *infiltrated*. I came because I wanted to give up smoking. My work with the police is separate. You can tell the others I wasn't well and had to leave.'

'Would you have come here if it wasn't for the police investigating us?'

'If I'd seen details of the programme, then yes,' George said.

'If you say so,' Shelley said, for the first time showing some emotion.

'If I were you, I'd make sure Troy goes out to speak to the police sooner rather than later, otherwise they'll be looking for him themselves. Where is he?'

'He's meditating alone and didn't want to be disturbed.'

'So, you pretended to the police he was with someone? Hardly a wise move.'

'I thought they might go away and come back later, which clearly they're not. I'll get him.' Shelley turned and walked away.

George went upstairs, collected her bag, and slipped out of the side door to the car park. As she drove away from the centre, a feeling of heaviness washed over her. Even though she knew it was for the best, having to leave wasn't easy. There was a lot of good going on, but the fact Troy used his position of power to seduce the recruits couldn't be condoned.

Whitney glanced at her watch for the tenth time in the last five minutes.

'Right, that's it. We're going to find him, now.'

They headed towards the main house as Troy Randall came out with Shelley Bates by his side.

'Chief Inspector,' he said, smiling at her.

'We'd like somewhere quiet to talk,' she said.

'My cottage. Shelley can come with us.'

'We wish to speak to you alone, and then we want to interview you next, Shelley.'

'Is this absolutely necessary?' Troy asked.

'Yes. If you don't agree, we'll take you in for questioning.'

'You can leave us,' he said to Shelley.

They followed Troy to his cottage.

'Would you like some herbal tea?' he asked once they were inside.

'Any coffee?' Whitney said.

'We don't have coffee here. It's addictive. We have herbal tea or water.'

'Nothing, thank you. We need to get on. Please sit down.'

Whitney and Matt sat on the sofa and Troy on one of the easy chairs. He leaned forward slightly, resting his arms on his knees, and stared at Whitney.

She got why George found him attractive, as there was definitely something mesmerising about him, even though he wasn't her type.

'What else do you need to know that I haven't already told you?' Randall asked.

'We understand you have sexual relationships with some of your recruits. Is that correct?'

Anger flashed across his face for a second and then he pulled himself together. 'Where did you get that information from?'

'It doesn't matter. Please answer the question.'

'I may have had relationships with some of the recruits in the past, but it's hardly a crime. They're not underage.'

'When you say *some recruits* does that mean more than one at a time?' Whitney asked.

'I don't see how this is relevant to any investigation.'

'Did you have a sexual relationship with Nicola, Hayley, Samantha, or Kelly?' she asked.

He paused for a moment, looking quite shifty. In fact, he looked very different when he let his charismatic persona drop.

'I may have with Samantha and Hayley, but not the other two.'

'You *may* have. Does that mean you're not sure?'

'It was just a figure of speech,' Randall said.

'And how long were you seeing these women?' she asked.

'For a few months.'

'When did the relationships end?'

'When they stopped coming to the centre.'

'So, you have sex with women living at the centre, and also those who live out and just come for yoga or other courses?'

'Yes,' he said, his shoulders sagging.

'Where would you meet up with them?'

'They'd come here, to the cottage.'

'Did they all know about each other? Know they were one of several sexual partners you had and that they were being used?'

'It wasn't like that,' he said.

'How was it like?' Whitney asked.

'My recruits know I spend time with certain individuals as part of their spiritual enlightenment.'

If she heard that phrase one more time, she'd ram it down the throat of the next person who uttered it.

She drew in a breath. 'What you're saying is that you have sexual relations with your recruits to help them on their journey. Is it only the attractive ones you target? Or does everyone get a turn?' She just managed to stop herself from mentioning George.

'No, of course I don't sleep with everyone. That would be ridiculous. I'm not a sexual deviant.'

'That's a matter of opinion, because from where I'm standing you take advantage of these women under the guise of spiritual enlightenment, when in fact you're using them for your own gratification.'

'I fail to see what this has to do with the deaths of the four women you're investigating, as I was only involved with two of them.' He leaned back and rested his hands behind his head.

Was he attempting to appear relaxed? It wasn't working.

'Does Shelley know about all the women you sleep with?'

'You'll have to ask her; I don't know.'

'Have you had sex with her?'

Could it be a crime of passion? Was Shelley Bates jealous of him being with other women?

'In the past we have, but not now, as she's my second-in-command.'

'Are you sure it's not because she's too old? Do you always go after the younger recruits?' Whitney pushed.

'I'm not answering any more questions without my lawyer present, because all you're doing is insulting me.' He removed his hands from behind his head and folded his arms in front of his chest.

Whitney glanced at Matt. She'd probably pushed this as far as she could.

'We'll leave you now, but we'll be in touch again soon. We're going to speak to Shelley.'

They left the cottage and went to Shelley's office. Whitney knocked on the door and entered. The woman was sitting at her desk, on the phone. She hurriedly put it down.

'Troy?' Whitney asked.

'Yes.'

'Did he tell you what to say?'

She coloured slightly. 'No, he just said you were on the way.'

'Of course he did,' Whitney said, narrowing her eyes.

Whitney and Matt sat opposite her. 'We've been talking to Troy about his sexual relationships with the female recruits. I understand that used to include you. Is that correct?'

'In the past, but not now.'

'How do you feel about him passing you over for the younger women?'

'I don't feel anything at all. It's just part of our spiritual enlightenment,' she said.

'Don't give me that crap. He's using spiritual enlightenment as an excuse to get into the knickers of all these women, you included. Were you jealous when he stopped wanting to be with you?' Whitney snapped.

Shelley averted her eyes. 'Maybe I was at first, but I've worked through it. I'm further down the path.'

'How long ago since you last had sex with Troy?'

'Four years,' she said immediately.

Had she been counting the days?

'Are you in love with him?' Whitney asked.

'Define love. It's not an easy concept,' Shelley said.

Whitney gave an exasperated sigh. 'You know what I mean. Are you in love with him?'

'Yes, but not in a sexual way. That's passed.'

'He had a relationship with both Hayley and Samantha. How did you feel about that?'

'Do you think it's connected to the murders?'

'That's what we're here to investigate. Do you?'

'Well, he didn't have sex with Kelly or Nicola.'

'Are you sure about that?'

'I think so,' Shelley replied.

'Do you always know when he's with one of the recruits?'

'I always know when he can't be disturbed, and when he's having one of his one-to-one sessions in his cottage.'

'And he didn't have these sessions with either Kelly or Nicola?'

'No.'

She didn't want to go over old ground and decided to end the interview.

'Thank you for your time. We'll see ourselves out. We may have further questions.'

They left, closing the door behind them.

'What do you think, guv?' Matt asked once they were out of earshot and on their way to the car.

'I think Troy Randall is a dirty little creep. I also feel sorry for Shelley Bates. She's clearly in love with him and has had to endure him sleeping with all those women. But I'm not convinced it's connected to the murders, because of Kelly and Nicola, which means we're still no closer.'

'But do you still think the deaths are to do with the centre?' Matt asked.

'Of course they are, we just haven't found out in what way, but we will.'

Chapter Thirty-Three

George walked into the incident room and was hit by the usual sound of people chatting and working. She'd only been away for three days, but it seemed much longer, and she was happy to get back to a place of familiarity. She'd spoken with Ross when she got home yesterday and explained she'd left early. She didn't tell him why, but she was certainly glad to hear his voice.

Whitney was standing by the board, staring at it. She wandered over.

'Good morning, Whitney.'

'How you feeling?' the detective replied.

'Pleased to be here. I hadn't realised how much I'd got sucked into the centre until I was away from it. It's ridiculous considering I was well versed in the practices of places like that, after all my research into them. But they still managed to lure me in.'

'What about the smoking?'

'I haven't even thought about having one.'

'That's not bad after only three days. Let's hope it continues, as that's what you wanted.'

'I'll wait and see. Certainly, I have no desire to have one at the moment, so something good has come out of this.'

'But that's the only thing,' Whitney said. 'We seem to be no further advanced than we were before. There's no evidence linking Troy Randall to the murders.'

'What about Shelley Bates?' George asked.

'She clearly idolises him. She knew about him sleeping with his recruits. But why would that prompt her to kill, especially as two of the women hadn't been with Troy?'

'Let's go over everything we do have, now that I have a perspective on the place,' George said.

'Okay. We have four victims, who were all recruits, but none of them lived on-site. Kelly was an undercover researcher.'

'Did you mention the research to Shelley Bates or Troy Randall?' George asked.

'No. Was there anything in Kelly's findings which could be linked to her life being in danger?' Whitney asked.

'Her findings weren't revealing in that respect. No mention of Troy's sexual activities. What else do we know?' George asked.

'Kelly spoke to the three dead girls when they were gardening together.'

'Did they discover something that put their lives at risk? Something they dug up?' George suggested.

'Well, considering there was three weeks between the deaths of Nicola and Kelly, wouldn't it have been mentioned in Kelly's notes?' Whitney said.

'I don't remember there being anything in there about the gardening,' George said.

'Could you check?' Whitney asked.

George's phone rang and she pulled it out of her

pocket. 'I don't recognise that number. I'll leave it.' She declined the call.

'What else do we know?' Whitney asked.

'What about Craig?' George asked. 'Did you interview him?'

'I didn't. I watched from the other room while Matt and Ellie did. We're still looking into his background. According to him, he went to see Troy Randall as a potential customer.'

George's phone rang again and she pulled it out her pocket. 'It's the same number.'

'Someone's keen to speak to you. Answer it. I'm going to have a quick word with Ellie.'

'George speaking,' she said as she answered.

'It's Shelley from the Wellness Spirit Centre.'

'Yes?' Surely she wasn't going to try to convince her to come back to the centre. The course didn't have much longer to run; it would hardly be worth it.

'I'm phoning because you work with the police,' Shelley said.

'Is there a problem?' George asked.

'I need to see you.'

'Why me?'

'I've discovered something, and I want to talk to you about it. I didn't phone the police directly in case they came here and I was seen talking to them.'

'About what?' George pushed.

'I'll explain here, in person.'

'Why can't you come to the station?'

'It will look too suspicious if I leave now. I'm meant to be working. It's the last day of the course.'

'Won't it appear odd if I suddenly turn up?'

'You can say you've come back to complete the course

and that you regretted leaving. I really need to speak to you today. I'm very worried.'

'I suppose I could. I'll need to clear it with DCI Walker.'

'Don't bring her with you.'

'She would keep out of the way,' George said.

'I don't want to risk it. Please come on your own. It's important.'

'I'll see what I can do,' George said.

'Thank you,' Shelley said as she ended the call.

George stared at the phone for a few seconds. What on earth was going on that she couldn't explain over the phone? She hurried over to Whitney, who was talking animatedly to Ellie.

'I need to speak to you urgently. I've just had Shelley Bates on the phone,' George said.

'We've got something to tell you first.' Whitney nodded to Ellie.

'I've been continuing with my background checks on people at the centre and, when looking at bank accounts, I discovered some inconsistencies relating to Stewart Cross,' Ellie said.

'The accountant,' George said.

'Yes. I managed to track down a bank account in his wife's name.'

'I thought she was dead,' George said.

'Yes, three years ago,' Whitney said.

'But the account is still active and there have been vast sums of money going through it,' Ellie said.

'Define *vast*,' George said.

'In the past five years, £10,000 a month has been going into the account. For the first two years it was used for medical expenses. Since then it's been fed out on a gradual basis to several other accounts in his name.'

'Do we know where this money came from?' George asked.

'A shell company whose directors' names are listed as Stewart Cross and his wife, Pam. From what I can work out, money has been transferred from accounts belonging to the centre to the shell company account as payment for services.'

'So, what you're saying is Cross is embezzling from the centre,' George said.

'That's what it looks like,' Ellie said. 'I've also found payments for a membership to a local sailing club.'

'Hence the rope he used in the fake suicides,' George said. 'It's all adding up.'

'Exactly. Something happened to put Cross on the back foot. The women who died found out about it,' Whitney said. 'Maybe they overheard something while doing his garden.'

'Maybe Shelley Bates has found out about it, too. She phoned and demanded I go out there straight away as she's discovered something important, which she's worried about. It's got to be connected to Cross; it would be too coincidental if it wasn't, and you know my view on coincidences. I suggested you came as well but she said no, as it would be too suspicious if you were seen there, too.'

'Okay,' Whitney said. 'But you're not going on your own, obviously. We'll need to put a team together.'

'Shall I go first to see Shelley and find what she's got to say, while you come along with the others to find Cross and question him?'

'I'm not putting you at risk. Listen up, everyone. We've got a strong lead for the murders. His name's Stewart Cross and he's the accountant for the Wellness Spirit Centre. He's been embezzling.' She walked over to the board and wrote his name. 'We're going there now. Matt, I want you, Frank, Sue, and Doug to drive to the centre, and if anyone asks, you're back to follow up on our enquiries. We don't want to alert Stewart Cross to the fact we're onto him.'

'Yes, guv,' Matt said.

'Cross's office is on the first floor. He also has a cottage in the grounds. The one to the immediate right of the main house as you're facing it. I want two of you to go there, and two of you to go to his office. Shelley Bates has asked George to go and see her, and I'm going with.'

'But she specifically said you're not to come with me as it will look suspicious,' George said.

'We'll go in separate cars, and I'll wait in the entrance while you go up to see if you can find Shelley in her office. Once you're with her, you can text me and I'll come up. That way she should be safe. Any questions?' Whitney asked.

'Do you want us to arrest Cross?' Matt said.

'No. Keep him wherever you find him. We'll interview him on site, initially. I don't want him to have the chance to get rid of any incriminating evidence.'

'What about a search warrant?' Frank asked.

'His house should've been searched initially, but we need to double-check that it was, and what was found. Ellie, check, please.'

'Yes, guv. It won't take long.'

After a couple of minutes, Ellie came over. 'His house was searched, but nothing of interest was found. That doesn't mean there isn't anything there, as they were looking for links to the murder victims, nothing to do with any financial irregularities.'

'He may well keep records on his laptop or computer. We'll requisition them,' Whitney said. 'Okay, everyone. Let's go nail the bastard.'

Chapter Thirty-Four

George pulled into the car park, got out of her car, and hurried around to the front entrance, acting as if it was perfectly normal for her to be at the centre. There was no one in the reception area, so she walked up the stairs and along to Shelley's office. She knocked on the door and peered in, but the room was empty. She texted Whitney.

She's not in office. Will check room course being held.

She recalled from the itinerary that this morning they were going to be having a group session with Dana. Shelley could be in there, as she sometimes sat in.

George went to the classroom and quietly opened the door. Unfortunately, everybody looked up as she popped her head in, and as she quickly scanned the room, she saw that Shelley wasn't there.

'Sorry, I'm looking for Shelley,' she said.

'I was told she's unwell and has gone back to her cottage for a lie down. Can I help?' Dana said.

'No, it's okay. I need to speak to Shelley. I'll see her another time,' George said, thinking what a ridiculous thing to say when she'd come all this way. She closed the door and left before Dana had time to reply. She went to the main entrance and texted Whitney.

Shelley at her cottage, not well, seems suspicious. I'm going to go there.

Within a few seconds Whitney texted back.

I'll meet you. Be careful.

George hadn't been to Shelley's cottage before, but she did know where it was. It was further away from the main house than Troy's and Cross's. She headed down the path, through the grounds and off towards the left. As she got closer to the cottage, she saw a car parked outside. It was Cross's silver Lexus. She took out her phone to text Whitney.

Cross's car outside Shelley's. I'll take a look.

George skirted around the bushes to the white wooden gate. She opened it and walked down the footpath to the house. If she bumped into him, she could make up an excuse as to why she was there. She tried the front door, but it was locked. She then stepped back off the doorstep and peered into the sitting-room window. She gasped. Cross had his back to her, but Shelley was tied up on the sofa. There was a knife resting on the table. She was about to step back, out of sight, when Shelley lifted her head, her eyes flickering with recognition.

George nodded her head in encouragement and then moved away. But she could still hear Cross's menacing tones echoing through the open window.

'I'll ask you one more time. Where is it?'

'I don't know what you're talking about,' Shelley said, her voice weak.

'You saw what happened to the others. The same will happen to you if you don't tell me where it is.'

'Where what is?' Shelley said.

'If you're going to play dumb, then let me elaborate.

You and your little gang of gardeners found a book in my garden and took it.'

'What book?'

'A small notebook itemising transactions over a period of years.'

'What sort of transactions?' Shelley asked.

'It doesn't matter. I want the book back.'

'I still don't know what you mean. Where was it?'

'Under the rosebush you removed when digging up my garden. I specifically told Randall to leave it because it was planted by my wife.'

'He didn't tell us that.'

'Whether he did or didn't, I don't care. I want my book back now, or you'll go the way of the others.'

'I don't know where it is. I don't even know if they found it. It might have been thrown out with the rubbish.'

'I find that hard to believe,' Cross snarled.

'It could still be buried.'

'I'm warning you.'

George pulled out her phone.

Cross here. Shelley tied up. He has a knife.

Almost immediately a text came back.

Get out, we're coming in.

George retreated down the path and hid behind the bushes. Whitney came towards her.

'Where are the others?' George asked.

'They're on the way,' Whitney said.

'How do you want us to handle this?' George asked.

'I don't want *you* to *handle* anything,' Whitney said. 'Just keep out of our way.'

'The front door is locked. You'll need to break in, unless the back door is open. There's a knife on the coffee table in the middle of the sitting room,' George said as the rest of the team arrived.

'Matt and Doug, go around the back and see if the door is unlocked. Radio in and let me know. We'll wait here,' Whitney said.

The officers left and within a minute radioed that yes it was unlocked. Whitney instructed them to wait until she gave the order and that they'd break in through the front door at the same time as they went in through the back.

Whitney, Sue, and Frank slipped down the path and stood by the front door, Tasers in hand. George followed behind. Whitney positioned her elbow against the glass and called 'now,' into the radio. She broke the glass, stuck her hand through, and opened the door.

They stormed into the lounge, closely followed by Matt and Doug. George stayed in the hallway.

'Stewart Cross, I'm arresting you on suspicion of the murders of Hayley Tennant, Samantha Lyman, Nicola Hurst, and Kelly Yeoman. And for the imprisonment of Shelley Bates. You do not have to say anything, but it may harm your defence if you do not mention, when questioned, something which you later rely on in court. Anything you do say may be given in evidence. Do you understand?' Whitney said.

George ran into the room and skirted around Whitney to where Shelley was sitting. She untied her. The woman fell into her arms, sobbing.

Whitney's Taser pointed at Cross. He glared at her as Matt removed the knife from the table, putting it out of reach on the chair.

'Yeah, whatever,' Cross growled as Matt handcuffed him.

'Frank, get the car and bring it here,' Whitney said.

George stayed with Shelley while Whitney and the others took Cross outside.

'T-thank you for rescuing me,' Shelley said, her voice

breaking. She wiped her eyes on the back of her arm. 'I was scared he was going to kill me. He saw me talking with Kelly and the others and wouldn't believe that I didn't know anything about the book that had gone missing. I had no idea what he was talking about. I still don't.'

'He was embezzling from the centre. I believe it was a book listing all the transactions,' George said. She hoped Whitney didn't mind her telling Shelley. 'But keep that to yourself for now.'

Shelley nodded. 'Okay.'

'When you phoned me to come in, was it about Stewart?'

'No. It was something else. I discovered that Ian, on the stop smoking programme, is really a reporter for the BBC and he's doing an exposé on us. I didn't want to worry Troy, because of everything else going on. I wanted your advice on how to stop him.'

'There's nothing I could have done. But right now, I think there's going to be enough publicity aimed at the centre. You need to rethink what's going on here, because you're going to be scrutinised to the nth degree.'

'There's nothing untoward going on.'

'Come on, Shelley. You think it's acceptable the way Troy behaves with the recruits?'

The woman shrugged and hung her head. 'I don't know.'

'Let's get you back to the centre,' George said.

'You go. I'm going to stay here. I need to be alone to think all this through.'

George left the cottage. The murders were solved, but what a mess was left behind.

Chapter Thirty-Five

'Matt, you're with me. George, you're listening, as per usual,' Whitney said. 'Cross's lawyer has arrived.'

As they left the incident room, Jamieson came towards them. She tensed. How did he manage to appear at all the wrong times?

'Do you have a moment, Walker?' he asked.

'We're on our way to interview the prisoner,' she said. 'Can it wait?'

Jamieson ignored her, instead looking over her head. Damn the curse of being short.

'Dr Cavendish, how are you?' Jamieson said, side-stepping around Whitney.

'Very well, thank you,' George replied.

'I'm glad to hear it. I understand you were involved in the operation at the centre. I take it nothing untoward happened to you?'

Whitney wanted to slap him. Could he be any more smarmy?

'I was there to give up smoking and, so far, it's been successful.'

'We really have to go, sir. What did you want to see me about?'

'It will wait. Come to my office after the interview.' He turned and walked off.

No doubt more work was heading her way now the investigation was coming to an end. But if it resulted in him getting promoted, it would all be worthwhile.

'Right, let's go,' she said.

When they arrived at the interview room, George left them to take her place and observe.

Whitney walked in, with Matt following. She placed her folder on the table and turned on the recording equipment. 'Wednesday the thirtieth of September. Those present DCI Walker, DS Price and—' She nodded at Cross and his solicitor. 'State your names for the recording.'

'Stewart Cross.'

'Tony Walsh, representing the accused.'

'Mr Cross, may I remind you that you're still under caution. Do you understand?'

'Yes,' he replied.

'I'd like to start with the murder of Nicola Hurst. Why was she chosen as your first victim?' Whitney asked.

'No comment.' He sat back in his chair and stared around the room.

'What had Nicola done?'

'No comment.'

'What about Samantha Lyman and Hayley Tennant?' Whitney continued.

'No comment.' He turned to his solicitor. 'How long do I have to sit here?'

'Until I've finished,' Whitney said.

'Leave that line of questioning,' George said in her ear. 'Ask about his wife. Some of the funds were used for her treatment.'

'Okay, Mr Cross. Let's talk about your wife.'

He glared at her. 'Leave my wife out of this.'

Whitney inwardly smiled. George had got him nailed. 'That's not going to be possible. We know that some of the funds you embezzled from the Wellness Spirit Centre went towards the treatment for her cancer. What treatment was this?'

'It doesn't matter because it didn't work. Thousands and thousands spent and nothing to show for it,' he said, shaking his head.

'Although I don't condone you stealing the money, I understand your motive. What I don't understand is why you continued doing so after your wife had died.'

'I deserved the money for putting up with Randall for all of these years. Who do you think is the brains behind the centre? Him? A financial thought would die of loneliness in his head. I'm the one who's made it a success, yet he got all of the perks. He was the one who had women falling at his feet. And did any of them look at me? Of course they didn't. I'm just boring old Stewart, who does the books. They'd rather be with superficial Randall and can't see behind his ridiculous façade. All that spiritual enlightenment is the biggest load of crap I've heard. And you know what, Randall came up with the idea one night over a few beers. I bet he never told his followers that.'

'He's on a roll and opening up. Now ask about the murders,' George said.

'But why murder the four women? Embezzling's one thing, but murder?' Whitney asked.

Cross glanced at his solicitor, who leaned in and whispered into his ear.

'It doesn't matter now. My life's over. I might as well tell them,' he said, turning back to face Whitney and Matt.

'That's a good idea,' Whitney said.

'I kept a record of all the transactions I'd made leading up to my wife's death in a small notebook. It had everything in there relating to paying for her treatment. When she died, I buried it under her favourite rose bush. They dug up the bush and took it. I couldn't risk them showing it to Randall and exposing me. They had to go.' His matter-of-fact tone surprised Whitney. She'd been expecting some show of remorse.

'What about transactions from after your wife's death, when you continued embezzling?' she asked.

'They're on my computer.'

'Let me confirm, you're pleading guilty to all of the murders.'

The solicitor leaned in and again whispered something.

Cross pushed him away. 'Yes. I'm guilty.'

'I'd like to ask some further questions. Where did you get the Rohypnol, which you used to drug your victims?'

'Why do you want to know?'

'To give us a fuller picture of what happened,' Whitney said.

'It's not hard. I found someone on the internet who supplied it.'

'Do you have their details?'

'Not any more.'

'Why did you inject Nicola and Samantha with the drug, yet put it in drinks for Hayley and Kelly?'

He shrugged. 'I thought it would be simpler, but actually it wasn't.'

'Could you explain further?'

'You have to get very close to inject someone. It wasn't easy. After doing it twice I decided to try putting the drug into a drink.'

'Did you do this in their homes or out somewhere?' Whitney asked.

'Their homes. I called to see them under the guise of wanting to discuss a surprise celebration for Randall. Stupid women just lapped it up. Thought it would put them in his good books.'

'How did you manage to spike their drinks if they were there?'

'I asked for a headache tablet. In both instances they left the room to find one.' He glanced at his solicitor. 'That's it. I'm not saying another word. So don't bother trying to make me.' He rested his hands in his lap and closed his eyes.

It was pointless continuing. He'd admitted his guilt. That would have to be enough for the time being.

'You will be escorted to your cell shortly.' Whitney picked up her folder and left the interview room. Matt followed. 'Arrange for someone to come and get him.'

She walked into the next room, where George was waiting. 'I think a celebration lunch is called for.'

'Agreed. Let's go.'

Chapter Thirty-Six

George ordered food at the bar and took their drinks to the table Whitney had found in the corner of the pub. The case had involved a tangle of secrets resulting in many red herrings. It was very different from the other cases she'd been involved in with the police.

'I can't believe he caved so quickly and pleaded guilty to all of the murders,' Whitney said. 'It was almost an anti-climax.'

'He's different from many serial killers. The victims were unfortunate collateral. Once the embezzlement had been uncovered, he came clean, because for him it was over. He has none of the traits usually associated with serial killers,' George said.

She certainly didn't consider him to be a psychopath. His murders were utilitarian.

'I wonder if the centre will recover from this? If Cross was the brains behind it all, Randall's going to be in trouble. Can't say I'm bothered about that, though. He's a creep,' Whitney said.

'According to Shelley, one of the participants on the

stop smoking course was an undercover reporter. They're going to be hit from all sides with bad publicity. My worry is what will happen to the recruits. They've been indoctrinated and are going to find it hard if the centre closes and they have to leave. There are help groups for people who have been inside cults so they can cope with the outside world. I might suggest it to Shelley.'

'But it might not close, so why speak to her?' Whitney asked.

'She knows it's all about to change. I want her to be prepared.' She took a sip of her beer. 'Have you seen Craig since he was interviewed?'

'No. He phoned, but I didn't answer.'

'Will you date him again?'

'I'll see him at choir rehearsals, but I'm not going to go out with him. It's too complicated and I have way too much on my plate at the moment with work and family.'

'But I thought you liked him.'

'I did. But not enough to fit him into my life. I'm going to live vicariously through you and Ross, instead.'

'Why?' George frowned.

'I'm joking. One day you'll get my sense of humour. Are you looking forward to the wedding? It's soon, isn't it?'

She'd been so wrapped up in the case it had totally slipped her mind.

'Yes, it is. I'd forgotten all about it. No. I'm not looking forward to it.'

'Not even as you're going with Ross?'

'It's going to be a chore. Being with Ross will make it less so, but not entirely,' George said.

'You call Westminster Abbey, the Imperial War Museum, and a hot sculptor a chore? I'll take your chores over mine, any day of the week,' Whitney said, as she she clinked her glass against George's.

GET ANOTHER BOOK FOR FREE!
To instantly receive the free novella, **The Night Shift**, featuring Whitney when she was a Detective Sergeant, ten years ago, sign up for Sally Rigby's free author newsletter at www.sallyrigby.com

A word from
Sally

Did you enjoy this book? You can make a big difference.

Reviews are the most powerful tools in my arsenal when it comes to getting attention for my books. Much as I'd like to, I don't have the financial muscle of a New York publisher. I can't take out full page ads in the newspaper or put posters on the subway.

(Not yet, anyway).

But I do have something much more powerful and effective than that, and it's something those publishers would kill to get their hands on.

A committed and loyal bunch of readers.

Honest reviews of my books help bring them to the attention of other readers.

If you've enjoyed this book, I would be very grateful if you could spend just five minutes leaving a review (it can be as short as you like).

Thank you.

DEADLY GAMES - Cavendish & Walker Book 1

A killer is playing cat and mouse……. and winning.

DCI Whitney Walker wants to save her career. Forensic psychologist, Dr Georgina Cavendish, wants to avenge the death of her student.

Sparks fly when real world policing meets academic theory, and it's not a pretty sight.

When two more bodies are discovered, Walker and Cavendish form an uneasy alliance. But are they in time to save the next victim?

Deadly Games is the first book in the Cavendish and Walker crime fiction series. If you like serial killer thrillers and psychological intrigue, then you'll love Sally Rigby's page-turning book.

Pick up *Deadly Games* today to read Cavendish & Walker's first case.

FATAL JUSTICE - Cavendish & Walker Book 2

A vigilante's on the loose, dishing out their kind of justice…

A string of mutilated bodies sees Detective Chief Inspector Whitney Walker back in action. But when she discovers the victims have all been grooming young girls, she fears a vigilante is on the loose. And while she understands the motive, no one is above the law.

Once again, she turns to forensic psychologist, Dr Georgina Cavendish, to unravel the cryptic clues. But will they be able to save the next victim from a gruesome death?

Fatal Justice is the second book in the Cavendish & Walker crime fiction series. If you like your mysteries dark, and with a twist, pick up a copy of Sally Rigby's book today.

※

DEATH TRACK - Cavendish & Walker Book 3

Catch the train if you dare...

After a teenage boy is found dead on a Lenchester train, Detective Chief Inspector Whitney Walker believes they're being targeted by the notorious Carriage Killer, who chooses a local rail network, commits four murders, and moves on.

Against her wishes, Walker's boss brings in officers from another force to help the investigation and prevent more deaths, but she's forced to defend her team against this outside interference.

Forensic psychologist, Dr Georgina Cavendish, is by her side in an attempt to bring to an end this killing spree. But how can they get into the mind of a killer who has already killed twelve times in two years without leaving a single clue behind?

For fans of Rachel Abbott, L J Ross and Angela Marsons, *Death Track* is the third in the Cavendish & Walker series. A gripping serial killer thriller that will have you hooked.

Acknowledgments

Lethal Secret was a very interesting book to write, and I enjoyed all the research into cults and how they operate. As usual, I couldn't have produced it without the help of many people.

Amanda Ashby and Christina Phillips, are my friends and critique partners. No book will ever leave my computer without them seeing it first. I would be lost without them.

Emma Mitchell and Amy Hart, my editing team, are invaluable. I'm so lucky to have them. Also, Stuart Bache, who produces amazing covers. Thanks for capturing the essence of the book so perfectly.

I'd also like to thank my daughter, Alicia, for her hours of help in brainstorming the plot.

Thanks to my Advanced Reader Team. This book is so much better for their input. Also, thanks to Barbara Woods Wright for her input which has been brilliant.

A special mention to my sister-in-law Jacqui for championing my books and being a surrogate mother to Alicia as we live so far away from her.

Thanks to my family Garry, Alicia, and Marcus for their continued support.

.

About the Author

Sally Rigby was born in Northampton, in the UK. She has always had the travel bug, and after living in both Manchester and London, eventually moved overseas. From 2001 she has lived with her family in New Zealand, which she considers to be the most beautiful place in the world. During this time she also lived for five years in Australia.

Sally has always loved crime fiction books, films and TV programmes, and has a particular fascination with the psychology of serial killers.

Sally loves to hear from her readers, so do feel free to get in touch via her website www.sallyrigby.com

Printed in Great Britain
by Amazon